It was Bryn's summer to be in Alaska. Would she come, as she had every five years? Memories of their last night together still clung to Eli's heart, like mud in a dog's fur. He sighed. He knew he needed to put that almost-romance to bed before he'd find the confirmation he sought for his relationship with Sara.

Bryn hadn't given him any hope in the following years. There hadn't been a single communication from her. And her intent, even during that visit had been clear: She wanted nothing from Eli Pierce other than a means of transportation. He was an old family friend, an old flame, nothing more. It was getting his heart to shut away the desire for more that was the trick. Maybe he'd ask his mom and dad when they got back from their summer road trip if they'd heard anything from the Baileys, but that wouldn't be until August.

He pulled the new Ford into the gravel driveway. Five vehicles belonging to clients in the bush were parked there and an old car with Anchorage identification. He put the truck in park and climbed out. A woman stood on the bank above the water, staring out at Fish Lake and the Talkeetna Mountains in the distance. One of the first sightseers to arrive for the summer? Probably wanted a ride around McKinley—

She turned then, at the sound of his truck door slamming shut.

And Eli felt as if he had been punched in the gut.

Bryn Bailey.

Pathways

ALSO BY LISA TAWN BERGREN

ROMANCE NOVELS
THE FULL CIRCLE SERIES
Refuge
Torchlight
Pathways
Treasure
Chosen
Firestorm

CONTEMPORARY FICTION
The Bridge

HISTORICAL FICTION
THE NORTHERN LIGHTS SERIES
The Captain's Bride
Deep Harbor
Midnight Sun

NOVELLAS
"Tarnished Silver" in *Porch Swings & Picket Fences*

CHILDREN'S
God Gave Us You
God Gave Us Two (fall 2001)

LISA TAWN BERGREN

Pathways

WATERBROOK
PRESS

PATHWAYS
PUBLISHED BY WATERBROOK PRESS
2375 Telstar Drive, Suite 160
Colorado Springs, Colorado 80920
A division of Random House, Inc.

Scriptures taken from the *Holy Bible, New International Version*®. NIV®. Copyright © 1973, 1978, 1984 by International Bible Society. Used by permission of Zondervan Publishing House. All rights reserved.

The characters and events in this book are fictional, and any resemblance to actual persons or events is coincidental.

ISBN 1-57856-462-X

Library of Congress Cataloging-in-Publication Data
Bergren, Lisa Tawn.
    Pathways / Lisa Tawn Bergren.—1st WaterBrook ed.
        p. cm. — (The full circle series ; 3)
    ISBN 1-57856-462-X
        1. Survival after airplane accidents, shipwrecks, etc.—Fiction. 2. Wilderness survival—Fiction. 3. Bush pilots—Fiction. 4. Physicians—Fiction. 5. Alaska—Fiction. I. Title.

PS3552.E71938 P38 2001
813'.54—dc21

                                                                        2001023379

Printed in the United States of America
2001—First WaterBrook Edition

10 9 8 7 6 5 4 3 2 1

To Cheryl, one of my oldest friends, rediscovered,
sister in the God who saves.
Thank you for praying me through this last year! I love you!

The place God calls you is the place where your deep gladness
and the world's deep hunger meet.
FREDERICK BUECHNER

Come to me, all you who are weary and burdened,
and I will give you rest.
Take my yoke upon you and learn from me,
for I am gentle and humble in heart,
and you will find rest for your souls.
For my yoke is easy and my burden is light.
MATTHEW 11:28-30

Part 1

Trailhead, 1991

CHAPTER ONE

Come on, Bryn. Come out in the canoe with me. You haven't been out of this cabin for two days. And it's summer. You can study later."

"No thanks, Dad," she said, turning her back to him and trying to concentrate on her anatomy textbook. The longer she could bury herself in her studies, the faster this trip would be over.

She heard her father, Peter Bailey, walk to the front window. "Come on, honey," he said, a slight begging tone to his voice. "The rain's let up. We haven't even been over to the Pierces' to say hello."

Thoughts of Eli Pierce flashed through her mind. People thought that Californians were snobbish. Eli wouldn't give her the time if he had the last watch on earth. They'd played together when she was at Summit Lake with her dad the year she was ten, but when she'd arrived over her fifteenth summer, the guy had avoided her like a bad case of barnacles on a barge. Sure he was handsome, but Bryn had better things to do than get snubbed by a small-town jerk. "I'm just fine where I am," Bryn said.

"Suit yourself," he said. She could hear the shrug of defeat in his voice.

She wondered what her dad saw in this place. It took hours to fly to Anchorage from Southern California, and a couple more to drive to Talkeetna. Then they had to take still another hour to get the floatplane loaded with their gear and fly in to Summit Lake. Bryn heard the door shut behind her father.

All day to get here. She turned over and looked at the two-room log cabin, built by her father twenty years before. Her eyes floated over the hand-hewn logs and white, crumbling chinking. She lay in the bedroom in back, which held a bunk bed on either side. The front room was reserved for a tiny kitchenette and sitting area. It was dark, with no electricity, and it smelled musty, like an old basement blanket at her Grampa Bruce's in Boston. Bryn had to read by the light of a kerosene lamp when it rained during the day. No wonder her dad hadn't been able to get Bryn's mother, Nell, to come all these years.

She closed her eyes as the hollow, scraping sound of her father dragging the canoe off the rocks and into the water reached her ears. She wished she were home working a summer internship at the hospital, heading to the beach, catching a movie with friends—anywhere but here. In two years she would be twenty-two, a graduate from college with a degree in premed. And she would finally tell her father that their days at Summit Lake together were to be no more. She would, after all, be an adult, no longer compelled to please her dad, despite her own desires. He'd have to accept that.

A pang of loss pierced her heart and she frowned, then sighed. Probably guilt pangs. The guy just wanted some quality time with his daughter. She could at least make the most of this trip with him. Appease him, share with him, make the proverbial memory together. Dutiful daughters did such things all the time.

Bryn tossed aside her textbook and shoved her feet into shoes, hurrying to catch him before he was too far out. Bumping her head on the top bunk, she grimaced. "Dad, wait!" she called, hoping he would hear her from outside. She rubbed the top of her head and rushed out to the front room, then out to the lakeside where her father was already nearly fifty feet out. "Dad, wait! I changed my mind!"

Her father turned and flashed her a white-toothed grin. He was dark and handsome—Bryn's roommate, Ashley, referred to him as "the sexiest man alive," which always made Bryn's skin crawl. No matter how others saw him, he was still just Dad to Bryn.

"Oh good, Bryn Bear," he responded, using her childhood nickname. "I was already missing you." The warmth and welcome in his eyes made her glad for her decision. It seemed his eyes were too often full of sorrow and longing these days, although she couldn't think of a reason for such emotions.

Bryn turned and ducked her head in the cabin door, grabbing her parka from the hook inside. Summers in Alaska were notorious for turning suddenly cold, so she always kept the warm coat at hand. She walked back to the shoreline, pulling her long hair out and into a quick knot. Her hair was the same color as her father's—Indian black, Peter called it—and they shared the same dark olive skin. Her nose was his too, straight and too long. But her eyes were her mother's—wide and a bit tipped up in the corners. Smoky brown, a boyfriend once told her. "Just like the rest of you," he had whispered. "Smoky."

He was long gone. She had seen to that. Keeping a straight-A average at the University of California at Irvine was no small deal, and he had been in the way, always wanting to party and go out rather than study. But she wanted to graduate and go on to Harvard, at the top of her class all the way. It took discipline and concentration to accomplish that. And vision. No man was going to get in the way.

The canoe crunched to shore again. "Push us off, Bryn Bear."

"Okay," she said, wrinkling her nose a bit when her boots got wet and the cold lake water seeped through her socks and to her toes. While they glided backward, Bryn balanced on the bow, then carefully climbed in.

"There's a jacket and paddle beneath the seat," Peter said from behind her.

"Thought I was goin' on a ride," she tossed back.

"If you ride, you paddle," her dad responded. "Can't make an Alaskan out of you if you sit up there like a Newport Beach priss."

She pulled out the life jacket, pausing to flick off a rather large spider, then put it on and reached for the paddle. Just then a bald eagle swooped low, his long wings spread wide, almost touching the surface as his thick talons clutched a trout from the waters across the lake. "Wow!" Bryn said.

"Isn't it something here?" Peter replied. "I never get tired of seeing things like that. If only your mother would share it with me…" His voice trailed away, as if the admission were too painful to tell his daughter.

"You always wanted to live here, didn't you, Dad?"

"Summers anyway. Your mother wouldn't hear of it. Wouldn't even come and see it." There was a shiver of anger in his tone, frustration, as well as pain.

"It is a bit…isolated," Bryn said, wondering why she felt compelled to defend her mother. She considered her father's words as she dug her paddle into the water. She had to admit that it felt good to be out on the lake, out from the dank little cabin.

"The solitude is part of what I love," Peter said, finally breaking the silence. "The first day Jed brought me here, I knew it would be a part of my life forever."

Bryn looked about them at the small, shallow lake, edged here and there by thick, swampy areas full of reeds, with thick-treed snow-covered mountains that shot up on all three sides. A river fed into Summit from the mountain streams to the south. "This place is *wild*," she said, shivering. "Mom would not like it."

He was quiet for a moment, paddling. "I know. There's something about being here—it's so…primary, basic. Not your mother's style at all. Reminds a person of who he is and who he wants to be." He dug in his paddle again, and Bryn remained silent, waiting for him to go on. "Jedidiah said to me once, 'The bush teaches a man about what he wants and what he needs, and the difference between them.' Every time I come here, I remember. And I leave rededicated to discovering it in Newport, too."

Bryn's mind flew from this thin-aired, low-maintenance hideaway to their rather ostentatious home in Newport. Her mother had made a career out of volunteering with the Junior League and decorating their home with only the finest furnishings and accessories. "How did you and Mom ever get together?" She looked over her shoulder to see his rueful smile.

"We were more alike once. In college, I thought…" His words drained away like the water off of his paddle. "At some point, your mother changed. I changed." He halted, as if trying not to say too much.

"She's been pretty mean lately," Bryn said, digging her paddle into the water again. "Are you two okay? I mean, your marriage and everything?"

He was silent for a long moment. "Sure, Bryn. We're fine."

Bryn licked her lips and kept paddling, searching the approaching shore for the Pierces' cabin. The sounds of sharp axes cutting through soft wood carried across the lake, as they had since morning, and she caught sight of Eli and his father as they stood around an old, dying tree. Built the same year as the Baileys', the Pierces' cabin had been completed first, then Jedidiah and Peter had moved on to finish the Bailey abode. All in one summer. "We were young then," her father would say wistfully. But there was something in his eyes, in the way he held his shoulders slightly back, as if still proud of the accomplishment, that made her ask him to tell the story again and again.

Peter Bailey had met up with Jedidiah Pierce, born and raised in Alaska, in the summer of '62, backpacking through Europe. In Germany, the pair had stayed at a youth hostel overnight and went out the next day to try the locals' fabled Gewürztraminer. Frequently wineries set up tents along the road, and the duo stopped at the first one they saw. It was only much later that they learned they had crashed a wedding party, and the father of the bride had them tossed out.

From then on, the men were like blood brothers, and Jed, having spotted the pristine site on a hike years before, brought his new friend to Summit Lake the following summer. Both purchased several acres from Ben White, who owned much of the land surrounding the water. Ben was an older man who had been living alone on Summit since 1953, when he was discharged from the army. His home was at the northern tip of the lake. No one else owned land on the lake or lived in the small mountain valley.

"There she is," Peter said from behind Bryn. "I'm always amazed that I can't see their place from the water until I'm nearly on top of it."

Deep in the shadows, the cabin did blend wonderfully with the trees, hidden behind a copse of alder and white spruce.

Jedidiah stood up with his son, ax in hand, panting. They had been working on felling an old-growth, rotten spruce that threatened their roof in the next winter storm. He wiped the sweat from his upper lip and took a step closer, grinning. "I knew that must be Peter Bailey who flew in," he said. "And he's got Bryn with him. Man, what a beauty!"

Eli met his father's knowing eyes.

"She was always like catnip and you the tomcat," Jed said in gentle warning. "Watch yourself."

"I don't think she's interested, Dad. The girl couldn't even manage to say hello last time I saw her."

"She was a kid then. Now you're adults. And that makes your dance a little more dangerous."

"What're you talking about?" Eli asked crossly.

"Can't you see it? Trust a father's intuition then. Just watch your step, Son. Listen to the Spirit's lead," he said, looking upward into the sunlight filtering through the dense alder and spruce boughs. He slammed his ax into the tree trunk and left Eli's side to greet his old friend.

After a moment, Eli began to follow. As he walked down the path, he tried to get a covert look at Bryn. When he saw her grin up at his father on the bank, it made him pause and almost trip. The girl, who had been a fox at fifteen, had grown into a classic Greek goddess, with long, lithe limbs and dark, swinging hair—an uncommon grace in every movement. And when she smiled, sweet heaven, it made his heart hurt and sail back to the year he was sixteen. The year she wouldn't even speak to him. Too good for him, he had supposed. Their childhood friendship plainly dissolved.

Forcing himself to leave the cover of the trees, he approached his father, keeping his eyes on Peter Bailey, not risking a fall on his face in front of Bryn. Eli shook Peter's hand firmly, noticed the look of admiration in the man's eyes, his glance down to his daughter. And then Eli had to. Had to turn and look at her, greet her. Like an adult, just when he felt a keening teen shyness he hadn't encountered in years.

Eli reached up for his grandfather's airman's cap and pulled it off his head, slipping it under one armpit. He forced himself to smile and look into her eyes—the color of a beaver's tail in water. "Hi, Bryn," he managed.

"Eli," she said with another smile and a short nod. "Your dad roped you into a trip to Summit too, huh?"

"Every summer," he said, wondering at her words. *Roped?* This place was heaven on earth. The kind magazine crews scouted for catalog shoots. Thoreau would have died a happy man after he'd seen a place like this. He glanced out at the honey glaze on the water, the deep forest green of the mountains, the snow at the peaks that was almost lavender. "What's it been, four, five years?"

"Five years," she said, confirming what he already knew. "Dad can only make it two years between visits here. Every five years is right on track for me. I mean, it's pretty… *rustic.*"

"Ah, I get it," Jedidiah said, giving her a warm hug. "Californian would rather be at the beach? You're a sight, Bryn. Pretty as a state-fair queen. You must be proud, Peter."

"Couldn't be prouder. And she's smart as a whip too."

"Dad—," Bryn tried, obviously embarrassed.

"Straight A's, at the University of California."

"Dad—"

"So focused on her studies she won't even look at the guys," he said, punching Eli on the shoulder.

"Dad!"

"What?" Peter asked innocently.

Bryn sighed and passed her father, shaking her head. "Dad still thinks I'm a deaf teenager," she said under her breath to Eli, "so that he has license to say anything that passes through his head. Sorry."

"No problem," he said, watching her go by, catching the scent of vanilla and green apples. Her shampoo? A lotion? She sat down on a chair on the porch and looked out at the lake.

"My boy has his pilot's license," Jedidiah said to Peter, clearly not wanting to be one-upped. "Has his sights set on his own operation out of Talkeetna."

"Great," Peter said in wistful admiration, as if he wished he were the one starting a company in Alaska. He clapped Eli on the shoulder. "That your de Havilland?"

Eli looked past him to the old, restored Beaver on shore, knowing full well that it was the only plane in sight. "She's mine."

"A beaut!" Peter said. "I would've had you fly us in had I known you were looking for work. Your operation will be all floatplanes?"

"Float*plane,* in the singular form," Eli said, following his father and Peter up the path to the cabin. "Maybe someday I'll have one outfitted with skis, take the tourists to land on the glaciers, up around Denali, that sort of thing."

"Talkeetna's hopping. Must be twice as many people in town this summer as compared to ten years ago," Peter said, as if hoping he was wrong.

"Yeah," Jedidiah said. "Have a seat, everyone. I'll get some coffee on." Through the open doorway, over his shoulder he said, "Princess Cruises bring busloads of tourists into town now. You should see them, walking through, completely oblivious to the locals trying to keep on with everyday life. It's as if they think they own the place. And the trash they leave behind!"

"You know what they say," Eli interjected. All eyes turned to him. "An environmentalist is someone who already has their own cabin."

Peter laughed. "That's a good one. It's true." He looked back out to the lake. "I never want Summit to be discovered, changed. This is our place. Ours." He almost whispered the last word, and Bryn studied her father as if confused. She clearly was not as enamored with the pristine Alaskan valley as were their fathers or Eli. But the way she leaned back against the Adirondack chair, her hair falling out of its knot like a curling oil slick along the Kenai peninsula... She looked as if she belonged there. At Summit Lake. In Alaska. Whether she knew it or not.

"Where's Meryl?" Peter asked as Jedidiah came out, a tray of coffee mugs in hand.

"She's taking this summer off. Said us boys needed some man time." He smiled and offered the tray to each before setting it on the porch floor. "Truth be told, I kind of like our reunions after a little time apart." There was a twinkle in his eyes. "So how long you stayin'?" he asked, directing the question to Peter.

"A month, if I can keep her here that long," Peter said, nodding at his daughter.

She paused for a telling couple of seconds. "I think I can last." She paused, obviously thinking. "You know, Dad, a porch like this would help a lot." Bryn looked around at the overhang that extended from the roof. "Allow us to be outside more. Keep us from getting cabin fever."

Peter nodded, looking around at it too, walking over to touch a post as if already doing measurements in his head. "Been a while since we've made any improvements to the old place."

"I could bring you some supplies," Eli offered. "Headin' out tomorrow."

"We could harvest the poles and crossbeams ourselves," Peter said, throwing Bryn a cocked brow of challenge. "I think the boards for the roof would have to be flown in," he allowed, gratefully accepting a refill from Jedidiah. "Not as young as I once was."

"Not ready to hew your own lumber?" Jed teased. "Gettin' soft there, city boy."

"Yeah, yeah. I'm not soft, just smarter. I'd rather spend my month building and hunting and hiking and canoeing, rather than harvesting wood. We'll maintain the integrity of the cabin with a few native elements," he said, looking at Bryn again to see if she was in on the idea, "and buy us some relaxation time by getting Eli to fly in the rest."

"You can do that?" Bryn asked of Eli, forcing his eyes to hers. "Fly in a load of lumber?"

"Sure. I'll strap it to the Beaver's belly, compensate for the weight, and bring it right to your door."

"Can I go with him?" Bryn asked suddenly, casting the question toward Eli as much as to her father. "To mail my letters, pick up some supplies I forgot?"

"Bryn, we just got here—"

"Please, Dad. I'll just be gone a day. And you said yourself this would be a good project."

Peter cast anxious, narrowing eyes from Bryn to Eli to Jedidiah. "He's a good pilot, your son?" he asked of Jed.

"You know as well as I do that bush pilots are the best of the best. And he was trained by a couple of old-timers."

Peter sighed. "All right." He looked to Bryn and shook his finger at her. "But you ever tell your mother of this and there'll be you-know-what to pay."

"My lips are sealed," Bryn agreed.

"It's not you, my man," Peter said to Eli. "My wife was very explicit about her desire to keep Bryn out of small planes as much as possible."

"I understand," Eli said. "Tomorrow then, Bryn. At eight?"

"I'll be ready," she said, and Eli wondered at the glint in her eye. Had she changed so much in five years?

CHAPTER TWO

*A*t least you're talkin' to me this year," Eli said, unable to hold it in any longer.

From his side view, he could see her lips moving and he motioned to his headset, reminding her that over the noise of the de Havilland's engine, little could be heard without the headset. Her face turned red at having forgotten his instructions, and she pulled the microphone down and said, "I could say the same thing."

His eyebrows shot up in surprise, but he had to concentrate on the plane as he ran through a quick flow check and eased the throttle forward, heading toward the north end of the lake. There was a slight chop to the water, perfect for taking off and landing. He turned the plane into the wind. The Beaver shot along the length of Summit, picking up speed, swaying a little, and then they were aloft, clearing the riverbed below by a couple hundred feet.

Eli chanced a look at Bryn and she was smiling, clearly enjoying the ride. He picked up his radio mike and pressed the button. "Talkeetna radio, this is Beaver-four-two-six-Alpha-Bravo. We're leaving Summit Lake and headin' home. ETA is 0930 hours."

"Roger that, Beaver-four-two-six-Alpha-Bravo." With Denali just twenty miles away, he knew they would encounter their fair share of air traffic, it being the height of tourist season.

Once they settled into the flight, circumventing the towering Mount Foraker and heading toward Gevanni Pass to the southwest, he spoke into the headset microphone again, talking to Bryn. "What did you mean by saying you could say the same thing?"

She faced him briefly, her look incredulous. "You were the one who wouldn't say more than two words to me five years ago."

"Oh no. *You* were the one who blew *me* off." They looked at each other for a long moment, and their smiles grew. Eli shook his head. "Guess we both assumed too much, huh?" He cocked an eyebrow at her. "And I guess I was in love with Chelsea that summer."

"Yeah, well, that's a good excuse. And we were kids."

It was funny, hearing her say that. Eli still felt like little more than a kid, just on the brink of adulthood. He sometimes looked at himself from the outside, shaking hands and talking like an adult, and yet he felt as if he were playing a role, pretending to be grown up. Getting his pilot's license, establishing a line of credit, and purchasing this old plane were all new territory for him. But there was something about Bryn that told him she was born old. Something exotic and knowing.

Like catnip to a tomcat, his father had said. How had he known?

Eli Pierce was like a cougar cub in a cage, Bryn decided, covertly looking at him. One minute playfully showing off his floatplane, and the next minute holding back for some reason, as if he were pacing. The combination was charming, she decided. Intriguing. And his declaration that he thought *she* had blown him off five years ago had her at once confused and relieved. Confused that they had gotten so off track and relieved that he didn't believe her to be beneath him, unworthy of his attention as an Outsider, a cheechako, as the Alaskans referred to those from the Lower 48. Her fears had been for nothing.

Because as much as she didn't quite understand Alaska and its draw for her father, she knew she wanted to belong. She wanted at least to find acceptance here. She had always needed approval from others, she realized, regardless of their roles in her life, regardless of how much she didn't *want* to need it, chafed against the need.

Bryn stared out the window at the miles of rolling forest passing by below them, mostly lime green birch and black, pointy spruce, if she remembered the names right. She admitted to herself that it was curious, her simultaneous need for acceptance and her solitary life. Was there something deep inside her that kept her from reaching out, joining the circle? Something that would incapacitate her for the rest of her life? She hoped it was just a phase, just this time of reaching for her goal of becoming one of the best physicians in the country. Once that was attained, surely she would make room in her life for deep friendships, soul connections.

She didn't want to become her mother, distant and angry, constantly blaming her childhood for her miserable adulthood. Nor did she care to become her father, wandering and searching for something intangible, something that would lead him to happiness. Bryn chanced another look at Eli. He and Jedidiah had a way about them, a peaceful aura that calmed those around them. Maybe that was what drew Peter Bailey to Jedidiah. Her dad wanted a part of Jed's secret, that sureness about his life. Could it be the place? Alaska? Summit Lake? Surely such certainty about himself had to come from more than a sojourn to the great outdoors. But what?

"Penny...your thoughts," Eli's tinny voice came through her headset, broken up.

"It would take many pennies for me to share," she said. "How long until we reach Talkeetna?"

"Twenty, twenty-five minutes," he said, glancing out as if able to pinpoint exactly where they were. There were few landmarks other than winding, silver ribbons of rivers among the miles of trees. Did he know this wild, seamless country so well that he could identify each tree? Perhaps it was such familiarity that made him seem so at ease. She wondered. As they got closer to town, they saw more dwellings—summer cabins and year-round homes. "Up ahead," he said, suddenly. He dipped the nose of the plane and then pulled off some throttle to lose some altitude. "See? In…pond, two o'clock."

She smiled as a bull moose raised his head—the living mantel for a huge rack of antlers—with slimy bottom sludge hanging from either side of his huge snout. He shuffled out of the water, disgruntled by their passing, and the de Havilland sailed by. "How many of those do you see from up here in a summer?"

"Train bait?" he asked with a grin. "A hundred or so."

"Train bait?" she chanced, feeling every bit the cheechako.

"Trains kill about forty every year in this area alone. They're slow, they're big, and they like the open track. Easier going than the forest."

The rest of the trip was spent in relative silence, with only air traffic control coming through their headsets.

"Talkeetna," Eli said with a toss of his chin. In five minutes they were landing on a narrow stretch of the Susitna River and, in another five, were tied up. "Want to come with me to the lumberyard?" Eli asked her. "I'll have to get my dad's truck to haul the wood. He leaves it parked at the church. I'll be gone for about two hours."

"No thanks. I think I'll poke around town and mail my letters, pick up a few things. Meet you back here at, say"—she pulled up a sleeve to look at her watch—"three o'clock?"

"That'll be fine," he said, staring into her eyes a moment longer than necessary as if he could see through her, ascertain why she was reluctant to spend time with him. She wasn't even sure herself, except that he seemed dangerous, too risky a diversion from her carefully laid plans. She looked away, busied herself with gathering her belongings, and pulled her backpack up on one shoulder. "See you then, Eli," she said.

"See you then, Bryn," he returned, nodding at her once. She turned away first.

As soon as she was talking to her mother on the phone, Bryn wondered why she had called. Maybe it was the vague longing in her heart, the pervading sense of displacement, missing home, wanting that security Eli seemed to have—

"Bryn? Are you there?" Her mother's voice jolted her back to the present.

"I'm here, Mom. We're doing fine. I'm just in Talkeetna for some groceries and then heading back to Summit. Is there…is there anything you want me to pass along to Dad?"

A long silence followed. "No. No, honey. Tell him I said hello. I'm going sailing with the Bancrofts tonight. It's always awkward to do that sort of thing without your husband. I tell you, I just don't understand why he has to go off to the end of the world every other year."

"Maybe you should come up and see—"

"Oh no. I have no need to go someplace that has no running water or a decent toilet or a telephone."

"We heat water on the stove for a bath every day. It's kind of fun actually," Bryn said.

"I'd rather have hot water at my disposal without lugging it anywhere. And listen to you! You sound as if you're actually enjoying it this year."

"I don't know if I'd call it enjoyment, but—"

"Are the Pierces still there? Have you seen Jedidiah's son?"

"Yes. He was sweet. We're getting along better than last time." She carefully held back the information that he had flown her to Talkeetna—her mother would never let Peter hear the end of it if she knew a twenty-one-year-old, just-licensed pilot had been in charge of her safety. There was no way to express in a way her mother would understand that Eli had a way about him that just made a girl trust...

"...that's good," her mother was saying. "Remember last time how crushed you were when that boy wouldn't say boo to you?"

"I was fifteen, Mom. I guess we had a misunderstanding. He was dating someone."

"Fifteen. My, it seems that was just yesterday. And now you're twenty. I miss you, honey. Want to come home? We could tell your father the truth—that you prefer being here in California to Alaska in the summers. He'd...understand."

He wouldn't. Her mother knew it as well as Bryn. "I don't think so, Mom," Bryn said gently. "I think...this will be good for me. Good for me and Dad."

"I...see," her mother said, a bit icily. Bryn had chosen. And it was the wrong choice, as if electing to stay was an admission of loyalty to her father over her mother.

"I gotta go, Mom. We'll send you a report in the mail in a couple of weeks. We're fine. Don't worry about us, okay?"

"A mother always worries," Nell said with barely disguised irrita-tion. "Take care of yourself."

"I will. You too." Bryn hung up the phone then, unable to rouse the words *I love you* from her lips with any semblance of honesty. She felt jumbled, confused, after her talk with her mom, as she always seemed to feel when they spoke. *Maybe this summer I can figure out exactly how I feel,* Bryn thought. *Maybe that's why I need to be here. To get my thoughts straight. To figure out where I belong. How I belong.* There was certainly time and quiet on the lake.

And Eli. He clearly knew who he was. "Comfortable in his own skin," as her Grampa Bruce would say. Maybe... No. She could never talk about such personal things with someone like Eli. He might laugh, or worse, feel sorry for her. *Poor, mixed-up Bryn Bailey.* Nobody at school thought of Bryn as mixed up. Everyone said she was so purposeful, focused. And she liked it that way.

She turned away from the phone, an open half stall against the side of Nagley's Mercantile, and left to mail her letters. She passed five college-age kids, probably river guides, who were laughing and playing around as they walked.

Suddenly she wished she were with Eli. Smiling and half flirting. Out flying or maybe hiking... Thinking about anything but her mother and her father and the widening abyss between them all.

What would it take to reach Bryn? Eli wondered, driving back to Talkeetna from Willow with Peter Bailey's wood and nails. When he entered town, he waved at the postmistress, walking with her toddler, then at Sheriff Ross. The tourists were out in force, and with Bryn not in sight, he turned down a dirt road to circumvent the crowd, heading back toward the river and his floatplane.

It took him twenty minutes to get the lumber properly secured under the belly of the plane. If Bryn didn't show up with too many purchases, they'd be perfectly balanced for the flight back to Summit. He rose, panting from the exertion of tightening the cinches, and wiped his hands on a cloth. He looked about for Bryn and spotted her approaching, only two sacks in hand—one a plain brown grocery bag and the other bearing the logo of a local T-shirt shop. It reminded him that she was only just passing through. Staying long enough to eat a few meals, but briefly enough that she needed a T-shirt as a memento. *Hang on to your heart, Pierce,* he told himself. *Pull back on the throttle.*

Two guys passed her and turned around to stare. She moved forward, oblivious to the strangers' admiration, focused only on him or the de Havilland. He couldn't tell which. There were some cute girls in town, but no one as amazing as Bryn Bailey. He knew it; those guys knew it. Bryn could be a model with her perfect features and long, shiny hair and curves right where a man appreciated them. A shiver ran down his neck to the middle of his back and out to his elbows and knees. What would it be like to take a woman like Bryn in his arms and kiss her? To feel her cling to him and press her lips hard against his? *Hang on to your heart, Pierce.*

She drew near and smiled shyly at him, her head slightly ducked. It made him want to hold her, to reassure her nameless, subtle fears. To kiss them away… *Hang on to your heart, Pierce.* The warning was clear, a holy urging from deep within, but he didn't want to hear it.

"Hi, there, pilot," she said, finally at his side. "I see you got the wood. All set?"

"All set. You can climb on in."

She paused on the float, one foot inside the doorway. "I was wondering, would you take me out hiking sometime this week? If you're not busy, I—"

"Sure. I'd love to." *So much for pulling back.* "I have a flying job over the next couple of days. How about after that?"

"Well, I gotta check my social schedule." She pretended to mentally mull over an intense calendar, finger to lip, eyes aloft. "Let's see, other than a promise to my dad for a daily canoe ride, I don't think I'm busy. So, Sunday?"

"Make it Monday. My dad and I hit church every Sunday morning, and that pretty much wipes out the day. Hey, you could come with—"

"That's all right," she said, climbing into the plane. "Monday will be fine."

"Okay." He climbed in behind her and buckled himself in, then grabbed the headset and put it on. He glanced at her, but she was staring outward, already quiet and thoughtful again. *Hang on to your heart, Pierce.* And this time the warning was as clear and alarming as a stall horn in the cockpit.

On Sunday evening Eli canoed over to the Bailey place to talk over the next day's plans with Bryn. She was out on the front stoop with her dad, holding a pole in place while Peter pounded in a long nail. With her hair up in a loose knot, soft tendrils falling to her neckline, and a body that in profile would make any man swallow hard, Bryn was as desirable as a mystery to a detective. And when she looked at him with those dark eyes that seemed to convey every whisper his heart longed to hear...

23

Eli wanted to know her—what motivated, moved, mortified, molded her. He forced his focus back to their project, suddenly conscious of Bryn's protective father and that he probably appeared to be gawking. *Am gawking.* The framework on the porch was almost complete, and appeared to be level and solid.

"Lookin' good," Eli called from the water, his eyes slipping back to Bryn. *The woodwork isn't bad either.*

"Thanks!" Peter greeted him. "Guess I haven't forgotten too much in the twenty-odd years since we built these places."

Bryn grinned at her father and then at Eli as he made his way ashore. "I think he was just waiting for my year to take this on," she said half accusingly.

"Hey, girl, it was your idea."

"So it was. But somehow I think it was yours all along."

Her father slipped his hammer into a belt loop and crossed his arms. "Now how do you figure that?" Eli picked up a rising note of tension and shifted, uneasy.

"I don't know… You've always been able to get me to do exactly what you wanted."

"Not me. Your mother maybe."

"Both of you," she said, picking a splinter from her hand. Eli noticed her nails were closely cropped, with small white half-moons on each nail bed. Perfect. Just like the rest of her.

"Hey, Bryn," he interrupted, not caring to be caught in the middle of a family disagreement. "I just popped over to talk about tomorrow. Want to head out early?"

"Sure," she said, still staring at her father. "We thought we'd go hiking, Dad. Okay with you if I abandon camp for a while?"

Peter looked from her to Eli, then back to her. "Just make sure you have the right gear and get back well before dark. Okay?" His focus was on Eli again, his intent clear. Alaska could be a dangerous place. *She's your responsibility, Eli. I'm trusting you.*

"No problem, Mr. Bailey," Eli said respectfully. He turned back toward the canoe, saying over his shoulder, "I'll see you tomorrow at seven, Bryn."

"I'll be ready." There was no hesitation, no qualm in her voice. She was brave and gutsy. He liked that.

"Good night," he said, already paddling away.

"'Night!" Peter called. Bryn was silent. And because she was silent, Eli knew he would be fantasizing about her whispering "good night" in his ear all evening. What was it about her? He stubbornly refused to look back toward shore.

For the first time since he'd started daydreaming about Bryn, Eli whispered a prayer heavenward. "Lord God, you have brought me to this place for a reason." He paddled deep and hard in a J-stroke, powerfully forcing the cedar canoe forward. "Help me to be your servant, to be who Bryn needs me to be, and not so focused on my most base desires." It was then that her declining his invitation to join them for church that morning came back to him.

Why hadn't he thought of it before? Peter Bailey had never been a believer, always telling Jedidiah that he lived a moral, if not a Christian, life. And that was enough. Memories of the two men sitting out by a campfire, debating theological questions, came back to Eli. Like father, like daughter.

He had assumed she was a believer. Hoped she was a believer. Hadn't wanted to think anything else, drawn into his attraction for her like...*a tomcat to catnip.*

The problem was that Eli was already rolling in the catnip.

"My dad calls you a bear magnet. Think we'll see one today?" Bryn asked, keeping up with Eli with some effort. It wasn't easy, at this altitude, but she was loath to admit it. There was an air of testing about Eli today, something she picked up the moment he collected her in the canoe. She wondered why.

"It does seem to be true—every time I go out I come across the closest bear. Must be something about my smell." He turned and grinned at her, handsome with a slight flush to his lower cheeks where the faintest stubble hugged his skin.

She raised her eyebrows, forcing her thoughts back to bears. "Great. So if we encounter a bear, Mr. Magnet, what are we supposed to do?"

"Grizzly, stay absolutely still. They perceive anything running away as dinner. If attacked, you play dead. If it's a black bear, you fight back. Don't try to climb a tree. They'll be right behind you, and trust me, they're better climbers. Grizzlies don't climb."

"Okay," she said slowly. "I'll just do what you do."

He smiled over his shoulder at her again. "Don't worry. I'm the bear magnet. You didn't put any citronella on, did you?"

She stopped, and he walked a few paces before stopping too, then turning around.

"You did?"

"Well, I had to do something to keep from giving these mosquitoes a unit of blood." She swatted around her head, suddenly hearing the high-pitched whine of the dreaded insect nearby. "Why? Don't tell me. Bears love citronella."

"Some bears." He frowned and Bryn frowned too, now truly

worried about a bear attack. Yet she was glad for the attention from Eli. There was a protective, loving way about him that made her feel more feminine, aware, alive.

"We're, what? Three miles out?" Bryn said, trying to return her focus to the task at hand. "Might as well get to the mining camp and then go home. Maybe the bears are in other territory today."

Eli scanned the horizon, suddenly all Eagle Scout. "Maybe. Just stick close to me."

No problem, she thought. It was about seventy degrees out, a perfect summer day, and Bryn concentrated on the beauty all about them rather than on her handsome guide or the bears that might want to eat them. Summit Lake lay on the western border of the Denali Wilderness, and from this vantage point, they could see much of Mount McKinley—which Eli preferred to call by the Athabaskan name *Denali,* "since that president from Ohio never even laid eyes on her"—and the rest of the Alaskan Range.

It was breathtaking—white peaks descending to dark silver-blue ravines and gullies, above green-brown tundra-covered "hills" that rivaled most of the Rocky Mountains in elevation. Bryn knew that many of the peaks were eleven to thirteen thousand feet high; Mount Foraker was over seventeen thousand; and McKinley, the queen, over twenty.

"What does *Denali* mean?" she asked, panting, following in Eli's footsteps.

"High One."

"That's appropriate."

"Highest point in North America," he said with a note of pride.

She stifled an *I know.* She wasn't stupid—she had scored 1490 on her SAT. But she sensed that he hadn't said it to be a know-it-all.

He simply loved this place. What was it about him that at once drew her—as though they had been lifelong friends rather than periodic acquaintances—but also repelled her—as if she were a complete cheechako?

"So you're premed," he said suddenly. "Want to be a generalist or a specialist?"

"Don't know. I have a few years to figure it out."

"I'd say," he agreed. "What makes you want to be a doctor?"

She mulled over his question, and the silence grew between them. Finally she said, "I think it's because I like to get to the root of a problem and fix it. Problems with the body almost always have a good reason for occurring, and a good solution."

He paused, letting her catch up to him, and opened up his canteen, then offered it to her. "You thirst, and you quench it. It's all very orderly."

She looked him in the eye, catching his obvious hint. "You don't care for the orderly?"

"I've found that my life isn't all that orderly. I want it to be, but it doesn't matter. It's messy and mixed-up and turned around every time I think I'm on the straight and narrow." He took a sip after her and then with the back of his hand wiped his lips. Bryn found herself staring at them a half-second too long.

"Isn't that aggravating?" she asked, taking a deep breath. She wouldn't let him distract her. "Don't you just want to make it right, make it straight, less messy again?"

"To some extent." He looked around, surveying the land like a one-man search party. "I've been spending quite a bit of time with Ben White. There's a reason my dad has been friends with him all these years. You should get to know him too."

She sat down on a nearby rock, her calves suddenly aching. "Why? My dad says he's just an old coot who's tucked himself away from the world. A religious fanatic."

"That's not how I'd describe him. Ben's wise. Smart. Caring. He's pretty remarkable."

"Because he raises bear cubs?"

"That's just part of the reason." Eli shook his head. "It's hard to explain. I'll take you to see him. He'll be back tomorrow. He's out on a Fish and Game assignment."

"What does he have to do with our conversation?"

Eli sat down on a neighboring boulder. "He writes a lot. He told me the trick to writing in a way that grabs readers is to note what is vivid and vital in life. And if you can take note of it and embrace it, whether you're writing about it or reading it, you'll enjoy it all the more." Eli looked at her steadily. His eyes were the color of the far hills, a hazel green. "When is life most vivid and vital for you, Bryn?"

Here, now was the first thing that came to her. She thought about sharing it with him but held back. He was right. Her days were not focused, not organized with a huge goal before her as she usually kept them, and yet she felt more…interested and…*whole* than she had in a long time. "It's a good question," she said instead, rising. "Come on. If we're going to get to that mining camp and back, we had better hurry."

Eli watched the thoughts pass through her dark chocolate eyes like a ticker tape through a stockbroker's hands. There was something moving her, changing her, making her think. She set off ahead of him, assuming their trail was dead ahead rather than veering to the right at the crags, moving on instinct. Was that how she always tackled a problem? Move forward and figure it out on the way?

"Uh, Bryn? We want to head over to the right. The camp should be about a quarter-mile farther."

"Oh. Okay." She modified her path immediately. "You asked me what makes me want to be a doctor. What makes you want to be a pilot?"

"You were up with me last week. You saw what fun it is, right?"

"Yeah. But what about the rest of the world, Eli? What about seeing Europe like our fathers did? Or China? Or New Zealand or Peru…"

"I'd like to see those places. Someday."

"Why not now? Have you ever even been Outside? To the Lower 48?"

"Twice. We went to see my grandparents in Chicago."

"That's it?" It was her turn to stop and study him. "Don't you ever wonder what you're missing? What's out there?"

He mulled over her question. "Guess not. Wasn't wild about Chicago. This is home, and I'm pretty sure it always will be."

She nodded but was clearly not assured.

"And flying… There's nothing else like it. When I was a kid, I wanted to be a hawk, circling, riding the wind. If I could spend all day in a glider, I'd be a happy man. The de Havilland and flying for a living is the next best thing."

He took the lead. "I might not have seen China yet, but I see something new every day. Isn't that what most people want from their work? Something new, to keep things fresh, interesting?"

"I suppose."

They crested the next hill and spotted the remains of a small mining operation—decomposing traces on the ground, a black, cavernous hole in the hillside, barely covered with metal fencing in a meager Forest Service effort to keep hikers and daring spelunkers out. There wasn't a whole lot to it. But beyond it, miles of treeless, green-gold tundra extended all the way to the base of the white mountains in the distance.

"This is it?" Bryn asked, staring down the gully to the sad remains.

"No," he said. He took her hand before thinking about it and waved to the horizon. "That's it." He stared outward, but his attention was on the connection between them. It felt so good, so right, that Eli suddenly didn't want the gesture to be casual; he wanted to hold her hand forever. He looked over to her.

She was gazing up with such a look of rapture that it seemed to Eli that she saw, really saw Alaska—the land he loved—for the first time. "Oh," she whispered, and her fingers tightened around his.

Bryn began to look forward to Eli's visits, his shy smiles and warm glances. So when he came over a week after their hike and invited her to go with him to meet Ben White, she agreed. Together they paddled up to Ben's cabin. His home was a bit more expansive than the other two Summit cabins, with a wraparound porch and wide windows on three sides. There were tidy wooden and stone steps that came down the hillside to the beach. Ben emerged as they neared and gave them a small wave, moving slowly, stiffly, to the stairs, to come and meet them.

"You all right, Ben?" Eli asked.

"Ah, fine. Just that darned arthritis acting up." He came closer and smiled tentatively at Bryn. "Must be Pete Bailey's girl. Spittin' image."

"I am." She reached out her hand. "Bryn. Bryn Bailey."

"Ben White," he said with a friendly nod. He was a short man, perhaps four inches shorter than Bryn, but compact and strong. About seventy years old. He was dressed in an old plaid shirt that had probably seen a decade of wear and jeans that had holes at the knees. But they were clean.

It was his eyes, kind and sagelike, that drew Bryn's gaze. "Come on up and share a cup of tea with me," he invited.

"That would be great, Ben," Eli said. He and Bryn moved forward, and Eli's hand moved to the small of her back, a polite gesture of pure masculinity. Women didn't go around touching each other there. She found herself wishing he wouldn't let it drop away. It was warm and comforting somehow. Oddly intimate.

"Have any bear cubs?" Eli asked Ben as they entered the house. The walls were plastered, making it lighter and brighter than the Baileys' cabin, and the floors were of wide, clear pine planks. She and her father had been debating the possibility of flooring their own cabin.

"Don't have any bears now. Those I went to see were dead before we could reach them. The guys down at Fish and Game tell me they're hoping to bring a couple by next week. Guess I'll be back to nursing a new set along."

"How many have you 'fathered'?" Bryn asked.

"Couple of twins. Several lone cubs." He set the pot on the stove, lit a match, and cranked the dial. A propane tank must be nearby, she surmised. He turned and reached for a few mugs from hooks and several boxes of tea, then set them on the table before her and Eli. "It's a crazy thing to do, but I enjoy it. Without me, those little critters would die. And there's a place on God's green earth for every one of them."

Bryn bristled at his mention of God. She remembered her dad's warning about Ben White, and she wondered if she would get the religious fanatic spiel now.

"Had a couple of problems with one young male," he continued. "He's wandered on over to Talkeetna and is liking the garbage smorgasbord rather than hunting. I have to figure out a way to get them used to hunting younger, so it's not such a shock. My females have done well, but this male—"

"How do you know he's yours?"

"Part of my deal with Fish and Game. I radio-collar them all. University tracks them for me. My job is to raise them up as a bear mother would. Wrestle with them. Take them out on walks. Show them how to dig for a spring covered with foliage or grub under a log, that sort of thing."

"How'd you get into it in the first place?" Bryn asked.

"Father was a vet and always fostering wounded or abandoned wildlife in New Hampshire. An owl with a wounded wing. A falcon. Ferrets. Anything you can name. We had a couple of bears when I was growing up. People brought him animals from all over the Lower 48. It became the family business." The teapot whistled, and he turned to take it from the stove and pour each a steaming mug. "Enough about me. How do you find Summit this year, Bryn? I wasn't around the last two times you visited. But I well remember the year you two were ten or eleven. Inseparable, you were."

She could feel the heat of Eli's embarrassment, but she concentrated on Ben. "It's pretty here. But a little...far away from everything for my taste."

Ben sat down and looked at her from over the rim of his mug. "Takes awhile. You'll see it eventually—what brings your father here."

"Besides a break from my mother?" It was out before she realized what she was saying, but there was something about Ben that invited confidences. His open kindness, lack of judgment.

He smiled and nodded, seeming to sense that now was not the right time for eye contact. "Alaska calls a body home. Your father's got it in his blood. I'd wager you'll soon have it in yours as well. Once it's in there, there isn't a way to get it out. No way to remedy the ache when you're away other than to visit. Or move here permanent."

Bryn smiled in confusion. "You make it sound like a disease."

"Some might call it that, yes."

He was puzzling, this wizened old man. She wondered what it was about Ben that her father had disliked, but for the life of her she couldn't figure it out. He was a genuine, sweet gentleman. Maybe Peter was afraid Ben would see into his soul as he was seeing into Bryn's. Afraid that he'd open up to the old guy when he wasn't ready to open up to anyone. Her thoughts floated until Ben brought another cup of tea.

They talked of Eli's blossoming business plans and his parents, about Bryn's studies, her mother in Newport, her grampa in Boston—it hit her then that Ben reminded her of her beloved grandfather. How she missed Grampa Bruce's smiling eyes and the way he would trace his old finger down her jaw tenderly when he was telling her something he wanted her to remember forever...

When their mugs were empty, Eli and Bryn said good-bye, promising to come back the following week to meet his "babies."

Eli followed Bryn down to the canoe, allowed her to get to the front, and then pushed off of a large rock without ever getting his boots wet. As they paddled away, he asked quietly, "What did you think?"

"About?"

"About Ben."

"I think he's a very nice old man. I don't know why my father doesn't like him."

"Why don't you ask him?"

"I might."

"Want to go fishing?" Eli changed subjects. "I can teach you an old Tlingit tribe method and catch you a passel of trout for dinner."

"Yes. I'd like that," she said. "But let's stop and get my dad's fly-fishing rod too. I want to try my hand at it."

"You got it."

CHAPTER THREE

*E*li was showing Bryn how to stand on the logjam and use Ben's dip nets to try to catch trout the way the natives caught chinook salmon on the Pacific rivers. Ben had handcrafted the nets years before; they weren't as effective as fly rods with the trout, but they were twice as much fun.

As Bryn stood spread-eagle over the rushing river, on top of logs that waved a little under her weight, she grinned. It was risky, this. With one misstep, she'd be in the frigid water and heading toward the lake through the small rapids. She couldn't remember the last time she had the tingle of anticipation running down her back, the relentless smile on her face from pure excitement. A dark form slithered toward her, and she dropped the long net. Too late. She studied the silver water a little farther upstream, hoping to give herself a better chance at dunking the net in time.

Across the water, Eli whooped with glee. "Got one! He's nineteen inches long if he's an inch!" he shouted. "Get to it, ya Californian. If you don't catch at least one, you don't get to eat tonight."

"I'm working on it," she tossed back, her eyes still on the water. *There!* She plunged her net downward so hard and so deep the hand-carved pole nearly slipped from her grasp. She gave out a little yelp, and Eli immediately responded in concern.

"Bryn?"

"I'm okay. Just missed a fish and almost lost the net."

"Don't do that. Ben'll kill us."

She glanced over at him and then did a double take. He was so cute, with his old airman's cap on backward. His hazel eyes studied her, and she deliberately looked back to the river. "Catch a fish, Bryn, or you won't eat. Don't lose the net or Ben'll kill us," she mimicked. "I can't win," she pretended to whine.

"You'll get the hang of it," he said. She could barely hear him over the water's rush.

Five minutes later, after several more failed attempts, she came up with her own prize trout. She hooted with glee, smiling over at Eli, and he grinned back at her. He was scrambling over the old silvered logs to get to her and help her with the fish when a shot rang out, from high up, in the direction of the glen over the ridge behind them.

Eli froze, then frowned. He studied the green peaks, and his head shook back and forth slightly.

"What was that?" Bryn said lowly.

He kept shaking his head for a moment. "That came from the area where the Dall's sheep have been grazing."

"Hunters?"

"Poachers, this time of year."

Bryn frowned.

"I'm going to go check it out. Stay here, Bryn. Or go back to the cabin."

"No way. I'm coming with you."

His head whipped around. "Not a good idea. I'm going to sneak up on them. If it is poachers, I want to get a good description so I can report them."

"Two witnesses are better than one."

Those hazel eyes studied hers. Fear, concern, and admiration all ran across his face. He paused a moment longer, then gave her a nod of assent. "We'll have to move quickly. Ready?"

She licked her lips. What had she gotten herself into? But as Eli gripped her hand in his and they made their way across the logs to the other side and began bushwhacking up the side of the mountain, across several streams, and through the forest, she smiled in satisfaction and anticipation. It was an adventure. Wasn't that why her dad wanted her here? To see Alaska in its natural beauty? Learn to love the land as he did? What better way to do that than to do some surveillance on a couple of lousy poachers?

A thousand feet up they paused and took deep drinks from the canteens at their waists. Another shot rang out, and automatically they ducked. Looking about, they saw no one.

"Over that next ridge," he said, gesturing toward a ragged, rocky hump another five hundred feet away, almost straight up. "We should be able to see them from there." They began moving again, slowing down over the loose shale and moraine left from the receding glaciers that had once dominated this valley. "Find your foothold and a handhold before you move," Eli told her sternly.

She swallowed a defensive retort, but she knew Eli was right. They were one handhold away from a long, prickly slide down the face of the mountain. The adventure was quickly becoming less fun. But she was determined now. Nothing was going to make her turn back.

In fifteen minutes they reached the ridge and scrambled on their stomachs to look over into the next shallow valley where the sheep loved to lounge about. From the Baileys' cabin they could often see their white forms frolicking in play or standing like statues as they grazed. Now the sheep were definitely on the move, making their way across impossibly narrow ledges, leaping five feet at a time, higher and higher, away from danger. Below them they could see two men hacking up an old ram, obviously intent on taking the head home as a trophy.

Bryn shivered. She didn't know if it was from the wind, omnipresent at this elevation, or from fear. "Do you know them?" she whispered.

"No," he said softly. She studied Eli out of the corner of her eye. His face was red and his jaw tensed. He was obviously enraged at the poachers, this invasion of his valley. There was something primal and all masculine in his demeanor that made Bryn's scalp tingle in anticipation. "You can't go out there," she said. "They're armed, Eli."

"Let's at least get a good description for the authorities; they look to me to be about in their midforties. Dark hair on both. By their duds, I'd guess they were Alaskans, not Outsiders. If one's an outfitter, he could lose everything."

Bryn nodded. What did she know? She had her own Eddie Bauer shirt and pants on today, purchased just before she came. "If they're from here, why poach? Why not wait until hunting season?"

"Maybe one's a hunter who wants a jump on the season and is willing to pay the right price. Or if they're both just poaching, they'll probably sell the head. The Chinese will pay a good price for the horns. They'll grind them up and sell the powder as an aphrodisiac. And they use the eyes as a supposed remedy for cancer. Or maybe they'll sell the whole thing, mounted, to a lodge somewhere. There're lots of ways to make money."

"Eli." She was staring straight ahead. One of the hunters had glanced their way, then abruptly stopped, as if he had spotted them.

Eli looked his way too. "Time to go, Bryn. Remember their

faces." Together they scrambled backward and rushed down the rocks below them. The sharp shale bit into Bryn's hands, and she winced as she was cut. If it hadn't been for her tough jeans, her legs would've been a mess too. They were nearing the bottom when a low voice yelled, "Hey! Stop!"

"Run, Bryn," Eli said. "We have to get to the trees. We'll hide there."

A shot rang out, and the rocks split five feet to Bryn's left. She froze, hands up.

"Keep moving," Eli demanded, taking her hand and yanking her forward. "That was just a warning. We won't get another."

She could hear the men running behind them, grunting and swearing. Slipping and sliding over the loose rocks as they had. The ground leveled out a bit, and Bryn welcomed the cool shade of the forest. They ducked low branches and dodged trees, sometimes side by side, holding hands, other times with Eli in front, breaking trail for her. He turned a sharp corner and rushed down a steep hillside. Behind her, Bryn could hear the men talking quietly. Eli disappeared in the foliage, and Bryn's heart leapt up to her throat.

She glanced around frantically. "Eli? Eli!" she called in a stage whisper. A strong hand grabbed her forearm and yanked her roughly to the ground. He covered her mouth with his other hand, preventing her from screaming, and pulled her deeper beneath the underbrush next to a decomposing log. "We can't outrun them," he whispered. "Hopefully, they'll think we went down this steep bank and give up on us."

They panted for air, trying to be quiet, hoping to gain control before their pursuers caught them. Five feet to their right, they heard branches breaking and the heavy breathing of the pursuing men.

They're right on top of us. Bryn pulled herself in a little more, as if she could shrink to the size of the log and disappear, and squeezed her eyes shut. Her ears pounded with her pulse, as if they could hear every last sound in the forest.

"Better a fine than a manslaughter charge," the taller of the two said to his companion.

"You're the idiot who cracked a shot at them. And Dall's fines are up to five hundred."

"It's my plane the feds would come after. I'd lose my license. Ah, they were just a couple of kids. Hikers. We scared them. By the time they get to a radio, we're outta here."

The other man kept panting, obviously thinking as he looked down the hillside. "By their tracks, it looks like they ran down this bank. We could check it out."

"And what are you going to do if you catch them?"

He didn't answer, obviously hadn't an answer. "Let's go," he finally said. They turned and made their way back through the forest. The cracking of branches and cones beneath their feet faded into the distance.

"I think they're gone," Eli whispered into her ear, his arms still around her. Bryn slumped in relief, realizing she had tensed up from skull to heel. Then she turned and gave him a long hug.

"That was scary," she whispered.

"I'm sorry, Bryn. I never should've taken you up there."

"Hey, it was me who pushed it. No apology needed." His face was a mere two inches from hers, and after the rush of adrenaline, the relief of escape, she felt a magnetic attraction to Eli. He was so handsome, and he had her in his arms. She tipped up her chin, inviting him to kiss her.

Desire rushed through his eyes, and he leaned forward, his breath hot on her face, as if he intended to answer that call. But with a rueful smile, he pulled away and rose, offering her a hand. "Come on. We better get back to the cabin to radio in a report on those guys."

Bryn tried to swallow, her mouth dry. She made herself smile, covering her disappointment. *What is it about this guy? He is so different! Why didn't he kiss me?* "Yeah. Better pick up Ben's nets too on the way," she said.

They slowly descended back to the river and divvied up the four fish for dinner. "I don't think they'll come this way again," he said, staring at her as if he wanted to say more. "Think they were from over the pass. Probably landed on a lake over there and hiked across, is my guess."

"Okay," she said, pushing a rock with her toe in an effort to find something to do with herself. "I had fun today, Eli. The fishing… Even our surveillance trip, up until they fired at us."

He grinned at her. "Me too. See you tomorrow?"

"I hope so. Let me know what the people in town say about the poachers."

"I will." He reached up then and tenderly ran two fingers down her jawbone, his eyes staring into hers. Abruptly he dropped his hand, turned, and walked away, heading to his side of the lake.

Nothing like a thousand yards of Alaskan water between us to cool things down, she thought, turning to head home. He obviously wanted to touch her, kiss her. What held him back? Where was the key to unlock the mystery of Eli Pierce?

When Eli took off in his plane a few days later, Bryn fought the loneliness as well as the admission that she was actually missing him. And when he was back at Summit, taking her up to the ridge to photograph the Dall's sheep, hiking, flying a couple times, Bryn knew that the spark she had felt the first time she saw him coming down from his cabin was growing into a billowing flame. The way he looked at her so tenderly, the way she felt when he was near, the way he tentatively reached for her hand—usually with the excuse to help her past a difficult area on a trail, but then he'd keep his grasp firm long past any real threat of slipping—it all left an imprint on her memory as clearly as a photo placed in a treasured album.

The thought of him made a warmth grow in her belly and spread up to her face. If he would only kiss her! Then she'd know that he felt more for her than simply friendship, respect, platonic love. Every guy she had dated had been eager to kiss her, trying to maneuver her into position at the first chance. But Eli…he'd had plenty of opportunities and each time had pulled away. What was his deal?

She dug her paddle into the water beside the canoe, on this day gliding to the north end to visit Benjamin White. Bryn, eager for Peter to give him another chance, had talked her father into going with her. Ben had brought home two black bear cubs the last time he was out on a job, and today Peter and Bryn would get to see them.

Ben came out onto his deck as the canoe crunched over the rounded pebbles of his beach. Often the waves blew from the south end of Summit Lake, ending on Ben's shore and working the rocks into gently rounded gravel, the kind people would put in the bottom of a fish tank in colors of a winter sky: gray and silver and black and white. Even now the waves lapped over the beach in a soothing wash and swoosh that reminded Bryn of the ocean on a mild day.

"Greetings, neighbors," Ben called, walking down to them. "Come to meet my new babies?"

"If we can," Bryn said. She stepped out of the canoe and accepted his warm, steadying hand.

"Sure, sure, come ahead."

Bryn turned to watch her father and Ben exchange awkward greetings. After shaking, Peter shoved his hands in his pockets and glanced over at Bryn with an I'm-doing-this-for-you look. Ben turned away first, to lead them up the stairs and inside the snug little house. It was a welcome treat to enter his home, which had gas for the stove and a generator for lighting and emergency heat. He kept it very neat and orderly. She knew that every three months Eli flew in a new propane tank for him from Talkeetna, removing the old one and taking it to town to refill. In the winter, he had an extra on hand in case Eli couldn't get into the high mountain valley. And today, like a counterattack against the gray afternoon, three lamps burned brightly.

The baby bears were in a pen in one corner. The coal-colored creatures were small and their coats thin. "Logging operation must've driven the mother away," Ben explained, picking one up. The cub wrapped his thick arms around Ben's, and nuzzled toward his chest as if wanting to nurse. "I'm feeding them round the clock."

"With bottles?" Peter asked, reaching to pet the thick fur.

"Yep."

"How're the two that you told us about before?"

"Macbeth is doing well. She's established her own territory. Hamlet is still a troublemaker, rummaging for food in the garbage. Birdfeeders are his favorite."

"What will happen to him?" Bryn asked.

"We're going to capture him next week and move him deeper into the wilderness. Hopefully so far that he won't find his way out. Want to hold her?"

"Yes." She accepted the tiny bear and stroked her black fur. "Ouch! Those claws are sharp!"

"Here," Ben said. "Let me get you her bottle. That'll keep her busy."

"What's her name?" Peter asked.

"Don't know yet. Livin' with them for a while before I christen them. Got to get to know their personalities. What can I get you two nonbear types? Coffee? Tea?"

They each accepted a cup of tea, and Ben went to the stove to pour steaming water—the pot was always on at his house—into mismatched mugs and added Lipton bags. "Tell me," he said from the kitchen. "What brings you Californians to Summit this year?"

"I think the question should be, 'What takes us away from Summit the other years,'" Peter said with a laugh. "But getting my wife up here has been a problem." His face sobered. Bryn could see that Ben's easy way was working its magic on her dad. "It seems I can't talk her up here, no matter how much I try," Peter continued.

"This country's not for everyone. And should only be for those who love her." He glanced at Bryn and then moved to scoop up the second bear cub. "This little girl isn't faring as well as her sister." The baby barely moved in his arms and only reluctantly accepted the bottle of formula. "Sometimes," he said, settling into a torn leather chair with the cub, "you can give a bear everything it could possibly need, but something still isn't right. Guess there's no real substitute for a mother, but a body can try." He looked up then, again at Bryn.

"Heard some hammers swinging down your way," he said, changing the subject.

"Yes," Peter said proudly. "Bryn and I are working on a small front porch. Someplace to escape the rain without having to be inside."

"I think we should cover it in mosquito netting," Bryn said, waving around her head at yet another bloodsucking insect. They were the worst thing about Alaska.

"That would be nice," Ben agreed. "I might consider that myself someday. Business good, Peter?"

"As always." Peter sighed and Bryn glanced at him. He was one of Orange County's top businessmen, working in banking, primarily acquiring smaller, local banks for the larger, national ones. "But sometimes I get so tired I think about chucking it all and coming here full time."

"What keeps you back?"

"A kid in college and a wife used to Newport."

"Dad, I thought you loved your work."

"Sometimes. More and more, no."

Bryn's eyebrows lifted in surprise. "I could get a job, Dad. You know I've offered—"

"No, no. Nell would never hear of it. I won't hear of it. It's enough of a job to keep up that grade-point. After you're done with premed, I'll let you foot the bill. That's what I'm waiting for. Then I'll look at my life again, reconsider my options. I can make it till then, honey. I've made it this far, haven't I?"

"Yeah. But I just never... Dad, I never knew you were miserable," she said softly.

He laughed shallowly. "Did I say I was miserable? Don't worry about me." He took a sip of tea and cast an embarrassed look toward Ben. "Please, honey, forget I said anything."

"There's something about Summit Lake that just makes a body think, isn't there?" Ben cut in, breaking the tension.

"I'll say." The cub had gulped down her bottle, and Bryn rose to put her down in the playpen.

"And what have you been thinking about, Bryn Bear?"

She glanced at her father, rolling her eyes at his use of her nickname in front of Ben. He knew she hated that. She supposed by his look of contrition, it had just slipped. "I don't know. Maybe taking another look at my life. It's good to just breathe the clean air up here," she said. "Have the chance to think at all."

A plane roared overhead, and Bryn jumped up to stare out the window and catch the Beaver's wings tipping in greeting. "Eli!" she said with glee. She glanced back and saw the men share a knowing look. But she didn't care. All she wanted was to be in that canoe, paddling down to Eli, finding out about his trip. She bit her lip, reminding herself that she had only another two weeks in Alaska. They would soon head home, to Newport, back to school. What would happen to their relationship then? How would she endure missing him then, when life resumed its frantic pace?

Bryn swallowed against a sudden lump in her throat. All at once, she understood her father's desire to run away to Alaska, to peace, to quiet.

She was becoming drawn to this place too—and more and more to Eli. She was falling in serious "like" with the man, she admitted. Eli's plane bounced atop the waves and then glided to a stop, turning halfway down, toward the Pierces' cabin. Bryn frowned. She was falling for Eli Pierce. Just what was she supposed to do with that?

Eli turned the plane toward his cabin, wanting to go directly to Bryn's. But it was time to call a halt to things, slow it down, make sure they both knew that what was happening between them was impossible. She would head home in two weeks and rip his heart out of his chest when she went. He had to put a stop to their relationship, keep it mellow, or he wouldn't survive. Even if she was to stay, Eli knew she wasn't right for him. She wasn't a Christian—he shouldn't have let it get so out of hand. And besides, she wanted to be a big-city doctor. He was a rough-and-tumble bush pilot. It could never work out.

But being back here, on the lake, with her just down the way was already pure torture. Everything in him wanted to rush to her, to pull her into his arms and run his fingers through that black-gold hair and kiss the lips that had been inviting him for days.

I shouldn't have come back. I should have stayed away. Lord, I can't do this. Why? Why give me a desire for a woman who doesn't know you? He thought he could feel God's distinct moving in his heart, in his desire for Bryn, his hopes for her faith, his efforts to model his own. But his baser needs were threatening. How could he keep a lid on the situation when everything about Bryn Bailey made him feel madly out of control?

Still inside the cockpit, he leaned his chest against the yoke and his head against the console, praying for strength and wisdom. His eyes were closed, so when his father knocked against the window, he jumped in surprise. Jedidiah opened the door. "Eli? Son, you okay?"

"Yeah, Dad. Just praying."

Jedidiah studied him for a moment. "Want to talk about it?"

"Yeah. That would be good."

"Come on out then. Sit a spell with me."

Eli climbed out of the cramped fuselage to the lopsided wooden dock. With the deep freeze every winter and the subsequent breakup each spring, keeping a dock in pristine condition was difficult. They had to pull it out of the water every fall, or they'd return in the spring to splinters after the ice chewed it up.

Jedidiah was pulling his boots off and gingerly setting his feet in the glacial water. "Ahh. It's a warm one today. The water feels good. Come and join me, Son."

Eli looked about them—it was maybe seventy-five degrees, indeed hot for the elevation—and then glanced down the lake. There were people—small in the distance—exiting Ben's cabin. Probably Bryn and Peter. He sat down beside Jedidiah and pulled off his own chukka boots and socks, then slipped his feet into the green blue water. He sucked in his breath as liquid cold met warm skin, then shivered.

"Must be Bryn Bailey that has your knickers in a wad."

Eli laughed under his breath. "That obvious, huh?"

"Haven't seen you this worked up since you met Chelsea Thompson."

Eli nodded with a smile. Chelsea Thompson. His sixteenth summer. The summer he thought Bryn thought she was too good to speak to him. Chelsea had been a close runner-up. A devout Christian, not to mention gorgeous… She had moved away just as they had declared their love. Just like what would happen with Bryn, if he were to tell her. "I don't know what to do, Dad. She lives in California. Likes it there. Plus, she's in for years of school, wanting to be a doctor and all. Wants to go to Harvard."

"Told you to watch yourself."

"I know it. I've watched myself fall for her like a trout for a hand-tied nymph."

Jedidiah laughed softly and clapped him on the back. "You could go with her. Outside. See some of this big, wide world. Find work as a pilot near her, see if it was leading anywhere."

The idea was alluring, and Eli was grateful to his father for allowing him the room, the freedom to explore the possibility. But he knew it wasn't right. "Can't do that."

"Because she's not a Christian?"

"Mostly, yes. I've gotta put a stop to it. Before it hurts her as much as it's gonna hurt me."

"Think she's not in as deep as you are?" They both looked down the lake to Bryn and her father, paddling south down the center of the lake, slowly getting larger the closer they came.

"Don't know. She's kind of closed-mouth about it. Another reason for me to be wary. She has something to work out. I don't know, maybe I'm wrong."

"Probably her parents. Mixed up a bit, I'd say. Bound to mix up their daughter."

"Peter Bailey is one of your closest friends. I've never heard you say something like that about him."

"He is a good friend. Haven't met many others that are as loyal. But those qualms you've had about Bryn are the same qualms I've had about her father. Man's been searching for a sense of place, a sense of who he really is and how he relates to the Father for years. I can't seem to ever crack that thick head of his enough to help straighten him out."

Eli nodded. It helped to be understood, to share some of his crazy feelings with his father. He was grateful that Jedidiah, and his mother, Meryl, were healthy and loving and devoted to each other as well as him. He wished someday he could find a woman who would love Jesus as he did. Without that deeper connection, there was something essential missing. If only he could find it with Bryn.

"Thanks, Dad," Eli said softly. The Baileys had turned their canoe toward home. Eli knew their voices carried over the water as easily as an osprey carrying a fish. "I needed to talk." It was clear to him; God wanted Eli to back away from Bryn, even though Eli, in his heart, wanted to move forward.

"Anytime, Son. I'll be praying for you. And Bryn."

Bryn knew something had changed in Eli. The way he rigidly held his head up rather than bending slightly forward when she talked to him, the way he crossed his arms or shoved his hands into his pockets—anything to avoid holding her hand again. He was drawing away, closing his heart to her. The idea made her feel oddly desperate, eager to recapture what had begun to unfold between them. What had put a stop to the dream, the hope for something dramatic and romantic and altogether desirable? The thing that promised to shake up her orderly world, that had already shaken it? He seemed relieved to depart for Talkeetna, mumbling his good-byes.

She suffered through Eli's three-day absence, wondering if it had all been a figment of her imagination, this budding romance, when he returned with the sudden appearance of a rainbow, showing up at her door with a sad smile and a bouquet of wildflowers. "Hey, Bryn. Wanted to know if you'd care to fly to Kenai with me tomorrow. See a little more of Alaska before you go."

Maybe he wasn't pulling away after all. Maybe he wanted to see more of her. With just a little more than a week left on Summit Lake, she was eager to spend any time she could with Eli, wanting to hang on to the thread of a promise with everything in her. Didn't people write letters, use the phone, keep up a romance from afar all the time? Wasn't it worth trying? She glanced back at her father, and he nodded once, his eyes just clearing the top of his book. "I'd love to. What time do you need to leave?"

"I'm going to meet with a few fishing operations down there, talk about how we might market ourselves together as a vacation package deal for tourists. Should get out of here, let's see, by six o'clock? I know that's early." He seemed to be relaxing the longer they talked.

"Six is fine. Want to stay for dinner?"

"Ah, no. I shouldn't. Dad's unloading the plane—we went home to see Mom—and he's planning a big return dinner."

"I guess I'll just see you tomorrow then."

"Okay. See you then." He turned to go. "Bryn, I..."

She waited, expectantly.

"Nothin'." He shook his head. "See you tomorrow."

"What time will you two return?" Peter asked loudly.

"Should be home in the twilight hours, sir. At least an hour ahead of nightfall."

"All right. Just wanted to know when to send out the search parties."

Eli smiled at Peter's pale joke, glanced at Bryn again meaningfully, and then turned to go. She watched him walk down to the beach to his canoe, feeling as if she were severing a physical thread between them. She shut the door and leaned her head against it, still seeing Eli's face, wanting to memorize him.

"You've got the bug, don't you, Bryn Bear?"

"Yeah, Dad. I think I do." She didn't turn from her position.

"He's a good kid."

"And he lives in Alaska."

"Well," he said, turning a page, "everyone needs a summer romance now and then. Maybe now you'll see why I love this place so much since Eli does too."

If only it were just a fling. An idle flirtation. Light and fun. But what was moving in her heart was like a tidal wave over a lagoon.

Eli flew low in the morning light, so Bryn could clearly see the small herds of caribou, the occasional Dall's sheep on the mountainsides, even a grizzly that rose up as if to wave at them as they passed over. Bryn shivered. "Hate to meet up with her on a hike."

"Most are as anxious to avoid you as you are them. Kind of a magical moment when you see each other, stare each other down, and then the bear rambles off."

"That kind of magic I'd like to avoid."

Much of the land looked lumpy with the heavy vegetation of the tundra that was beginning to change color. They passed over rounded, ancient mountains and younger, more jagged peaks, and a snowline that was getting lower with each passing storm. Autumn arrived early in Alaska.

"Unreal," she said to herself, awed by the beauty.

"Or the most real thing you've ever seen?"

She didn't answer, hadn't an answer.

Soon they sailed past groves of birch beginning to turn a pale yellow, over braided Atlantic blue rivers, beyond sublime ponds where the sound of their plane's engine raised hundreds of birds—

pintails and red-breasted mergansers and sandhill cranes—to flight, and by thick forests that seemed impenetrable. At times the mountain peaks stood clear and bright in the early light of day. Other times they were clouded in, dark and brooding and ominous.

"You hope to build a business with these people you're visiting?" she asked, breaking the silence at last.

"Yep. K2's got Talkeetna pretty well hemmed up," he said, referring to the biggest floatplane operation in town. "Need to get some fresh blood. If I don't, my flying might just be a hobby. I'll have to find some other way to make a living."

"I hope it goes well," she said, tentatively taking his hand. It was warm, her own fingers frosty in the cool plane.

"Me too," he said, smiling briefly at her. Then he moved his hand away, back to the wheel.

By the time they reached the Kenai Fjords, set down, and tied up, it was time for Eli to get to his first meeting. "I'll find us some lunch and a rental boat for this afternoon," she volunteered.

"All right," he said with a little surprise in his eyes. "There's a place just down the street," he said, nodding past her. "I'll meet you there in a couple of hours, okay? I should be done with all my meetings by then."

"Sounds good."

"Bryn…you'll be okay? Hanging out by yourself?"

She furrowed her brow in playful agitation. "I'm a big girl, Eli Pierce. You go do your business, and I'll be fine."

"All right. The rental shop. Two hours."

"The rental shop. Two hours. See you then." They paused, close together, and once again Bryn wondered if he would kiss her, just a quick one. But he was already turning away, striding down the street.

He was a picture, all natural good looks and masculinity amid this otherworldly setting. Sighing, she turned and began walking.

The Kenai Peninsula was remarkably different from the rest of Alaska. Almost entirely supported by fishing, the town was full of houses that were tall and thin and close together, reminding Bryn a little of the East Coast. In the protected coves, porches often extended out over the water on stilts, and the homes were painted bright red or silver blue or yellow in gay contrast to the woods and rocks about them.

Bryn spent an hour ducking into a few tourist shops with clerks who had a slightly desperate look to their faces, as if they knew there were too few days left of the summer and still too few dollars in the cash drawer to make it through the winter. The entire town seemed a bit dilapidated and depressed, showing the wear and tear of a diminishing economy and overfished waters. Still, Bryn found it charming and enchanting to be walking among people again after three weeks in relative isolation, even if she felt more the cheechako here than in Talkeetna. Many of Russian descent, fishing folk were a different breed—toughened by the salt spray on their faces, undaunted by the freak storms that could rob them of their boats, their livelihood.

She stopped in a store and purchased smoked salmon and halibut, crusty French bread, cream cheese, and a jug of homemade apple juice, probably imported from someplace like Oregon. She also bought a *USA Today* dated two days ago and then moved on to the rental shop. In short order, she had secured a sturdy rowboat with an even sturdier motor, the proprietor assured her. Then she settled onto a park bench at a lovely overlook, opened her paper, and waited for Eli Pierce to return.

When Eli found her sitting across from the rental shop, he believed his heart actually hurt to look at her. Maybe it had been a mistake to invite her on this trip. He'd planned to use the time to break the news to her that "they" could never be. But his heart ached at the thought.

Dressed in a lavender cotton turtleneck and black leather jacket, she looked smooth and sophisticated. Her hair was loose and shimmering in the slight breeze as she tried to read her ruffling paper. She was so beautiful. So smart. Probably used to a paper delivered on the day it was dated. She could never be happy in Alaska. And moreover, he didn't belong with her if she didn't share his love for the Lord and his love of the land. She was highly educated, going much farther than his own associate's degree. A doctor. *A doctor.* What right did he think he had to even consider being more than a friend to her?

They were a mismatch, from sock to hat. From the inside out. That was what he told himself anyway. Tried to tell himself to get a grip. To move forward with his plan to tell her good-bye. Not just for the summer, but forever.

She glanced up, looking along the fjord beach line, and finally to the street and Eli. He smiled, and she smiled back, her eyes mysterious and beckoning. He walked forward, like a sailor careening toward a dangerous shoal, yet unable to do anything else.

"How did it go?" she asked, folding up her paper and standing beside him. Her eyes were bright and happy, and an hour in the seaside sun had kissed her cheeks with pink.

"It went well," he said, stuffing his hands into his jean pockets. "All three of them were interested. We'll talk about it more next month and do some serious planning—maybe even a little joint advertising come spring."

"That's great news!" she exclaimed, throwing her arms around him in an exuberant hug. "I'm so happy for you!" She started to pull away, but he succumbed then to the relentless desire to hold her. He pulled her to him tightly, moving to cradle her head against the nook beneath his chin, feeling the heavy, long strands of silky hair beneath his hand.

"Oh, Bryn," he said, almost in a moan. "Oh, Bryn."

She looked up at him then, her eyes the color of a fall leaf-fire's smoke, the invitation to kiss her present again. Her lips parted, slightly, beckoning him. He closed his eyes against her beauty, against the vision of her, and tipped his head back a little, trying to pull away, knowing he must.

"Kiss me, Eli," she whispered. "Kiss me."

He shook his head, a tiny motion at first, then stronger, gaining momentum until he could release her entirely. He sighed heavily and dared to look at her. "I can't."

"Why not?" she asked, her look incredulous. "You clearly want to. I want you to. Why not?"

"Because." He licked his lips and swallowed hard. "Because a kiss means more to me now than when I was sixteen. Because a kiss is a seal, a declaration of love. A proclamation of it. It means something to me, Bryn."

"It means something to me, too," she said, wrapping her arms around him again.

"No. No, Bryn," he said, pulling her away from him. "I can't. I can't do this. You and I are not right. You belong someplace else. I belong nowhere but here." He shook his head sadly, nearing tears.

"I brought you here to see more of Alaska and to say good-bye. Not to get things rolling again."

"Oh," she said, her face showing the blows of his words. "I had thought... I had hoped... Oh." She glanced up at him, her eyes brimming with tears.

He closed his eyes to the gut-punch of inflicting pain on her. Of bringing her anything but joy and light and peace. "I'm sorry, Bryn. I wish it were different. I wish we were older, that we had a chance. But right now, we're too different and heading in opposite directions. Don't you see? It's hopeless."

"Hopeless," she mumbled back, nodding a little. But her eyes— those dark, clear eyes that he had begun to read so well—her eyes were still full of hope. Hope that he would change his mind, hope that he was mistaken, hope that there was a way for them.

But there wasn't.

Part 2

Higher Road, 1996

CHAPTER FOUR

*B*ryn Bailey left for Alaska again four years, ten months after she departed swearing she would never return. This time she was alone. She wasn't sure what she was going for, what she wanted from her visit; she only knew she was supposed to come. That it was *right* to come.

She considered that it might be a pathetic attempt to feel closer to her father—conspicuously absent for her fifth visit to the lake— but then put the thought out of her mind. It's what her therapist would say.

"You sure you'll be all right up there alone, Bryn Bear?" Grampa Bruce asked her as they walked toward the gate in the airport terminal in Boston. She took a step away at his use of her father's nickname for her. She studied him, but he walked along as if he had said nothing unusual at all. He was aging quickly. Since when had his shoulders slumped so severely? And his step had lost its spring and become more of a shuffle. She hadn't spent nearly enough time with him since she'd come to Massachusetts, she realized with regret.

She blew out a quick breath and ran a tender hand over her grandfather's shoulders. "I'll be fine, Grampa. Will you?" Thinking of him alone, with no other family nearby, she worried about him. Bryn's grandmother had passed away over a decade earlier. She knew he still missed her, and yet after her death he had charged forward, embracing his life and making the most of it. He was the darling of his neighborhood, making friends with the old and the young alike.

"Ah, I'm always fine. You'll rest there, then? In Alaska? You've gotten no sleep at Harvard. Your grandmother worries after you." There it was again, evidence that his mind was slipping away.

"I'll get rest there." She bent and kissed him on his leathery cheek, all wrinkles and sagging skin. "It's so quiet on Summit, I won't be able to sleep the first night. Then I'll sleep like the dead."

"I'd still feel better about it if your father was going. You've never been there alone."

"I'll be fine, Grampa. Dad has his new life. I'm going to go and discover what I'm supposed to do with mine."

Grampa Bruce placed one hand on top of his cane and then the other hand on top of that. "You going there alone to punish him, child?" His brow furrowed.

"No. I'm going there for me. I can't explain it. I just know I'm supposed to be there. I guess it's Dad's fault. He was the one who insisted I go every five years. Now I can't seem to get it out of my head."

"Or your heart. Maybe it's God who is calling you there, Bryn. Have you thought of that?"

"No," she answered simply. Grampa Bruce always required total honesty. He could see through people as clearly as the airport x-ray machines had examined her bags. "I think I just know that it is the one place I can go where I can find some sort of peace."

"Yes, yes," he said, his brown eyes studying her. The lids sagged at the corners, showing red, tender inner flesh. His irises were a bit cloudy, but his intent was clear. "Peace," he nodded. "See if you can find the Source of peace."

Bryn gave him a wise look. "There you go, Grampa Bruce. Always trying to evangelize me."

"Just be open. Promise me that."

"I will, Grampa." She bent and kissed him again and, with a last farewell smile, turned and handed her ticket to the gate agent. She took a long, deep breath and entered the Jetway. Medical school had chewed her up and spit her out. She simply could not face anything else without a break, a total break. And Summit Lake was about as far from Harvard as she could get.

As she rode in the taxicab up the highway from Anchorage, through the awe-inspiring Matanuska Valley—wide and flat for miles and banked by towering green blue snowcapped mountains—into the heavily forested hills of the Susitna, with gasp-worthy peaks, she took a long, deep breath. She found more reassurance and peace in this place than she ever could in Newport Beach. Particularly when her mother was in the throes of despair and looking for a constant sounding board.

The cabby turned off Highway 3 at an abandoned real estate office and headed toward Talkeetna. To Bryn's left was a magnificent, perfectly still lake—a picture postcard—lined with pointy black spruce, and in the distance, the Alaskan Range made its appearance, suddenly bigger and closer. Not much farther Bryn passed a small lake that opened up toward the Talkeetna Mountains with a lovely hand-carved sign advertising a floatplane service run by…

"Wait!" she cried, leaning forward in her seat. "Please. Go back."

The driver silently pulled over and made a U-turn. "That float-plane service?" he inquired over his shoulder.

"Yes." Bryn peeked out one window and then the other, trying to read the sign even as they were moving. ALASKA BUSH: FLOATPLANE SERVICE, the sign read. ELI PIERCE, PROPRIETOR.

Eli.

Her mind raced back five years to that day outside Seward, when Eli told her he couldn't, wouldn't, be involved with her. Didn't want her. Didn't need her. What at one time had been a bone-crunching pain was now merely a twinge. He had been right, of course. It was the wrong time; there was no way they could have been together. They had flirted, had a summer fling. He was simply being sensible.

Eli Pierce, proprietor. He'd done it. Built his de Havilland into a full-fledged business. She needed a ride to Summit. Who better than her old neighbor? Maybe he'd cut her a deal. She had the cabby pull into the parking lot along the highway and wait while she walked to the small log cabin she assumed was the office. Below her, on a tiny lake, was the Beaver, with its perfectly proportioned pontoons, thick high-lift wings, big flaps, and powerful engine. She remembered Eli telling her it was the ideal plane for getting into and out of small bays and short lakes at the higher elevations, especially with people or cargo to haul.

She raised her hand to knock on the door, hesitated, then rapped four times. There was no answer. Bryn checked her watch—eleven-thirty—and sighed. She'd taken the red-eye to get here and was eager to finish her travels to Summit. Where could he be? This wasn't the way to run an efficient operation—*Sunday.*

It was Sunday. And Eli Pierce, the most moral man on the planet, was most certainly at church. She smiled and headed back to the taxicab, picking up a brochure from an outdoor display, reading in a whisper as she walked. "Unguided Hunts—Remote Lake and

River Fishing—Rainbow Trout, Four Species of Salmon & Northern Pike—River Floating—Backpacking (Drop Off & Pick Up)—Flight Seeing Glacier Tours and Flights Around Mount McKinley in Denali National Park—Wildlife Tours (4 Years Experience)."

Bryn rode the rest of the way to town and had the driver canvass the few church parking lots, ending up at the Christian Center. She was sure she saw Jedidiah's truck out front and supposed the Pierces were inside. "You can drop me off here," she told the cab driver.

"Sign says it started an hour ago."

"It's fine. I have a friend inside. He can take me where I want to go."

She thought about going into the church, but told herself that the service was probably just ending, that she would disrupt things. But most of all she was afraid of feeling...weird. She hadn't been inside a church since she was a kid with her grandparents.

So Bryn sat down on the front bumper and perched there, waiting for Eli to emerge. She could hear singing, and it sounded so sweet and fervent, she almost wished she were inside to better listen. She fidgeted, crossed her legs, uncrossed them, leaned her elbows on her thighs, chin in hand, then crossed her arms and leaned back. She turned slightly sideways, so he'd see her best side first.

What are you doing, Bryn? She blew air out from between her lips, angered at herself for posturing—her preparation for flirtation, attraction. Eli Pierce was likely to be involved with someone else by now. Or married. Whatever there had been between them was over. And she did not want to feel the pain she had felt five years ago, never wanted to feel such agony again. She needed a pilot and a plane to get to Summit Lake. That was it. Nothing more. But the idea of seeing him again had her heart pounding, and she couldn't resist running a hand over her hair as the church doors opened and people began pouring out.

When Eli emerged, smiling and speaking animatedly with an attractive young woman with dark blond hair, her racing heart seemed to skip a beat, then pounded forcefully, robbing her of air. She fought off the desire to bring hand to chest, not wanting to appear as taken as she was. Maybe he was seeing the blonde, maybe he was in love with her, maybe he wasn't available even to take Bryn to Summit today. Maybe they had plans for brunch or something.

He spotted her then and came to a full stop. The woman next to him looked from Eli to where he was gazing, then back again, her smile quickly fading. Eli began walking again, shaking his head and grinning.

"I knew I'd find you here," Bryn said softly, smiling.

"Didn't know I'd find you here. I mean, I knew it was your summer but…"

She sat there, staring at him, wondering if he could read her mind. If he knew how good it was to see him, that it brought her a combination of pure, manic joy and agonizing pain all at once.

He opened his arms to her then, and she immediately slipped off the bumper and embraced him, inhaling his scent of cinnamon and pine and a tinge of airplane fuel. Eli held her for a long, tender hug, then pulled away. "Uh, Sara, I'd like you to meet an old friend, Bryn Bailey. Bryn, this is Sara Cussler. She's a river guide, new to Talkeetna this summer."

Bryn tore her attention away from Eli to the pretty woman at his side, tall and slender. She had hair the color of caribou, eyes the color of the Chulitna River, and a healthy glow that reminded Bryn of a warm sunset. Outdoorsy and attractive and no doubt a Christian—

and checking out Bryn as clearly as Bryn was checking her out. Her lips curved into a welcoming smile, but her blue eyes were suspicious, had reason to be suspicious. Because as much as Bryn had prepared herself for this moment, for seeing Eli again and guarding her heart, she found her skin tingling where he had touched her, as if he had left hot handprints on bare flesh.

"I need a ride to Summit," she said to Eli, taking a half-step away, wanting it to be clear to Sara that that was all she wanted from him, that she did not intend to interfere. "Saw a nice lookin' operation on Fish Lake."

"That would be mine," he said, grinning and nodding. "Happen to be taking Sara to Summit today. I could give you a lift."

Bryn swallowed her disappointment that Sara was coming too, calling her heart foolish for hoping for anything else. She licked her lips and forced a smile. "Great. What time are you guys leaving?"

Eli looked at Sara for the first time since laying eyes on Bryn. "What time, Sara? In an hour or so?"

"Sure. After we pick up cinnamon rolls. Want one, Bryn?" Her tone was friendly, but her eyes conveyed anything but warmth.

"That'd be perfect. I need to grab some groceries too. Is it okay that I'm intruding?"

"No problem." Eli came around to open the truck door for them, gesturing for Sara to enter first. As she ducked inside, Eli's eyes found Bryn. "It's...it's good to see you," he said lowly.

"It's good to see you, too, Eli. We'll have to catch up sometime."

"I'd like that," he said, then brushed past her toward the driver's side of the cab.

Bryn didn't dare look over at Sara, certain she would appear as jealous as Bryn herself felt about her. *Stupid, Bailey,* she told herself.

You're being completely stupid. Back off. You're here for you this summer, not to reclaim Eli. And you have no right to him anyway. Suddenly all she wanted was the safety of the taxicab, the reminder that she was a cheechako, and the subdued smell of old cigarettes—anything to make her forget the spicy, outdoorsy aroma of Eli Pierce.

"So tell me about Bryn Bailey," Sara invited, her tone carefully neutral. They had dropped Bryn off at the mercantile for supplies.

Eli smiled over at Sara and took her hand with his right. They had been friends from the start this summer, and dating for a couple of weeks. "She's an old family friend. Her dad and my dad bought places on Summit the same summer. They met in Germany. It's a long story."

"I have time." She crossed her arms, and Eli could feel her eyes on him. A slight flush rose up his neck.

"Bryn has come to Alaska every five years since we were kids. Last time I saw her was in 1991. Her dad practically dragged her up here. I'm surprised she came alone. I wonder where…"

"And?" Sara asked impatiently, pulling him back to the point of their conversation.

"And…we were friends, that's all. Did some hiking, some canoeing, some flying together." He pulled the truck over, across the street from the bakery, and looked at Sara. "I'll be honest with you, Sara. I wanted to have something more with her; she wanted more with me. But we were just too different. Not to mention that she lived in California and I lived in Alaska. Now she's in Boston. And she's not a believer."

"But if she had been?"

"If she had, something more probably would have happened between us. But there was still the major obstacle of distance."

Sara nodded, her eyes searching the park before them. They were on the edge of town, near the river. She nodded again, as if mulling over his words, but then simply smiled. "I'll go talk to the guys, see if there's someone who wants to take my day trip tomorrow so we can spend more time together at the lake. Meet you back here?"

"Sure. I'll go get the rolls." He watched her turn to let herself out the door, and wanting to reassure her, he reached for her once more. "Sara, there's nothing between Bryn and me. We're old friends. That's all."

"Uh-huh. I'm not staking a claim, just curious. We're just *friends* too, right?"

"How long you here for?" Eli tossed over his shoulder to Bryn. He had seated Sara beside him in the cockpit, wanting to make her feel like the priority. After all, he had invited her out to the lake to be with him.

"Couple of months," she called out. Eli caught Sara's meaningful glance as he focused on the instrument panel again. It was clouding up quickly, and Denali was already behind a thick curtain of gray. He'd follow up with Bryn later. Right now he had to concentrate on getting to Summit safely and not setting off any more alarm bells for Sara. Sara was a fine woman and a fast friend, just his type; he didn't want to mess up with her. They'd just started to really connect. There was the potential of something sweet between them... Something like what he had once with Chelsea Thompson. Something big. *Yeah, something big.*

He nodded at Joe, another pilot, who gave the prop a pull and pushed the plane out to the water. Bryn had two huge duffels with her this time and several bags of groceries. Eli ran through their combined weight one more time and, satisfied that they weren't overloaded, cruised out to the end of the lake, radioed Talkeetna's air traffic control, and, when cleared, took off.

The trip to Summit took about ninety minutes, and much of it was spent listening to the roar of the engine and watching the fast-moving, low-lying clouds move in on the Susitna Valley. "You okay?" he asked Sara.

She nodded quickly, her wide eyes never leaving the front windshield. "Fine. How long till we reach the lake?"

"Another ten, fifteen minutes."

"That cloud bank," she said, motioning toward the wall of silver before them, directly over the mountain pass. "We're going through it?"

"Yes. We'll be fine. I've flown through stuff like that plenty of times."

She nodded again, a bit too eager to agree. He glanced back at Bryn, who stared wordlessly out at the tundra beneath them. She was more beautiful than ever; the five years had given her the gift of more pronounced curves and a mature look that enhanced everything right about her. But there was a touch of mournful sorrow in her eyes, and the crow's-feet at the corners seemed deeper, the shadows beneath, darker. She was plagued by something unhappy. He cleared his throat and stared ahead again.

Ben always said Alaska was filled with people who were running either away from something or toward something. If Eli were a betting man, he would wager she was running away. But from what? Where was her father? Coming in soon? His questions would have to wait until he could return to Summit, without Sara.

They dropped Bryn off at her cabin while the heavens softly rained, reminding her of flour coming from her grandmother's sifter.

"You going to be okay, Bryn?" Eli asked after bringing her duffel bags up to the cabin. He looked troubled, as if he wanted to say more but knew he had to get back to the plane and Sara.

"Oh yeah. You hop in; I'll push the plane out."

"Okay. Let me know if you need anything, all right? We'll be here until tomorrow evening. I'm coming back next week with supplies for Ben. He's home. Radio me in town if you need something."

"All right," Bryn said, thinking about him and Sara alone in that snug little cabin across the way. *"Here until tomorrow evening." Surely Eli and Sara wouldn't...* She resolutely pulled the hood of her parka up, and they ran back to the plane. She smiled as Eli's face reappeared in the cockpit window and she called, "Thanks for the lift! See you around!" It was none of her business what Eli Pierce did or didn't do these days. Never mind that she couldn't even get the man to kiss her five years ago. There had been plenty of others who had been willing in the interim. Unfortunately, none of them seemed worth her while. Not like Eli.

She pushed them off again, and Eli ran up the engine and motored across the perfectly still lake, marred only by the tiny raindrops and the wake behind the plane. Within minutes, they had landed on the other side.

Suddenly Bryn felt bone-cold and very alone. Sighing, she made it up the beach and under the protection of the porch roof she and her father had built. Bryn ran her hands up the nearest pole, her eyes scanning the length and breadth of their work. It was holding up well. "Oh, Dad," she whispered. It made her ache inside to recognize how lonely she was, how different Summit was without him.

She knew she had come here to feel closer to him, to remember when he was still trying to reach out to her. But she had also come here for her. To look forward, to find rest and rejuvenation and direction. It was a challenge to spend two months on Summit alone. And a good one. From the looks of things, Eli wouldn't be around much, with Sara in the picture and tourist season soon coming to its zenith. It was up to her. To figure out where she had been, where she was now, and where she was going.

Bryn fished for the old key in her pocket, slid it in the lock, and then pushed on the lever. The door creaked open. Even her father hadn't been back since they had left, pestered by her mother, plagued by an intense work load, then caught up in his new...

She hauled one heavy duffel into the sitting room and then the other and her groceries. The fire was laid in the wood stove, just as they left it—"I like to know it's here, ready for me to come and light it," her father had said upon their departure—and thankfully, with a quick strike of the match, the dry tinder immediately blazed to life. She left the cabin to gather more wood, pulled from beneath the higher, wetter logs. She dumped her armload beside the stove and set about unpacking.

Within a week Bryn had settled into the cadence of her days, beginning with stirring the coals in the stove, adding wood, uncovering the jar of sourdough starter, and dumping two-thirds of it in a bowl. She put three heaping teaspoons of flour back into the jar, added some lukewarm water, stirred, and capped it. If she did it every time, Ben had told her, she could have sourdough forever.

Bryn wasn't wild about the taste, but it allowed her to have fresh bread and pancakes and biscuits on a daily basis, and made her feel somehow less the cheechako. She had been given her starter by Ben, who had been given it by another, who had been given it by another. Who knew how far back the origins of it were? She smiled, thinking of the miners and trappers who had first settled this land, bringing their white man's concoction with them. After a sourdough summer, maybe she wouldn't be considered an Outsider at all.

Conscious that a week had passed since Eli and Sara had roared down the lake, taking off just as the mild summer storm lifted, Bryn jumped at every unusual sound. She was waiting for his return, she acknowledged to herself. Hoping for his return, like a stupid school-girl with a crush. *Get a grip, Bailey,* she told herself. This summer was about her, not about rekindling old flames. *I need a project,* she decided, sliding biscuits in the oven. After three overly crispy, overly blackened attempts, she had finally mastered the needed heat of the fire to perfect her baking. In twenty minutes, she'd have them out to accompany her maple bacon, sizzling in a pan, and fried eggs. She ignored the cholesterol count. *When in Rome...*

Project. What could she do? She looked around the cabin. She'd already added a couple of rough-hewn shelves. Made them herself by carefully following the instructions in a pioneer-era guide she'd dis-covered in the back room. She picked up the book and thumbed through it. *A fireplace.* In the book there was a river-rock fireplace and step-by-step instructions on how to construct it. Wouldn't her father love a fireplace? Love knowing that there was not only a wood stove for heat but also a real fireplace, with a hearth and chimney and a crackling fire, ready to be enjoyed? She supposed there was a part of her that still wanted to please her dad, connect with him, however angry she might be. And yet she could do this for herself, too. To expand her mind, keep her hands busy.

She looked to the end of the cabin. There was no window to contend with—the fireplace would add charm to the structure. It wouldn't have to be huge. Bryn smiled. It was the perfect job. There was only so much reading and fishing she could do. The hard, manual aspect of it would be cathartic. *That's it.* After breakfast she would begin to gather rock, a process that she guessed would take at least a week. Later she'd paddle down to Ben's to ask his advice and input. Maybe he'd even help get her started or pitch in during the times she would undoubtedly need another set of hands. Eli certainly appeared unavailable. She quickly turned her thoughts toward breakfast.

She flipped the bacon and placed it on her plate, then added the eggs. Her dinner the night before had been a cup of beef bouillon and cold biscuits, so breakfast smelled heavenly. She sat down with her meal, ate quickly, and then geared up for the task at hand, gathering a canteen of water, some smoked sockeye salmon—Squaw candy, the natives called it—and the last biscuit in the pan, as well as her father's fly-fishing gear. Bryn laced up her hiking boots and set off for the south end of the lake, toward the trout spawning area where Eli had fished with her, and then to an ancient, dried-up riverbed full of stones that were perfect for fireplace building.

It was perhaps a half-mile away, and the weather was great for hiking. The sun was out and warmed her skin with the hint of true summer in Alaska, though it probably only hovered around sixty degrees. She wore thick twill chinos to protect her legs from the underbrush and mosquitoes and an old lavender turtleneck sweater that had always reminded her of her last summer in Alaska. While at the river, she planned to fish. If they weren't biting, she would scout for a few perfect rocks to begin her collection.

She had just settled in to casting, feeling the rhythm of the line, when she heard the metallic whir of a prop plane in the distance. Within sixty seconds, the Beaver cleared Gevanni Pass and came into view, flying low over the length of Summit Lake. It was Eli. She waved as he passed by, and he tipped his wings, then swooped up and around to prepare for landing. She resisted watching the whole process, concentrating on her casting, which was suffering dreadfully from the distraction.

Bryn selected a silvering spruce carcass, and the shadow it cast into the silver blue waters, as a likely hiding place for a rainbow trout, and placed her fly directly over it. She had a bite within seconds. The fish ran, trying to take the line beneath the safety of the old tree, but Bryn pulled the rod up and walked with it, trying to set the hook and bring it out at the same time. In another minute the fourteen-inch fish was flapping and flipping over on the hot, dry stones, his mouth opening and closing as if hoping he could get one more ounce of the ice-cold water. "Sorry, buddy," she mused, crouching and pulling the hook out. "You're going to be dinner."

At least she hadn't forgotten everything her father and Eli had taught her about fly-fishing, regardless of the fact that it had been five years since she held a rod in her hands. *Still got it, Bailey,* she smugly told herself. If she caught any more, maybe she could invite Eli over for dinner. Or build a smoker and dry the meat for another day. Or maybe borrow Ben's old nets and try that method again. She grinned. She felt alive and vital again, as if every pore on her skin was open wider, every nerve a bit more aware, her eyes bigger, her focus sharper.

She put more oil on the fly and worked the area for another twenty minutes, but the fish she had caught appeared to be the only one under the old tree. Bryn walked upstream, fishing all the while, but still there was nothing. After twenty minutes, she climbed over a logjam and stopped suddenly. Nerves she thought were awake turned into an electrical system carrying live voltage.

Straight ahead was a mother grizzly. Swallowing slowly, as if the bear could hear even that, Bryn froze. Her eyes moved to the right, where a cub played in the shallows of the river with a flopping, not-quite-dead trout. "Only three kinds of bear will attack," Eli had said once, "a sow with a cub, a bear with a kill, or one with a bad attitude." She was considering where to go, what to do, when Eli's low voice sounded behind her. "Stay absolutely still. Don't look back. Keep your eyes at her feet."

But his arrival alerted the mother bear. She stood up on her hind legs, a frightening eight feet tall. She raised her mammoth head, sniffed the air once, and then without further warning charged.

She came fast, impossibly fast, and Bryn's first instinct was to turn and flee. Only Eli's command to stay right where she was kept her feet frozen in place. "Eli," she cried under her breath, watching the bear rush them as if she was in a movie theater and none of this was real. But it was real.

"Duck and cover your head and neck," he said quickly. "If she attacks you, play dead. Remember, play dead. Do not move."

"*Eli,*" she cried again, as if he could stop the oncoming bear. When the grizzly was twenty feet away, Bryn curved into a ball and covered her head and neck, feeling as if she were in third grade, doing an earthquake drill at school. *If only I had a desk to protect me,* she thought, her mind spinning wildly. They were going to die, die there together on an old riverbed of Summit Lake. *Duck and cover. Play dead. Stay still.*

But Eli was not still. He had taken off over the rounded rocks toward the far bank. Shouting and waving his hands to draw the sow's attention and make her chase him. Protecting Bryn. It worked. The bear quickly changed direction and charged after Eli. The confused cub cowered for a moment by the logjam and then tentatively lumbered after his mother.

It was quickly obvious that Eli could not outrun the bear. In horror Bryn watched as the grizzly took him down with a swift rake of her huge paw. Eli plunged to the grassy bank, disappearing behind her massive brown form.

"Eli!" Bryn screamed, starting to run toward them and then hesitating. What could she do? *"Eli!"* she screamed again.

CHAPTER FIVE

*T*he bear moved to his side, and Eli turned and hit her full in the face with pepper spray. The bear backed off, mewling like a newborn cub and rubbing her eyes with a furry brown arm. Eli rose and sprayed her in the face again, yelling wildly, and the combination of disorientation, confusion, and lack of sight made the sow turn and run, her fat cub close behind.

Eli sank to the ground, his face a grimacing mask of pain. It was then that Bryn saw him cradling his ankle and the bright red trail of blood seeping down his jeans. "Eli!" she yelled. "I'm coming!"

When she reached him, she pulled up his pant leg to expose his leg. His ankle was already swelling, probably sprained, and there were multiple, deep lacerations in the flesh where the bear had raked her claws across him. "We have to get you to the cabin. I can treat you there."

Eli only nodded as he accepted her help up, and they began making their way back to his canoe.

"That was an incredibly brave, incredibly stupid thing to do," she said, huffing with exertion. Eli's arm was around her shoulders, and he winced with each step. She could almost feel the pain herself each time he dragged his leg across the stones.

"Told you I was a bear magnet. Lucky for me I had a doc to save," he said through clenched teeth. They were close to Eli's canoe, but he was losing a lot of blood and was growing weaker. "Think I'll have to call you that, after you stitch me up."

Bryn's mind was not on nicknames. "What do you weigh, two, two-twenty?" she pretended to complain.

"Two-twelve," he answered softly.

She looked up at him, studying his eyes, the sickly pallor of his skin, the sheen of sweat that coated it. "Eli? Gonna make it?"

"Going to…make it," he said with determination. He stood up a little straighter as if to take weight off her shoulders, stepped forward, dragging his left leg behind…and immediately fainted. He was too heavy for Bryn to catch, and she stumbled forward when he fell. Worse yet, his head hit a rock on the way down. She shuddered as she heard bone meet granite.

"Eli!" Quickly she turned him over and grimaced as blood rolled down his face and into his eye. Wanting to cry, she looked up at the sky and yelled, "What do you want from me? A little help! I need a little help!" Her eyes ran from Eli's canoe, just twenty feet away, down the lake to the north end and Ben's cabin. He was out in his canoe, already paddling hard toward them, apparently having heard her cries. "Benjamin!" she screamed at the top of her lungs. "*Ben!* Hurry! I need help!"

She turned back toward Eli, opening first his left eyelid and then the other. She fought to remember all her medical training. The pupils looked good. It was dangerous if one was larger than the other. But Eli's were both normal.

"Bear attack," she said through her tears, when Ben finally reached her side. "We were trying to get back to his canoe when he passed out."

"Easy, easy," he said to her tenderly, looking Eli over for himself.

"It's not too bad. I'd bet that wound at the head is mostly superficial."

"I don't know, Ben. He's still out. I was hoping he'd rouse by now."

"All right. You're the doctor. What do we do next?"

Bryn took a deep breath and surveyed Eli as if he were a nameless patient in the teaching hospital. She assumed he was suffering from a concussion. Her next concern was the blood he was losing down his leg. "If we can get him to my cabin, I can stitch him up."

"Done," he agreed.

Together they moved Eli in a woolen blanket that Ben had in his canoe to Eli's wider, more stable vessel. Working quickly, she wound an extra T-shirt around his leg and tied it as tightly as possible to help stanch the flow of blood. Then they climbed in and started paddling for Bryn's cabin, the closest shelter. She had medical supplies there—a full kit of bandages and medicines. Even some emergency surgery necessities she had brought with her from the hospital. Bryn was thankful for her mother's insistence that she be prepared for "the worst."

By the time they neared the cabin, Eli awakened as if from a nightmare, disoriented, his forehead dripping with sweat.

"Eli! Eli, it's okay," Bryn soothed, turning to talk to him while Ben kept paddling.

Eli grimaced and groaned lowly. They soon made it to shore and carried the man up to the front room. Ben stoked the fire while Bryn attended to Eli, first cutting away his jeans to expose the entire lower half of his leg. "I think your ankle is just sprained, Eli."

"Better stitch those wounds fast, girl," Ben directed.

Bryn cut off the top of a small plastic bottle of saline and began irrigating the wounds. Then, with trembling hands, she covered them with Betadine. Eli winced at her first touch, and she pulled back.

"Go on," Ben coached. "He can take it."

Bryn's eyes flew to Eli's face, clenched in pain. He opened them briefly and nodded at her. "Go on," he agreed. Bryn swallowed hard and quickly cleaned the long, deep lacerations and soon moved to inject twenty cc's of lidocaine along the gashes.

It took her an hour to put in the sixty stitches, and she was actually relieved when Eli passed out again after watching her poke and pull the 3-0 Silk as she sewed the gashes shut. She paused to check his pupils with her penlight.

"He's fine, Bryn."

"Appears that way," she responded. "Just passed out again, I guess." She cast a worried glance in Eli's direction and resumed her stitching. Before long, Eli was sleeping fitfully, on top of an old bearskin rug—appropriate, Bryn mused—and covered in a Hudson's Bay blanket.

"Think we ought to radio for a helicopter to take him out?" Bryn asked.

"Nah. He's survived worse. Besides, you've given him better care than old Doc Towne would've."

"We could have him sent to Willow instead of Talkeetna's clinic. He'd get good care there."

"No. I tell you, he's been through worse." Grunting from the effort, he went down to his knees and gently, quietly pulled Eli's shirt upward. There, at Eli's side, were four foot-long scars, red and angry even though they were obviously several years old.

Bryn gaped. "What happened?"

"Year after you and your dad left last. Eli and I were out hunting, and the griz came out from nowhere, charging us. Eli got off a round, hit him right between the eyes."

"That didn't kill the bear?"

"One of the thickest formations of bone, right there," Ben said, gesturing between his eyes. "It just made him madder."

"Eli shot him again?"

"Yep. Hit him in the shoulder, but he just kept coming. To make matters worse, I missed too. He was on top of us before we could say lickety-split."

"What are you two doing checking out my chest?" Eli teased with mumbled words, suddenly coming to.

"Giving you a further exam," Bryn tossed back. "Didn't know you had other bear wounds."

"Stitched the boy up myself," Ben said proudly.

"That's why the scars are so ugly," Eli muttered.

"That's why I knew you couldn't do any worse," Ben added. "Didn't take me near as long though," he teased her.

"Why didn't you take him to town?"

"You learn to do for yourself in the bush. Basic survival medicine. If it's bad, really bad—for instance, when your life is hanging in the balance—that's when you call for help. Not before."

"Bush code of honor," Eli mumbled, already drifting back to sleep.

Ben moved to sit on a chair again. He nodded at her, lifting one brow in appreciation. "You got the right stuff, girl. Not many women could've done what you just did."

"I guess I can rise to the occasion." Still shaky from the whole experience, she found pride in the moment. "I'd still feel better if Eli was seen in a hospital."

"We'll ask him when he comes to," Ben said, settling the matter. "I'd say that it's his call."

"I'm his doctor," Bryn said, lifting her chin a little.

"That you are," Ben said with a smile that said he was remembering their last summer together.

"That…what Eli and I had is over, Ben. We're just friends."

"Uh-huh."

"We—oh, think what you like. I'm telling you the truth."

"Right. Better go and fetch my canoe before the breeze changes direction and I have to paddle upwind again." He rose to go. "I'll check on you two tonight."

"Aren't you…aren't you afraid you'll run into that bear again?"

"This is bear country more than it is my country. Been living side by side with them for decades now. You surprised that sow, I'd wager." He grinned and raised his hands. "You don't surprise them, you don't threaten their cub or their dinner, and they'll never lay a paw on you." He looked her over. "Don't let this bad time keep you inside, Bryn. Summit has a lot to show you."

She was mute, thinking how scary it would be to go back to that riverbed and wondering what Ben's words meant. What would Summit teach her? Was it that obvious, her dissatisfaction with life? Her casting about for direction? For happiness?

The shutting door awakened Eli again. "Ben go?"

"Yeah. Said he'd be back tonight to check on us. Eli, I think we should get you to town. To Willow, where they can check you out."

"My head okay?"

"I think so. I'd guess it was a mild concussion. As Ben thought, the wound above your eye seems mostly superficial. Freaked me out with all the blood coming down. I didn't even have to do stitches there. A few butterfly strips and it should heal all right."

"And my ankle?"

"Think it's probably a bad sprain."

"Then that settles it. Not much more they could do for me in town. And it gives me a chance to see if you're going to be as fine a doctor as I always thought you'd be."

She turned away and poured herself a cup of tea, then sighed. "First sign of infection, I'm radioing for help. Animal wounds can be nasty."

"Deal."

"I want to keep an eye on you, so you'll be here for a few days. Need to let…anyone know?"

"I'll radio my office. Cancel my flights for a week." He didn't mention Sara Cussler.

Bryn checked her watch. "Another hour and I'll give you more Tylenol. How's the pain?"

"Been through worse."

"When?"

"Car accident, Denali, when I was seventeen. That broke my arm in three places. The bear attack with Ben. He stitched me up and then hauled me out on a stretcher over very bumpy ground. Took us eighteen hours. Ripped up this wrist water-skiing in Illinois," he said, raising his right hand. "And when I was eight, a neighbor kid shot me in the thigh."

"Shot you?"

He smiled at her reaction. "Clean through. Lucky for me he missed any major arteries."

"I'll say. You Alaskans have it rough."

"We're tough."

"Or accident prone. You want some water? Some tea?"

"Tea would be good." He shifted and winced.

"I'll get you some tea and then a pail of lake water to ice down that ankle."

"I could get used to this. Service with a smile. A doctor who looks like a dream. A—"

"Don't." Bryn steadily looked at him. Wanted to squelch the beginnings of flirtation, for both their sakes. "Don't, Eli."

The next day Bryn fried some fish and prepared a luncheon salad of fireweed greens dressed with sugar and vinegar. She could feel Eli's eyes upon her as she moved between the skillet on the stove and the small table beside it. A crackling fire roared in the stove, and the fish were cooking quickly.

"You're a good doctor," he said at last.

"Think so?"

"Know so."

"Sometimes I wonder." She wiped her hands on a cloth and looked over to him. He had his ankle elevated on a crate, and his face was bruised. Blood from the lacerations was still seeping through the bandages. "You don't look so hot."

He ignored her barb and continued to study her. "Where's your dad this year, Bryn?" he asked softly.

She turned back to the stove, pretending to fiddle with the fish. "He had other plans."

"But you still came. I thought the only reason you came was because of him."

"Used to be," she said, cocking her head, her eyes still on the browning breadcrumbs that coated the trout. She didn't want to be staring into his hazel eyes, knew he'd pull the truth from her before she was ready to share. He was her patient, not a boyfriend. She didn't need to saddle him with her sob story about a wandering father.

"And now?"

"Now I thought I'd come and see Summit on my own. See it through my own eyes, not my father's."

"You seem tired."

She let out a hollow laugh. "Yes. Medical school was rough. Harder than I anticipated."

"Think you'll like it, being a doc?"

"I think so. I didn't kill you," she tossed over her shoulder.

"No," he said slowly, gently.

"Fish is done," she said, scooping the long forms from the pan and setting them on two dinner plates. When he didn't respond, she looked up. "Eli?"

"Yes." He rose clumsily and limped over to the table. When she set his plate down, he took her hand, his touch electric in intensity. "Bryn?" He waited until she met his gaze.

She hoped her eyes answered him. She couldn't risk this again. What did he want? Surely he didn't think they could pick up where they'd left off, not with five years in the interim, not with Sara Cussler in the picture.

Abruptly he dropped her hand. "Smells great," he mumbled.

*

"What's your middle name, Doc?" he asked Bryn the morning of his third day with her. They had spent a long afternoon beside the crackling fire in the stove, talking, sharing tidbits from each other's lives.

"Skye," she answered tentatively.

"Bryn Skye Bailey. Pretty."

"Thanks." She paused thoughtfully before going on. "Listen, I'm going to go out. Look for some stones. For my fireplace."

"Back to the riverbed?"

"Yes." She pulled on her parka and grabbed her fishing rod. "Maybe catch us some dinner."

"You're not afraid?" he asked mildly.

"Back in the saddle and all that," she said with a quick shrug. "As Ben says, it's more a bear's country than mine. I'll just make *lots* of noise. And carry this," she said, smiling back at him as she motioned to his pepper spray like a game-show queen.

"Armed and dangerous," he mused, obviously flirting. What was it between them? It was as irresistible as a frozen, isolated, perfectly smooth pond to an old ice skater.

"Need anything before I go?"

"I can get it if I need anything. Oh, got any more books to read?" Eli had gone through two novels and her pioneer guide in the three days he had stayed with her.

"You're voracious," she said, moving to the bedroom shelves to see what else she might scrounge up.

"I love it when you use vocabulary words on me," he flirted.

"Eli—"

"All right. How 'bout a Bible?"

She paused. "No...I don't think we've ever had one up here."

"Oh."

She ignored the meaning behind his slow *oh* and grabbed the first three books she could put her hands on. Suddenly she just wanted out of the cabin, away from Eli, away from the uncanny sense that he knew where she fell short, knew what she was missing. It was galling. "Okay. You have books, you have water, you have wood to feed the fire. Anything else?"

"No. I'll be fine. As I said, I can get it."

Bryn turned to go, but Eli caught her wrist in a firm grasp. Her eyes flew to his thick, masculine fingers that grew more gentle as she paused, to the handsome face of her patient. "Take care out there, will you?"

"Sure," she said flippantly, pulling her hand from his grip. It was happening again. This thing between them. Bryn stopped at the door before closing it behind her. "You're making good progress, Eli. There's no sign of infection, and you're able to move about some now. Maybe…maybe it would be a good idea for us to get you situated at your own cabin. I could come over to check on you, still make your food…"

"Oh. Sure, Doc. Maybe tomorrow?"

"Tomorrow," she said with a nod, then shut the door firmly behind her as if to punctuate her decision like a solid, rounded period to a sentence.

Bryn hiked back to the riverbed, as irritated with Eli as she was worried about the bears. He had no right to start things with her again. What was he thinking? What about Sara? *And who does he think he is, asking for a Bible as if every household, even cabins, had to have one?*

She was on a spiritual journey of her own, taking it in her own time, exploring in her own way, thank you very much. Her grandparents had always been devout Christians; her parents, not so much.

She had med school friends who were Buddhist, Jewish, Muslim, Unitarian, far-right Christian—the whole gamut. What was it about Eli that made him think he had it all nailed down?

And why was she so defensive?

She shouted and sang, not wanting to surprise a black bear, a brown bear, any color bear, scouted out the immediate area, then settled in to fish where she had caught her last trout. That fish had been forgotten on the bank in the wake of the attack, perhaps picked up by bears or an eagle or another scavenger. This day, Bryn intended to fish and cook what she caught, come bear or high water. She had a hankering for fresh food, anything fresh.

She unhooked the nymph and drew out the line, preparing to cast. Two weeks out at Summit and she was already salivating at the thought of broasted chicken from Boston Market or a tossed salad from the local delicatessen. It didn't take long to grow weary of canned beans and corn and tuna and smoked salmon. What she needed was some couscous. That would be great.

Her daydreaming only made her lack of luck at the river all the more aggravating. Four hours later, she gave it up, heaving a stone into the water with a cry of frustration.

"Teaching her a lesson?" came a voice behind her.

She whirled. It was Ben. "What is it about you people? Eli snuck up on me three days ago, and now you."

"Sorry. You okay?"

"No. No, I'm not. I'm hungry and I'm tired and I can't seem to catch a thing."

"I had better luck," he offered calmly. "Caught a whole string of them this morning. Left a few at your cabin for you and Eli. He sent me down to check on you."

"I don't need to be checked on."

"Said you'd been gone for hours. He was worried."

"Well, I'm fine, thank you. Ben." She added his name in a milder tone, hoping to soften the sharpness of her retort. She sighed. "I'm sorry. I'm all riled up."

"Can see that. Want me to listen?"

Bryn sat down on a large, rounded boulder the color of a pigeon along a beach boardwalk and sighed again. "Maybe."

Ben reached for her rod, hooked the fly on the bottom ring, laid it gently beside her, then perched on another boulder nearby. "I'm all ears."

Bryn took a deep breath, puffing out her cheeks and letting it out slowly. Where to begin? "Dad's in Peru. He took up with a woman twenty years younger than he is, almost my age. My roommate, in fact. Divorced my mom and retired early. They do nothing but travel. I think they're even thinking of starting a family together." She let out a humorless laugh. "Can you believe that? If I ever have any kids, they'll have aunts and uncles the age of most cousins."

Ben raised his eyebrows in surprise. He nodded sagely, his hand to chin. "As long as I've known your father, he's been a seeker. Always searching for something that will make him happier. I'd always hoped he'd discover it here." When she didn't speak, he went on. "You're looking for the same thing, girl. Happiness. But happiness is not something you *get* to. Those who are happy enjoy the getting-to-it-ness of life. Life itself breeds joy. If you see it in the right light. And if you see it in the light of the Father's eyes—oh yes, my, that's when life is sublime."

He let her ruminate over his words for a moment. He hadn't condemned her father or her. "You and Eli. You're Christians. Is that what brings you happiness? That sense of peace I feel around you two?"

"I'd guess that's on target. It's the foundation, sure. But happiness is a choice mostly, Bryn. It's a choice. Deepening my walk with Jesus makes me a better man each day. Opens my eyes to the light that the Father sees us in. But becoming a Christian doesn't mean everything is easy, that we're only brought joy. Take Eli, for instance."

"Eli?" she asked warily.

"Yes. That boy has loved Jesus for years. He's a good man, a solid man. Jedidiah and Meryl have good reason to be proud. He's got a job he loves, lives in a place he loves. But the woman he's been in love with for years—not saying who that is, mind you—doesn't share his beliefs. That keeps him away from one of the things he wants most in life. Makes him miserable every time he thinks about it. He's tried to get past her, tried with everything in him, but it's hard."

"There are more obstacles than faith between us, Ben."

"Right. But God has a funny sense of humor. An interesting way of leading us down the winding path, if we're careful to listen to him."

"He'd speak to me?" The thought had never occurred to her before. "I mean, I know there's a God. I'm that far anyway. But I don't know if I'm ready to swallow that he'd send his Son to die for me. Don't know if Jesus is really who he said he was. Maybe he was just a teacher. A good man who—"

"Listen to me, Bryn Bailey," Ben said carefully. "Jesus Christ is either who he said he was or a complete fraud. He himself gave those around him no room to think otherwise. He is either the Son of God—our Savior—or he is a madman." Ben stood. "Look it up. Start with Romans. Decide for yourself. You're a reader, a scholar. Maybe you'll find a bit of that Happy Road you're seeking."

"I don't have a Bible here," Bryn admitted.

"Yes you do. Brought Eli's over from his cabin. Thought he might be missing it."

"How'd you…? That's quite a coincidence."

Ben smiled, his gray eyes sparkling, his wrinkled face kind. "That's one of the first lessons you learn as a believer, Dr. Bailey. There is no such thing as coincidences. Only divine appointments."

Bryn cooked the trout as she had planned, watching them. When she flipped them, she added the fresh carrots and, at the last minute, the canned okra. She seasoned it all and covered it with a lid before taking a seat at the table.

"You're quiet tonight," Eli offered, sitting in a chair in the corner, his leg on an upended box.

"Had a talk with Ben today."

"Oh."

"What does that mean?"

"What does what mean?"

"Your *oh*. You always say that word when you want to say more but are holding back."

"I do?"

"Yes."

"Oh." He caught himself and they both smiled.

"You asked where my dad was this year, Eli."

"I know."

"You do?"

"Yeah. My dad got a postcard from your father. From Peru."

Bryn sighed. "Did Ben know?"

"No." He seemed curious about her question. "So, what did you and Ben talk about?" he prompted.

"My dad, for one." Just saying that much out loud left her feeling vulnerable.

"I'm sorry, Bryn. It's gotta hurt, to have your folks break up."

"Yes." She rose, lifted the lid on the pan and fiddled with the fish, suddenly wanting something to do. "Maybe it's the plight of only children, huh? It becomes all the more important that your family stick together, however miserable they might be."

Eli shook his head a little. "Can't speak to that. My parents, thankfully, have always gotten along."

Bryn nodded. Ben would probably tell her it had to do with their faith.

"You missing him?" Eli asked softly.

"Yes," she said, pushing against the sudden ache in her throat. She tried to stop the tears, but it was too much. The day, the week, being here… She couldn't fight the tears anymore and broke down, hating being weak and blubbering in front of Eli.

She could hear him moving toward her. "You shouldn't—," she said.

"Shh." He gathered her in his arms. He smelled of wood smoke and leather and something faintly spicy. She cried then, relaxing into his embrace, making his shirt wet from her tears. It felt good to be held, to be cared for, and his chest was solid, his arms around her so strong. She felt safe and warm.

"Bryn," he said.

"Wh-what?" She looked up at him, suddenly longing for him to kiss her, to make her forget her inner pain.

He leaned back, his arms pulling away. "The fish. I think they're burning."

"Oh!" She grabbed the pan from the burner and raised the lid. "They were going to be so perfect!" He didn't respond but instead moved to her side, his eyes upon her. More cautious now at exposing herself, she couldn't bear to look back at him, to offer her lips to him again and have him pull away as he had before.

"They'll be fine," he said soothingly. He wiped a remaining tear from her cheek and tenderly tucked her hair behind her ear. "They'll be just fine, Bryn."

Bryn helped Eli move to his own cabin the next day, and from there he radioed his office to tell his assistant it would be a few more days before he could leave Summit. Bryn carefully avoided his eyes as he talked over the CB, probably so he wouldn't see her look of confusion or hurt or sorrow at the mention of his departure, Eli guessed. Quietly he asked his assistant, Jamie, to call Sara Cussler and tell her he'd be phoning within the week. Then he signed off.

"She won't like it, your being here," Bryn said, folding back the blanket on his bed.

"Why not?" He knew. He wanted to see if she would verbalize it.

She finally met his eyes, and her lost-little-girl look threatened to take him to his knees, make him apologize, and hold and kiss her until those brown eyes sparkled with the knowledge of joy and peace. Bryn Skye Bailey moved him as no other woman had in his entire life. Why oh why did she have to be so lost? She had to find herself before they would ever have a chance. And coming across her again, when he'd finally stopped dreaming about her at night, when he'd finally met a nice, sweet girl like Sara, was a cruel coincidence.

There is no such thing as coincidence, Ben always told him. *Only divine appointment.* But Eli was having a hard time believing that this was a God thing. His Lord was loving and full of grace and peace and joy. What Eli felt for Bryn was torturous, like a bed of nails.

"You *know* why she won't like it, Eli," she said, fluffing a pillow.

"Quit. Quit with the bed, Bryn. I'm not going to bed," he said, grabbing her arm. "I'm back here because we both know I can take care of myself."

"Well, what are you going to do with yourself?" Gently she pulled away from him.

"You don't want to stay for the afternoon?" he asked carefully. "Keep me company?"

"No. I think we need some time apart now. You have your own books here. I need to get back to my fireplace project. Ben's coming over this afternoon to help me cut the hole and build the frame for the arch."

"Okay. Just keep that pepper spray ready in your pocket if you go looking for more river rock."

"Now that, you can be sure I'll do," she agreed, finally smiling up at him. "Good-bye, Eli."

"Good-bye, Doc. Thanks for your help."

She turned, her eyes bright with tears again. The smile slid from his face as she approached, stood on tiptoe, and kissed him on the lower cheek. "Thanks for saving me from that bear," she whispered, pushing a grin through her tears. And then she turned and walked out, leaving him feeling as cold and bereft as an orphan on the streets at midnight.

CHAPTER SIX

ryn read the whole book of Romans that week. While some of the words were hard to believe, she found herself drawn more and more to them. They spoke of grace and of a God who cared deeply, intimately, about his creation. The words soothed her, helped her begin to see a hint of God's forgiveness, not only for herself but also for her father. Yet while the words moved her, she longed for some tangible evidence that what she read was true. Perhaps it was the scientist in her wanting everything orderly. But this faith business seemed anything but orderly.

She visited Eli every afternoon to check on his progress, but she was relieved when she saw the de Havilland take off without a formal good-bye from Eli. She knew he would be back. Right now, she needed to be alone. The dizzying attraction was too intense when they were together, too great to deny when she was alone. She was on the precipice of something big, and she needed to find it on her own, with a clear mind.

Her therapist would say all her woes stemmed from her mother—needy and dysfunctional apparently. That was all fine and good, but Bryn was ready to move on, not wallow in the past.

Bryn followed a path that Ben had pointed out to her beyond the cabin. The path led into the high country and, after a couple of miles, the Alaska Range. In awe, she squinted against the bright white of the High One and her sisters. The snowy fields and glaciers were blue white, like an old woman's hair, and where the shadows deepened, the snow changed to a blue as royal as in the American flag. Bryn uncapped her canteen and drank deeply, appreciating the vista and the solitude.

She thought about her life. She was a competent doctor, she supposed. Bryn Skye Bailey was pretty competent at everything she did. But would doctoring make her happy? Ben's words—"Happiness is not something you get to. Those who are happy enjoy the getting-to-it-ness of life itself"—returned to her. Being up here, alone, happy with herself, felt right. She was embracing what Summit Lake could give her this summer, not concentrating on what it couldn't. Like Eli. She felt a twinge in her belly as she acknowledged that in every direction she turned she encountered a beauty that maybe one in a thousand people would ever see. She counted it a blessing.

Blessing. A word Ben would use.

She thought about her father, who had come too, perhaps seeking the same thing she now sought. Maybe he had even asked Ben and Jedidiah similar questions. But her father was in Peru, or maybe Ecuador or Colombia by now, traveling with his fiancée through Central America. They planned to marry when they reached Mexico. Bryn wouldn't attend.

Her father certainly seemed to be wandering, searching for something, even after all these years. Maybe he thought he'd discover it by traveling the world, or with Ashley, the proverbial younger woman. Perhaps going through the process of having another child when he was in the latter half of his life would give him a piece of eternity, a vital piece of *life,* that he was missing. She doubted it. All his searching just led to more searching—what was the point of that? She looked back to the majestic, powerful mountains. Perhaps Ben was right. Perhaps Alaska did hold the answers for her, if only she would be quiet enough to hear God's whisper.

The thought surprised her. Just when had she started listening for God? Longing to hear his voice?

⁓

"Sara, I—"

"Look, Eli," she turned around, staring at his crutches. "I get that you were hurt, that you had to stay put for a while. But it was with *her*. With Bryn."

"Nothing happened," he said, hating the high, defensive tone his voice had taken.

"Didn't it?" She raised a brow.

She stared at him until he looked down at his foot. "You were out on a rafting trip. I didn't think you would worry."

She nodded knowingly, then switched to shake her head. "You don't owe me anything, Eli Pierce. We started something. I'm just glad we both found out before it went too far."

"Found what out?"

"That you're in love with Bryn."

"I'm not! I was once. I'll admit it." She didn't respond, just stared at him with her deep blue eyes. "Sara, it's over between Bryn and me, not that anything ever really started. We're friends, that's it. We're too different, on two separate paths—"

"That keep intersecting."

"Yes, but she's not a believer. You know how important that is to me."

Sara sighed and laid a hand on his chest. "Eli. You don't have to convince me. You have to convince yourself. When you can do that, come back around. You're an honest man; I'll trust you. Until then"—she lowered her forehead, looking at him from the top of her eyes—"stay away. Please."

He grabbed her hand, wanting to hold her there.

Her eyes softened. "Please," she repeated, pulling at her hand slowly as if she wanted to give him another chance.

He released her. "I'll be back around, Sara," he promised. He settled the airman's cap on his head again, determined to do right by her. Convince himself, as she said, then come back and convince her. She was too good, and what they had was too special, for him to mess up. He just had to get Bryn out of his head, as Sara was asking him to do. It was only fair to Sara. And to himself. In the meantime, he hoped Sara wouldn't slip away forever.

"I won't be waiting, Eli," she warned, then turned and walked away.

A week after Eli had left, Bryn shared a bonfire on the beach with Ben. She had shown him the progress she had made on the fireplace, and he was going to help her with the tricky process of cutting away the wall without hurting the structure.

"I need more mortar," she said, watching as sparks flew upward and dissolved into the inky black sky. She remembered that her father once told her that they went all the way to heaven and became stars like those that carpeted the darkness at night. "I've already gone through the Quick Crete you gave me. Can you ask Eli to bring you some the next time he flies in supplies? I could also use a pound of cornmeal and sugar. And a pepperoni pizza. I don't care if it's cold."

"Sure. Don't want to radio him yourself?"

"Nah. It's better this way, us remaining apart. When we're together, we can't seem to be anything other than *together.*"

Ben nodded and sat quietly. He poked the fire, sending even more sparks toward Cassiopeia. It was a glorious night. What was it about this place? It seemed to reach out to her. She recalled her time on top of the mountain, and her sense that God was trying to speak to her. "When did you become a Christian, Ben?"

"Korea, 1952. Nothing like being pinned down by sniper fire, your buddy dead beside you, to make you take a good, long, hard look at yourself and the ever after."

"I didn't know you went to Korea."

"Yeah. I'm a few years older than your dad and Jedidiah."

"Why didn't you ever marry?"

"Not a ton of women who are ready to live in the bush."

"Would you have lived closer to town, in Talkeetna, for the right one?"

"I suppose," he said, grinning over at her, the dancing light of the fire bouncing along his face. "If it had been the right woman. But I don't meet a lot of good women out here. I guess I could always start reading the personal ads." He chuckled.

Bryn smiled.

"I don't suppose a pretty girl like you has ever looked over those ads."

"Oh, I have. Two or three times. When I'm especially lonely."

"What kind of ad would've made you pick up the phone or e-mail or whatever you kids do to contact each other these days?"

Bryn thought about it, took a sip of her cocoa. "Tall, handsome,

single pilot with a yen for the outdoors seeks brunette to share cama-
raderie and quiet kisses." She blushed, and Ben laughed softly. He
reminded Bryn so much of Grampa Bruce before his memory started
fading that she found herself sharing the most intimate of thoughts.

"Ah, love. You two are like unbound lobsters in a butcher's fish
tank."

"What happens when they're unbound?"

"They rip each other to shreds. Don't mean to, of course. It's just
their way."

"That's a pleasant thought."

"Sorry. The funny thing is, when lobsters are in the ocean, where
they're supposed to be, it doesn't play out like that. I mean, at least
not for the males and females."

"So you're saying that if Eli and I were someplace different, we
wouldn't be killing each other. We could be mates?"

"It's not Summit that's tearing you apart, Bryn," he said gently.
"It's where you are, here," he said, motioning toward his heart.

Bryn sighed again. She seemed to do a lot of that, sighing. "I
know, Ben. I know. But I'm getting there."

⁓

Eli flew to Summit Lake on his monthly supply run for Ben. He
knew he had to see Bryn, see how she was doing, show her how well
his leg was healing. Ben had radioed in for a pepperoni pizza—a
rather unusual request—and some additional supplies beyond his
typical order. Eli knew they were for Bryn. He also knew Ben would
ask him to deliver them. He landed on the choppy, silver lake and
expertly beached the de Havilland on Ben's shore.

Eli watched as Ben came out of his cabin, waving and ambling down the stairs to help unload. Eli jumped out of the plane, leaned back inside the fuselage, and pulled out the pizza. "Haven't known you to ever have a hankerin' for pepperoni."

"Pshaw," the man retorted, turning half away and waving a hand. "Not for me. Gastritis city. You know as well as I it's for the pretty girl down the lake."

"You'll have to take it to her," Eli said. "I can't see her. It's not good for us, Ben."

"No," he said. He studied Eli as if he was a wounded bear that he needed to treat. "It might hurt a little bit, but it will all be worthwhile. Maybe not this summer. But down the road. You'll see."

Eli sighed and tossed the cold pizza back in and grabbed a crate instead. He raised an eyebrow as he passed the shorter man. "Don't go matchmaking, Ben," he warned. "We've tried. It's not going to work."

"Maybe," the man said, taking another box and following behind.

"She's not a believer," Eli said, huffing a little as he climbed the steps.

"Yet."

"She lives in Boston."

"Right now."

Eli reached the porch and set the crate on the railing, turning to look at Ben. "You know somethin' I don't?"

Ben stared at him, set his box on the rail, and looked out at the lake. "Don't know anything really. Just a feelin' I've got. Always had it around the two of you."

"We always get that feeling too," Eli said, going inside. "And it always sets us on the road to heartache." He put Ben's supplies down on the kitchen table, and Ben did the same.

"Sometimes," Ben said, placing a hand on his shoulder, "Heartache leads to ultimate healing. The girl wants what you have, Eli."

Eli glanced at him.

"Yes. Inside. She wants to know the Lord. She's on her way. But sometimes it takes an awful lot of pain to tear down the walls. Take me for example." He moved back to the porch door to go and grab another load. Eli followed, stooping to pet a lone cub in the pen in Ben's living room. "I'd been listening to the platoon parson ramble on about Jesus for a good seven months. Had to be in a Korean swamp, bullets singing by my ears, my buddy dying in my arms, before I was ready to walk with him."

"So who's going to die for Bryn to see the light? Me?"

Ben raised a brow, his eyes twinkling. "Hope not. Like to see you two married. A few little cubs of your own."

Eli laughed and shook his head, following Ben down the stairs. "That, my friend, is about as likely as the northern lights appearing at midday."

Bryn hauled more rock inside, sweating from the labor. She was almost to the ceiling. With a little more mortar, she'd reach the top, and all her work would then be outside, where the mosquitoes would do their best to eat her alive.

"Not much use living anywhere a mosquito wouldn't even choose to live," Ben had defended. He had helped her cut away the logs and build the flue form, as well as the arch support, which still remained. It would be there until she was done, and then she'd know for sure if the project was a success. *If it all comes crashing down…* She shuddered at the thought. Not after all that work! She still had the outside of the chimney to complete. It would take some work—she only had a few weeks left at the lake. But she felt certain she could do it.

She stood back and wiped the sweat from her forehead. *Dad would be proud.* He'd love the real fireplace. It gave the cabin a snug feel, and being able to see it complete, with a fire crackling inside, made her feel just a bit closer to him. She imagined the mantel where she'd built a support form. She moved her hand to shoulder height. She would place her treasures on it—that plaster casting of the wolf print she'd taken, the driftwood "sculptures" she'd collected from shore, the various items she'd found over the summer.

The sound of the de Havilland drew her to the window. Eli. He was back, after being gone from Summit for a couple of weeks. She wondered how his leg was faring. More important, she wondered if he had brought her pizza. She smiled and looked down. She was a mess. Good. The last thing she wanted to do was look attractive. The messier the better. Maybe she ought to smear some of the rock dust over her face.

No. She was who she was. Looked the way she looked. Eli had made his decision. Besides, she had work to do. He would show up when he was good and ready. And she would go on with this day without him, just as she would return to Boston in a few weeks and resume her life without him.

They were simply not meant to be.

With some trepidation, Eli paddled across the lake with Bryn's supplies—mortar, coffee, sugar, cornmeal, and the pizza. He could see her, moving outside the house, probably working on her fireplace.

When Bryn Skye Bailey went after something, she went after it big. And opened herself up to a very big fall. *Like us,* he mused. As he drew closer, the hot early-August sun high in the sky, he could see her in a long-sleeved T-shirt and jeans, her olive skin glistening in the sun, her ponytail half undone, smudges of gray stone dust on her arms and even on her forehead. She wore leather gloves, and as she leaned down and took another load of rock inside, she pulled her head back once with a smile of greeting.

When he beached the canoe, she came outside. A squirrel chattered madly from a nearby branch, as if telling him to go away.

"When Pizza Town says they deliver," Bryn said, "they mean *deliver.*"

"Yes," he said with a chuckle, stepping out. "That will be forty-five dollars and fifty cents, ma'am."

Bryn's smile grew larger. "A deal, I tell you." She took the box from him and opened it up, groaning in pleasure. "Pure heaven. Worth any price."

"Cold pizza? Must be a desperate bush woman."

"I'd say," she answered. The squirrel scolded from above them again, and a pine cone dropped nearby.

"New friend?" Eli asked.

"Ishmael," she introduced, then shrugged. "He's mad because I've filled all the holes in the roof and he has to find another home this fall. Come in. Come see my fireplace. You'll forgive me if I don't offer you a piece of pizza? I'm going to nurse this all week."

"No problem." He ducked through the low doorway and walked over to the fireplace and short hearth. "Doc, it's…" He paused to run his hands over the stones, impressed with their perfect placement and her choice of the rocks themselves, varied in color and, from the looks of them, gathered from all around Summit. "It's beautiful."

Bryn smiled broadly and pulled off her gloves. "Ben says that too many people do parts of jobs, not the whole thing from beginning to end. Gives a body a sense of satisfaction."

"Wise man, our friend."

"Yes." She looked Eli in the eyes, almost searchingly. "Ben is a wise man. We've had some good talks..." Her words trailed off as if she wanted to say more, and Eli wondered just what Ben and Bryn had been discussing.

She opened the pizza box, took out a cold slice, and bit into it as if it were manna from heaven. She turned her wide, grateful brown eyes toward him. "Mmm. Thanks for bringing this. I owe you big."

"Nah. Check out your stitches. I still owe you." He propped a boot up on the nearest chair and lifted his khaki-colored cargo pants. "Nice work, eh? Dr. Towne was most impressed."

"Not bad for an emergency treatment."

"Towne called them perfect."

"He's easily impressed. How's the ankle?"

"Still a little sore when I do too much. Nothing that some Advil doesn't whip in an instant."

"Good, good." Her pizza seemed forgotten in her hand as she stared at him.

"I'll go get your other supplies," Eli said, suddenly aware of the electricity in the room. He motioned with his thumb over his shoulder and firmly tucked his other hand in his pocket.

"Great," she said softly, decidedly returning her attention to the pizza. "Need some help?" she asked, then took another big bite.

"Nah. Take a load off, enjoy your dinner. I'll just bring this stuff up to the cabin and be out of your hair."

"You have to leave right away?" Her voice was soft again.

"Yes," he said, too fast, too defensively. "I mean, yeah. Jamie has me scheduled for a sunset flight tonight out of Talkeetna, and I have a full couple of weeks ahead."

Bryn nodded. "I need to pull out of here in a couple of weeks myself. Can you come pick me up on the twentieth?"

"Sure. I'll put it on the schedule," he said over his shoulder, walking out. Suddenly he couldn't get away from Bryn fast enough. The woman was as dangerous as a tarpit to a saber-toothed cat.

———

The afternoon before Bryn's departure Eli returned to the Pierce cabin, bringing his mother and father with him. He couldn't keep himself from pacing in front of the deck window, looking out across the lake.

"Go see her," Meryl encouraged, taking his arm and looking out the window with him. "Before you wear a rut in the wood floor."

"I can't, Mom. I can't be with her. It will just make things worse. The best thing to do is stay away." He resumed his pacing.

"You'll have to see her tomorrow."

"Yes. But I'll just pick her up and drop her off in Anchorage. Knowing she's on her way out will help me keep a lid on things." He walked over to the stove and poured himself a steaming cup of coffee. The weather had changed over the last week, from a hint of autumn to full-fledged fall. At the narrow edges of Summit, there was even the thin sheen of ice, testimony to cold nights and the coming onset of winter. The tundra's fireweed had turned a brilliant red and had topped out its bloom; the locals called it the "red flag of winter."

"I always forget how beautiful it is here," his mother said, still at the window. She looked on down the lake, where Jedidiah had canoed to see Ben. Eli rejoined her at the window, as drawn to the vista as a June bug to light.

"Sure you shouldn't go on over there?" she asked. "Say your good-byes, so she doesn't haunt you for the *next* few years?"

"It isn't going to be like that again, Mom. We didn't spend as much time together this summer. She had some things to work out, inside, for herself."

"Did she do that?"

Eli thought about Bryn, about how she had completed the fireplace by herself. He could see the chimney rising from the trees. And Ben had told him that she'd taken to hiking again, even after the bear attack. She definitely seemed to be moving forward, not wallowing in the pain of her father's desertion. Eli thought about their last conversation, when he'd brought the pizza. She'd wanted to tell him something, and there had been a hint of excitement in her eyes. "Maybe. I think so," he finally replied. He took a sip of coffee. "And tomorrow, she heads back to Boston."

He turned away from the window. "We're just not meant to be, Mom. I've given up on it. Don't go gettin' my nose back to the scent."

Bryn couldn't sleep. It was her last night here, and she had bedded down in front of the fire on top of the bearskin rug, waiting to get sleepy as the flames danced before her in hues of crimson and sapphire and aspen yellow. But sleep wouldn't come. She supposed it was Eli being right across the lake but failing to come and see her. Or memories of Ben's sweet good-bye hug, the most tender grandfatherly embrace she'd had since Grampa Bruce had hugged her at the airport.

Ben had made her feel whole and loved and worthy. And he had opened her eyes to God's unfailing love for her, even though she still longed for some tangible evidence, some proof she could cling to in the days ahead. But she realized it didn't matter. Faith was about not always having proof. Besides, the peace in her heart spoke pretty loudly. Yes, it had been a good summer for her in many ways, regardless of what had or hadn't transpired between her and Eli.

The bright third-quarter moon rose, sending rays of silver light through the front window, calling her. She glanced at her watch, turning to see its face in the light of the fading fire. Two o'clock. She looked back to the window, sighed, and rose, pulling on a wool sweater, jeans, and parka over the long underwear she had recently taken to wearing to bed. Outside, the lake was completely still, the mountains' reflection brilliant in the water. It was irresistible.

Bryn pulled up her hood and turned the canoe over, shoving it into the water. One last good-bye to the lake her father had once loved, the lake that had now captured her heart. She paddled outward, toward Eli's—no, to the center, she corrected herself—so she could get a 360-degree view. The reflection of the moon on the Alaska Range's white peaks illuminated them all around her. She was halfway out when she heard a soft whisper.

"Doc?" came Eli's quiet voice. "That you?"

She pulled her head back, jumping slightly in her surprise. Then she laughed to herself. "Yeah, it's me, Eli."

He paddled toward her and, when he glided alongside, reached out to grab the edge of her canoe. "Couldn't sleep either?"

"No. Too much on my mind. And it was too pretty outside."

"Yeah. Know what you mean."

They sat there together in silence, drifting a little, staring all about. In the distance—up north toward Denali—a faint green light streaked across the sky, then another and another, like a giant artist making his first strokes on a naked canvas. "Eli—"

"Yeah, I see it, Doc."

As they stared in awe, the neon-green streaks connected and then grew in a sinuous, undulating wave, coming south, rolling onward like a wave across the sea. "Oh, Eli," Bryn gasped. She had seen the aurora over the years, but nothing as brilliant as this.

The lights continued to dance, rolling with a faint stroke of white across the bed of green like wind in wheat. And then, at the bottom, the streaks turned a faint red. Minutes later, that red grew more vibrant, and the light changed direction, cascading downward in what Bryn could only describe as the gossamer wings of angels. Even more breathtaking was the bright scarlet hue those wings took; the closer they came to Summit, the deeper they became. "Oh, Eli," Bryn repeated.

Tears coursed down her cheeks, and a joy bubbled from deep inside her—a joy she had never known before. Surely this was like the kiss of God. A gift. A miraculous gift. She could not take her eyes from it. She felt embraced, surrounded, blessed from above. This was the tangible she had craved, and God in his goodness had given it to her. Undeserving as she was.

"My father would say they're sixty miles away, the product of a solar wind stream," she mused. She could feel Eli's gaze upon her but could not draw her own eyes away from the arcs and bands and rays and filmy draperies that surrounded them.

"What would you say, Doc?"

"I'd say this is the breath of heaven," she said, weeping all the more.

Eli looked upward again. "Ben calls it an angel walk, when they come down like that. That we're seeing them descend, the multitudes from heaven."

Bryn nodded. She had been given a vision from heaven, had seen the hand of God. "That's right," she whispered. "I can see why he'd say that."

She looked up again and cried even harder as the lights continued in their dance, celebrating over her. Bryn grinned through her tears. *Thank you, Father. Fill me. Make me your own. Teach me! Show me!*

Eli seemed to sense her need for quiet and remained still in his own canoe, staring upward too. At long last he reached out and brushed his fingers over her cheek. "You all right, Doc?"

"Better than ever."

"This been a good summer for you?"

"The best, Eli, the best. You were right, you know." She looked at his handsome face, outlined by moonlight.

"About what?"

"About God being here, showing himself to me, talking to me." Bryn looked skyward again, and wiped her cheeks, but the tears kept coming. "Eli, he's here. *Right here.* With us."

Eli paused, obviously surprised by her revelation. "Always has been, Doc. Waiting."

Part 3

Homeward Bound, 2001

CHAPTER SEVEN

*B*ryn couldn't believe she was back in Alaska, regardless of the fact that it was her year to be here. If she hadn't come, something would be missing, something integrally wrong in her life. At least she wasn't heading back to Talkeetna or Summit Lake this year. She was going to steer clear of Eli Pierce. He had occupied enough of her dreams—day and night—for the last decade. Besides, he was probably married with two kids. No, this year she had a new goal.

A full-fledged doctor now, as newly minted as a 2001 quarter, Bryn had elected to come to Alaska with Housecalls, a relief organization that would fly her to remote bush families or communities to tend to their medical needs. It was how she would spend the summer; then she would return to the Lower 48 and look for that perfect job that every new physician dreams of. But serving Alaska's people for a summer was a way of giving back, returning a part of the gift she'd been given five years ago in 1996. The summer she'd first known she was a chosen child of God.

She turned her thoughts to her hospital buddies—friendships forged over the last five years. When she had gone home to Boston after her summer on Summit, it was as if something inside had burst loose, and she felt free for the first time to join in and meld with others. That summer had changed her life in many ways. She shook her head in awe. "Thank you, Lord," she murmured, looking skyward from an Anchorage taxi.

She was glad her Grampa Bruce's mind had been clear enough to know she had embraced Jesus. It was the happiest she'd ever seen him, the day she'd shared her news. He'd suffered several small strokes in the intervening years, rendering him incapable of caring for himself. It broke her heart every time she saw him, made her yearn for heaven for him. Where he would be whole again, fully functioning, his eyes as keen and bright as they once were. When he would be reunited with his beloved wife, gone now these last fifteen years.

In short order the cab pulled up outside a dilapidated building that looked like an old warehouse, half refurbished. A hand-painted sign outside read HOUSECALLS, and a light shone through a window. Bryn paid the cab driver and got out. "Wait until I make sure someone's here," she said. Obediently the cabby waited, the engine roughly idling.

When the knob turned, she waved at the driver and he gave her a dismissive flip of one hand and drove away. Bryn turned back to the small front room and closed the door behind her. When no one appeared, she called out, "Hello? Anyone here?"

"Coming!" a male voice called from the back. He emerged through a hallway and smiled as he turned the corner, a tall man, as dark as Bryn, with handsome features. About her age, too.

"Hi, I'm Dr. Bryn Bailey," she said, reaching out her hand.

"Ah, Bryn Bailey," he said, taking her hand in his and covering it with his other in a warm gesture of greeting. "I'm so glad to meet you, Doctor."

Even after her years as an intern and resident, Bryn was still getting used to the title. "And you are…?"

"Oh!" he said, his eyes smiling at her. "I'm Doc Carmine Kostas, in charge of this most impressive operation," he said, waving about at his humble surroundings. *Greek and a sense of humor,* she mused. *It just might be a romantic summer after all.* "Come on back," he invited, already on the move. "We'll sit in my office."

She followed him down the hallway, past a couple of people who were talking on the phone in cubicles, past a conference room lined with maps and a whiteboard on an easel.

"We run a pretty lean operation," Carmine said. "Thus the lack of a receptionist. We want to make sure we get as much of our donated dollar as we can out to the people who need it. So we set up each volunteer doctor in his own location, with his own phone or radio and supplies. We're"—he waved his arm to indicate the office—"simply the conduit of information. Once your area's people find out you're around—and believe me, word gets out fast—they'll come to you direct. At that point, you only contact us on a weekly basis to ask for needed supplies and to report on the week's activity."

"How many doctors do you have this year?"

Carmine sat back in his chair and steepled his fingers in front of him. "We have fifteen this summer. Five year-round." He glanced back at an extensive map of Alaska, with sections divided by different colors. From what she had studied, she guessed it was divided up by native tribes.

"So, Doc Kostas," she said gamely, "where are you sending me?" She had thought about being stationed someplace very isolated, prepared herself for it. Maybe up on the Arctic Coast, in Barrow, serving the Eskimo population, or out on the Alaska Peninsula, with the Aleuts. Or maybe—

"Talkeetna," he said, smiling as if he were Santa Claus bestowing a gift.

"Excuse me?"

"Talkeetna. We have a new outpost there. There's a clinic that's growing in case you have an emergency, a small hospital in Willow—"

"Ex-excuse me?"

Carmine's face fell, his eyes betraying disappointment at her reaction. "What? Have you been there? It's incredible! It's one of the best locations in the field—"

"I can't go to Talkeetna," Bryn said, shaking her head. "Doc Kostas, please. Send me someplace else."

"You're crazy, girl! I'm telling you, there's not a better place to be in Alaska come summer—"

"I can't! I can't go there."

The director leaned back in his chair, clearly puzzled. "Want to tell me why?"

Bryn sighed. "Not particularly. Let's just say I have some history in Talkeetna that I'd like to remain a fond memory, not a trip back in time."

Carmine studied her, looked upward, then to the map. After a long moment, he turned back to her. "No, it won't work. The two other areas I could assign you to already have better doctors in the field"—he raised his hands up as if to guard himself—"not a comment on your medical skills. They know the native languages." He gazed back at the map. "Shannon is near Wainwright; she speaks Inupiaq, and Eric is going to an outpost east of Bethel and speaks Yupik. The rest of my doctors are established with their populations, having at least been to their regions in previous summers. No, the only place that makes sense is Talkeetna, Bryn."

"Why there? You said yourself that there's a clinic in Talkeetna and a hospital in Willow. I thought Housecalls was all about serving—"

"Serving people in the bush," he said, nodding. "With the popularity of Denali on the rise, more and more people are moving to the bush country near the park and visiting bush families that take in overnight boarders. We get some state funding—"

"I'm sorry," Bryn mumbled. "I can't go there. There must be someone else who could."

"Are you saying you're not going to join us if we send you there?"

Bryn's mind went back to Boston, to the three hospitals that had expressed interest in her, that she had put on hold in her desire to serve Alaska's people. "I don't know."

"What happened in Talkeetna that was so bad?" Carmine asked gently. "Want to talk about it?"

"No," Bryn said, shaking her head and sighing. "I don't want to talk about it. Nothing happened—nothing bad, that is."

"Then what's the problem?"

Bryn studied his dark eyes and mulled over her dilemma. "Guess there isn't one," she sighed. "I suppose I'm just meant to be there every five years."

"Every five years?"

"Never mind. Where will I stay?"

Dr. Kostas rose to pull a file from his cabinet and then sat back down. "Looks like we've secured a great little cabin on the Talkeetna River, right outside of town. Not a half-mile from the airstrip and two, three miles from the anchorage of our floatplane contractor."

For the first time, Bryn dared to think of that angle. "And...who will be flying me to see patients in the bush?"

Dr. Kostas looked through several pages in the file folder. "Here we are. Leon Wilmot and Eli... What was his name? I just met him last fall. I swear I'm losin' it." He laughed at his lack of memory and scanned the remaining copy. "Nice guy. Eli—"

"Eli Pierce."

Carmine's dark eyes met hers with surprise. "You know him?"

Bryn laughed softly, shaking her head. "Ever hear, Dr. Kostas, that God has a funny sense of humor?"

"Yes," Carmine responded with a tentative smile.

"Well, he does. I'm living proof."

⁓

Eli spiked a volleyball over the net, grinning at Sara Cussler, who was on the opposite team and nodding at him in admiration. They had kept in touch over the last five years, and she had recently moved back to spend the summer in Talkeetna, ostensibly because she missed the place, but Eli knew it was to see if they could figure out what they might have together long-term. It was looking promising. She was into hiking, had learned to love flying, even helped him at the fledgling outreach center at the church. Today they had drummed up a crowd of river guides from several rafting companies, as well as a huge group of young people for a mean game of volleyball.

"Come on, Eli," a kid complained on the opposite side. "Quit sparing your girlfriend. You're killin' me."

"Can't send a pretty girl like that a zinger," he tossed back, wiping his upper lip.

"Bring it on, Pierce," Sara taunted. She wasn't one to sit back and be treated like a girlie-girl. She still had it. The gumption he admired.

Not to mention an athlete's body and a heart for Jesus. Eli was a happy man. Life was looking up.

When the game was over, they all retreated to the fellowship hall for sodas and snacks. "You're going to go broke if you keep doing this," Sara said, gesturing toward the piles of chips and cookies and pop that would be gone within the hour. He pulled her into his arms and gave her a sweaty kiss on the cheek. She wrinkled up her nose in distaste.

"It's good for them. Good for me. If I can raise a little more money, we can have ourselves an indoor basketball court. Maybe even yearly sponsors, so someone else can buy the snacks once in a while."

"You're a good man, Eli Pierce," she said, admiration shining through her blue, blue eyes.

"You're a good woman, Sara Cussler," he responded. "I'm glad you're here, back in Talkeetna."

"Me too." She moved closer and hugged him tight. "Can you take me to the lodge? I'm on in an hour." She had taken a job working the front desk at the Talkeetna Lodge.

"Sure."

"Great. I'll go clean up and change."

Eli dropped Sara off for her shift, smiling as he drove away. Lately he had been praying about whether he should propose, move the relationship on to permanent status. She hadn't been here long, but she had made it clear she was ready. And Eli thought he might be ready too. Almost. Another couple of weeks and he was sure he would get the confirmation he sought through prayer, the blessing he hoped for.

It was time to settle down, start a family. He was thirty-one, business was good, and he had enough money saved to buy land and build a house. And he wanted a woman in his life who would partner with him on the project and not just choose flooring and paint colors. He wanted a partner to work alongside him, hammering nails, pouring concrete, selecting rock for a fireplace.

Wrong image, Pierce. Over the last five years he had convinced himself that any fantasy of a life with Bryn Bailey was exactly that—fantasy. It was better to stick with reliable, sweet, fun, faithful, steady Sara than a fantasy girl from his past. Yes, it was time to settle down. Almost. He just needed... What? What was it he was waiting for?

He drove his truck down the road to the office, where it sat on the highway along the edge of Fish Lake. It had been busy already this summer. He'd dropped a few hunters and fishermen off in the bush and made flyovers every day, looking for their signs that they were ready to be picked up. Some had cell phones with them for the same purpose. And today he was supposed to meet the doctor from Housecalls that he would ferry to the bush for medical emergencies and routine checkups.

A doctor. It was Bryn's summer to be in Alaska. Would she come, as she had every five years? Memories of their last night together still clung to his heart, like mud in a dog's fur. He sighed. He knew he needed to put that almost-romance to bed before he'd find the confirmation he sought for his relationship with Sara.

Bryn hadn't given him any hope in the following years. There hadn't been a single communication from her. And her intent, even during that visit, had been clear: She wanted nothing from Eli Pierce other than a means of transportation. He was an old family friend, an old flame, nothing more. It was getting his heart to shut away the desire for more that was the trick. Maybe he'd ask his mom and dad when they got back from their summer road trip if they'd heard anything from the Baileys, but that wouldn't be until August.

He pulled the new Ford into the gravel driveway. Five vehicles belonging to clients in the bush were parked there and an old car with Anchorage identification. He put the truck in park and climbed out. A woman stood on the bank above the water, staring out at Fish Lake and the Talkeetna Mountains in the distance. One of the first sightseers to arrive for the summer? Probably wanted a ride around McKinley—

She turned then, at the sound of his truck door slamming shut.

And Eli felt as if he had been punched in the gut.

Bryn Bailey.

Bryn had expected the old leap in her belly when she first saw him but not the accelerated pulse rate, the sudden cold sweat. Was she actually scared to see him again? She forced a smile and walked across the grass to meet him. "Hello, Eli," she said softly.

"Hello, Doc." He pulled her into his arms for a warm, if a bit awkward, embrace. When he dropped his arms and pulled back, a question ran through his eyes. "Need a lift to Summit? I wondered if you'd come this year."

"No. I mean, maybe at some point. I'd like to get to Summit for a weekend or two. I'm actually here on official business."

His eyes, such a soft hazel, narrowed in confusion. "Official?"

"Yes. I'm the volunteer doctor for Housecalls this summer. And as fate would have it, I've been assigned to Talkeetna."

"Y-you?"

She nodded, acknowledging his shock. "What are the chances, huh?"

"You didn't request it?"

"No. I was thinking they'd send me up near Barrow or out to the Aleutians." She reached into her coat pocket for Carmine's paperwork. "Doc Kostas said there was a guy named Leon who had agreed to fly me around too. Housecalls covers all your expenses. But I'm sure you know that."

"Yeah. I met Carmine last summer." Eli crossed his arms in front of him. "He was up fishing. Decided then to establish an outpost here. There are quite a few people who live in the bush over the summer. People who are used to medical care."

Bryn raised her eyebrows, pursed her lips. Why did she get the feeling that he thought she had orchestrated all of this? "Guess I'll be their doc."

"Guess so." His eyes remained on hers and she stared back, refusing to look away first. He had aged nicely, the high mountain air giving him the ruddy complexion of a cowboy on the range, his customary three-day beard growth more full, more manly now. A fine, light-brown stubble covered his square jaw line and that sweet dimple in his chin. He was a handsome man, no doubt about it.

"You married yet?" she asked suddenly.

"Not yet," he said in a tone that implied he might be soon. "You?"

"Not yet," she returned, smiling. "Met lots of people over the last five years, but not the right guy."

He nodded, obviously trying to resist smiling too, then sobered. "I'm back with Sara. Things are pretty serious."

She nodded again, feeling like a child's toy with a bobbing head. "Good to know. I don't want to intrude, Eli. If you'd prefer that I fly with this Leon fellow—"

"You say that now. You've never flown with Leon—it'll curl your hair."

Bryn's eyes widened in surprise. "He's safe?"

"Most of the time," Eli said, smiling again. "Where are you staying?"

"On the river. On the edge of town."

"That's convenient. Won't be the same as Summit though."

"Nothing's like Summit."

She thought then of that last night together, when the aurora borealis had shone so brightly, and by the look on Eli's face, he was remembering too. That night when, as Jonathan Edwards wrote, she felt "wrapt and swallowed up in God." She looked out over Fish Lake and then back to Eli. "Been there much yourself this year?"

"A couple of times."

"How's our cabin faring? How's Ben?"

"Your cabin is in good shape. Ben? Ben never seems to change. Has a new bear cub already."

The mention of bears sent Bryn's mind back to the grizzly, to Eli saving her, to longing glances by the stove as he recuperated in her cabin.

Another car roared into the driveway, sending gravel flying. "That's my client," Eli said, obviously relieved to be given an excuse to end their conversation.

"You'd better go. If you want to rethink your commitment to Housecalls, I could call Carmine, tell him you'd changed your mind. There's probably another operation in town that could—"

"No. No. I made a promise to Housecalls, through September. I'll honor that."

"Okay," Bryn said, raising her hands. If there was one thing Eli

Pierce certainly was, it was honorable. "Just remember I gave you an out."

"Don't need an out, Doc," he said softly. But she believed he did. If he wanted to stay with Sara. If he wanted things to remain serious with her. Because it was happening again. That relentless *passion* between them. She knew it would take everything in them both to avoid it all summer long.

"She's here? In Talkeetna?" Sara asked, alarm running through her morning blue eyes.

"Yeah. Didn't ask for the assignment. Actually asked for something else. But was sent here."

"And you're going to be her pilot?"

Eli licked his lips, measuring his tone, his words, desperate to reassure Sara but be honest too. "Yes. Me and Leon."

Sara sighed, walked to the front window of her tiny rental home. "And she's living here, in town. Not Summit?"

"Yes. When she's not out on assignment. Bryn said she'd like to get to Summit Lake a couple of times this summer, but she's here on official business. I'd guess Housecalls will keep her fairly busy, on the road quite a bit."

"With you."

"Or Leon."

Sara shook her head. "I don't like it, Eli. I mean, I just have to be honest. Last time—"

"Last time I was still hung up on her."

"And now?"

"Now? I'm hung up on you." He smiled at her and she leaned into his chest, accepting his embrace. He breathed a sigh of relief.

"I don't want to lose you, Eli."

"I don't want to lose you, Sara."

She leaned back and stared up into his eyes. "Then watch yourself." She shook her head once. "I can't take another breakup. We just got things going again. Everything is right, you know? This is it."

Eli nodded. "I know." He wished he were ready to propose, that he could assure her with a ring on her finger and a wedding date. She was right for him in so many ways. He thought the world of her, cared for her deeply. Maybe even loved her. His parents liked her, and she loved Talkeetna, was ready to settle here.

Everything *was* right. In his head, it all lined up. Why wouldn't his heart tell him so too?

Bryn arrived at her cabin and opened the back door. It was a small seventies A-frame, built right on a bend in the Talkeetna River. She could hear the river's rush, even from inside, and decided it would be a pleasant and soothing sound, especially at night, much as the waves on Summit's shore had been to her over summers past.

The carpet was an outdated avocado shag, in need of a good washing, and the pumpkin-colored couches, stiff and uncomfortable, had a layer of dog hair on them. Bryn decided that the first thing she would do, after unpacking her bags, would be to give the cabin a thorough cleaning. Make it hers. At least for the summer.

She climbed up the wooden steps to the loft and was pleasantly surprised to find nice, wide-planked pine flooring, a log bedframe with a firm queen-size mattress, a matching pine chest of drawers, and end tables. The owners, clearly, had invested more in the bedroom than the rest of the house. She threw her duffel on the bed and walked to the huge picture window. On either side of it were smaller windows, which she immediately cranked open to let in the sounds of the water as well as some fresh air.

In the back of the loft bedroom was the lone bathroom, a simple shower, sink, and toilet arrangement but with newer-looking tile. She returned to the more dismal downstairs. The kitchen was a galley setup, long and narrow. But it would do. After all, she was only cooking for one. And when home, she would spend lots of time either on the deck, overlooking the water, or up in the luxurious bedroom. Not a bad way to spend the summer, she mused. Much better than her friend Annie getting used to her first summer in New York City or Jeff in St. Louis.

She walked out the patio doors and surveyed her view of the river and the Alaskan Range beyond. *Not half bad.* To be fair, not really bad at all.

CHAPTER EIGHT

*E*li had traveled far and wide in the last five years, but nothing was like home. He rolled the de Havilland into a steep bank and surveyed the land like a king taking in his domain. New York had been crazy; Beijing, otherworldly; Rio, hedonistic; and Israel, holy, even amid the constant strife.

Bryn had once asked him how he knew he was supposed to be in Alaska when he'd never been anywhere else but Chicago, and now he knew. He wasn't one of the Alaskans that were running away from something; he was home. This was it. This broad, beautiful Susitna Valley, the mountain ranges that showed themselves to him in surprising ways—the High One, often veiled in clouds and then clearing like a looming warrior emerging from the fog, the miles of birch and spruce, the herds of caribou, the grizzly and moose. He took a deep breath. This was home.

The tourists with him asked about the clear-cutting and expressed the normal Outsider belief that no trees should be harvested at all, never mind their penchant for pine tables and paper and disposable napkins. They asked him to name the mountain peaks as they passed, mountains that Eli had dreamed about when away—*Mount Deception, Mount Brooks, Mount Silverthorne, Mount Tatum, Mount Carpe.*

And even cheechakos like them—people who had squealed in delight over a moose sighting that was actually a musk ox from a commercial operation outside Talkeetna—hushed in awe of their beauty. The morning light cast deep shadows on the western slopes while the eastern angles glowed with a soft, peachy hue. The mountains at lower elevations, those that slept at the high peaks' feet, were a soft maroon.

The tinny voice of Leon came over the radio, interrupting the blessed silence. "Beaver-four-two-six-Alpha-Bravo, this is Alaska Bush. You out there, Eli?"

"Alaska Bush, this is Beaver-four-two-six-Alpha-Bravo. Go ahead, Leon."

"I've got a trio here wantin' a trip around Denali and a doc from Housecalls wanting a lift to Shubert Lake."

Eli pursed his lips, thinking. "Is the Housecalls trip an emergency?"

Leon apparently turned away from the radio to ask, then said, "Kind of. The family there called in, asking for assistance. Said they had an uncomfortable meeting between an ax and a thigh."

Eli frowned. "I'm headin' home now. I could take the tourists if you'll take Doc Bailey to Shubert."

"Gotcha."

"And Leon?"

"Yeah, boss?"

"Take care, will ya?"

Leon paused for a moment, and Eli could almost see his expression of puzzlement. "Always, boss," he finally replied.

"You folks can make yourselves comfortable," Leon Wilmot said to the tourists in the small cabin that served as Alaska Bush's office.

"Eli will be back in about half an hour. He'll refuel and then head out with you for your sightseein'. You, Doc, I'll escort to Shubert."

"How far is it?" Bryn asked, suddenly remembering Eli calling Leon something like a "crazy old pilot."

The short, wizened man was already moving out. "C'mon, Doc. You got your first patient waitin' on ya," he said from the open doorway.

Bryn followed him down the bank to the docks, to a Cessna on pontoons. He opened the door to enter, caught himself, and stepped back to assist her in. Jamie came down the slope to give the prop a good pull and help them cast off. The Cessna, like the de Havilland, was tight inside, and Bryn struggled to get situated with her bulky Housecalls bag and an overnight duffel. "Sure you don't mind dropping me at Summit after this trip?"

"No problem," Leon said, smiling at her with teeth that were in sore need of a dentist's care. "We won't be but seven miles from Summit."

"That's what I figured from the map. I'd be happy to pay—"

"Please. It's my pleasure, Doc."

It had been a week of twiddling her thumbs and plowing through the latest Oprah pick. The thrill of finally seeing a patient, to do what she had come to Alaska to do, charged through her veins. She had been about to scream, what with her constant thoughts about Eli, here, in his home turf, and memories of them together at Summit driving her to distraction. She had just called Carmine, asking if it would be okay to spend a long weekend up at the lake, when the emergency call had come into headquarters.

"Go ahead and go," Carmine had encouraged. "We can radio you there and pick you up at the lake if necessary."

Leon nodded at Jamie, who cast off their mooring line, and he headed out toward the end of Fish Lake. A gray swan and seven cygnets scattered in the wake of the prop wash, hustling into the safety of tall, yellow-green reeds. And then Bryn and Leon were motoring down the lake at increasing speed, the highway and Alaska Bush coming into quick view. Bryn's hand tightened around the other, but she willed herself not to scream. The plane lifted at the last possible moment, clearing the cabin by twenty feet—twenty feet that felt like two.

"You got grit, Doc," Leon said with nod and a cracked-tooth smile. "Gotta love a woman with grit."

Bryn struggled to find her voice. "I'm in Alaska now, aren't I? And I've done my years as a cheechako. It's time to do as the natives do and fit in."

They landed on a pristine robin's-egg blue lake, just a mountain saddle over from Summit. It occurred to Bryn that it might have been there that the poachers had once landed their own plane. A white-faced, winter-worn woman greeted them at the shoreline and, trailed by two small children, led them up to the tiny two-room cabin where they made their home. In the back bedroom, a man was trying to sit still, trying not to writhe in the obvious agony he was enduring, and a broad bandage was soaked through with bright red blood.

"First things, first," Bryn said, taking control of the situation. "Mr. Jurrel, I'm Doctor Bailey. We'll get you feeling better right away or ferried out of here to Willow."

"Want to stay here," he said through clenched teeth.

"That's up to me to decide," Bryn answered. She bent to unzip her Housecalls bag, searching the compartments for lidocaine to ease the man's pain, 3-0 Vicryl to sew up the first, deeper layer, 3-0 Silk to close, Betadine, and an antibiotic ointment. "Had a tetanus shot in the last seven years, Mr. Jurrel?"

"Four years ago," he gritted out.

"Good. You're up to date. How'd this happen?" she asked, still looking for the 3-0 Silk while trying to keep the man's mind off the pain.

"Chopping firewood. Stupid. Stupid of me. My boy came up... wanted to help. All of a sudden he was in my line of swing and...tried to avoid him. Hit me instead." He managed a rueful smile, and Bryn realized with a start that he couldn't have been any older than she was. This country had a means of aging people that was startling. Tough, mean, long winters. Only the narrow shoulder seasons of spring and fall and the delightful summer kept them at it, kept them all holed up in Alaska. If it was only winter, they'd all run from here screaming. But those other seasons made it all worthwhile.

She quickly cut away the bandages Mrs. Jurrel had applied and efficiently injected lidocaine along the wound. "You did good work here, Mrs. Jurrel," Bryn said with a smile of encouragement. The woman had enough to deal with in her two rambunctious children.

"The wound's clean. The ax missed anything important, lucky for you," she said, noting the proximity of the femoral artery, half an inch from the cut. "Looks to me like you're going to need about twenty stitches, some cleaning up, and bed rest."

"Told ya we didn't need to radio in," Mr. Jurrel said to his wife.

"You did the right thing," Bryn interrupted. "You talk tough now, but you wouldn't want to suffer these stitches without anesthesia."

Thoughts of Eli, memories of stitching him up in her cabin, tumbled through her mind—broad, strong hands; tender hazel eyes. But he was not hers to dream about anymore. He was Sara Cussler's. And Bryn had every intention to stay out of their way. No one would ever claim Bryn Bailey as the cause for unhappiness again. Not if she could help it.

"I have some whiskey somewhere," Mr. Jurrel said with a pained smile.

"You just sit back and let modern medicine do its duty," Bryn said, placing a gentle hand on his shoulder.

They were taking off from Shubert Lake when a second visit request was made from Housecalls. There had been a cave-in at the old Lone Gulch gold mine, where, Leon informed her, operations had recently been started again.

"When it rains it pours," Bryn said with an assenting nod to Leon's unspoken question. "This is what I came to do."

Leon banked the plane, wing to sky, and headed off toward his new coordinates. "The only problem," he said so softly she almost didn't hear, "is a good landing site."

Bryn licked her lips and stared out the window. *Please, Lord, I am here to serve you and the people. Please get us there in one piece.* She didn't care to be in an accordion-like crash, her body one with the earth. But eventually she relaxed. The Cessna's loud hum had almost lulled her into napping when Leon took a sudden dive toward land.

Bryn sat up straighter, frightened, but the old man let out a shout of glee. "Just wanted to wake you up, Doc," he teased.

"I'm awake."

Leon flew low over the mine site, tipping his wings at the frantic man on the ground who waved a red flag. The mine was little more than a dark hole against a naked mountainside with three outbuildings. They surveyed the impossibly short, boggy arm of the river nearby as their landing strip. Leon banked and made another low run.

"Leon—"

He held his hand in the air, shushing her, staring outside at what Bryn hoped wouldn't be their own site of catastrophe. He banked the Cessna again, this time going over the waterway and reeds and mud like a pro golfer judging how far it was to the tee. When he pulled up and banked, then banked again, Bryn couldn't hold her tongue.

"Leon, we can't make that."

"Sure we can, Doc. Just close your eyes if it scares you."

He came in low again, just a few feet above the rolling tundra, making Bryn fear that it would be the land and not the water that would kill them, that it would take hold and grab and flip them into a cartwheel, or worse, a dead stop. But onward they rolled, the engine slowing, the nose up, so that as soon as they hit the nearest bank, Leon had the plane in the water, madly working to slow it down, the far bank almost upon them.

At the last possible moment, he made a high-torque turn, and Bryn let out a little scream, finally shutting her eyes. It was then she realized they had come to a full stop, the back ends of the floats neatly tucked on the muddy bank.

"You okay, Doc?"

She fought for breath. "Fine," she managed. "Fine," she said again, as much to reassure herself as to convince Leon, who was already out the door.

The man with the flag met them at the riverbank, his booted feet sinking a few inches into the sludge. It had rained here recently, maybe accounting for the cave-in. The man, who introduced himself as George Schwender, shouldered Bryn's Housecalls bag and hustled her to the largest of the outbuildings, which served as a temporary triage unit.

When he opened the door, five men spilled out, and Bryn quickly entered to examine the injured miners. The first had a compound fracture of the forearm that would require surgery; the next was suffering from a wound to the eye and would also need surgical care; the third and final victim was still unconscious, possibly with a broken neck. Bryn's eyes widened as she gazed from one patient to the next. "These men all need a hospital, not an emergency medic. I can stabilize them, but they need to be taken to Willow."

"Didn't know it was so bad when we called," George said, hands in his pockets. "We were still gettin' them out. Would've asked for a helicopter to airlift them, but you were so close—"

"Fine," she said, waving her hand to shush him. She looked at Leon then. "How long would it take to get a chopper here?"

"Probably come from Anchorage. Hour, hour and a half. Depends on what's avail—"

"These men don't have that long," she snapped. "They need to be in a hospital in under two hours or we might lose him," she said, nodding at the unconscious one. "I'll need you to make two stretchers to get them to the plane and out of here. The guy with the bad eye can probably walk, right?" She waited until he nodded slightly, and then she went to work, doing her best to stabilize them for the miserably long and bumpy ride back to town. She had seen the gray bank of clouds moving in as clearly as Leon had.

She edged toward the unconscious man first. "Has he been conscious at all since the cave-in?" she asked.

"Yeah. Complained of pain in his neck. He was thrown backward when it happened. Couldn't get up and walk out of the mine," said the nearest man. "Said he couldn't move his legs."

Bryn wrapped his neck in a plastic collar from her bag, trying her best to immobilize his spine. Who knew what damage his fellow miners had done in moving him to the mess hall. "Okay, now when we move him to the stretcher, our goal is to keep his back as straight as possible."

She moved on to the man with the broken forearm, which was at an odd angle at his side.

"Hi." She looked in his eyes. "I'm Doctor Bailey." For a moment his gaze connected with hers in a nod before the pain of his injury reclaimed his attention. "This is going to smart," she warned. Then with a quick movement she reduced the fracture, snapping it into place. The man screamed in agony, and all eyes moved to Bryn. "I'm sorry," she said, looking in her bag for a portable metal-and-foam splint. She quickly wrapped his limb and surrounded the support with an Ace elastic bandage.

"His leg? Why do you think it's broken?" She directed her question to the crew boss, still a little ashen and wide-eyed over her quick movement. "George!" Bryn shouted.

"Uh, he couldn't put weight on it. Said it hurt like all get-out."

They were probably right in their assessment, but without an x-ray, a broken tibia was tough to tell. She rummaged for her other splint and wrapped his leg too. The man moaned. She drew up a hundred milligrams of Demerol and gave the man a shot in the rear to ease his agony.

Turning to her last patient, she said, "Looks like your eye's in a bad way." The man remained silent while Bryn fashioned a disk out of a plastic foam cup and taped it over his seeping eye. She was in no position to extract anything inside and then close the wound in the middle of the Lone Gulch mining camp. It was better to send him to the hospital. As she wrapped gauze around his head, she gently probed his zygomatic arch. He winced, even with the Demerol in his system.

"That bone could be broken. Tell the doc when you get there. They'll x-ray it. You'll be fine."

"Am I gonna be blind in that eye forever?" he finally said.

"I hope not. They do amazing things these days. We'll say a prayer for you. For all of you." She rubbed his arm in encouragement, and then they moved the patients out to the plane.

They were at the Cessna before Bryn realized there would be no room for her to go, not if Leon wanted to get off that slender band of water. He had already taken the two backseats all the way out of the fuselage to make room for the other two on stretchers and to reduce his total cargo weight.

"Guess I'll have to come back for ya, Doc," Leon said, helping the man with the wounded eye in first, to sit beside him up front, in the cockpit. "Won't scare him so much since he can't see that approaching bank," he whispered to Bryn.

She half laughed and shook her head, turning to get out of the way as the men brought the other victims aboard. Leon led her off to a small stand of spruce and pushed a gun of cold metal into her hands. "It's loaded. You know how to use it?"

In shock, Bryn turned over the Colt and studied it. Her dad had taught her to use firearms as a girl, hoping she might one day be a hunter as he was. "Yeah. I can use it." She supposed it might come in handy here, in a mining camp.

"Good," was all Leon said, returning to the plane. Bryn tucked the gun into her waistband, underneath the back hem of her coat.

If Leon could just manage to get off safely and over the mountains to Willow in time, they all might make it. Again Bryn cast her eyes to the gray sky.

"Hey, at least you packed," Leon said, eyes twinkling as he dumped at her feet the bag she had intended for Summit. "I'll be back when I get these guys situated and the weather clears."

Bryn licked her lips again, staring at the grizzled old pilot, suddenly fully aware that she was in a mining camp full of perhaps twenty female-starved men, miles from civilization.

"You'll be all right, Doc. Have you got any money to gamble with?"

Bryn thought about it, remembered the twenty she always carried in her shoe. "Twenty bucks."

"That'll get you into the game!" a miner yelled behind her as Leon shut the fuselage door and grinned even more widely. Leon gave her the thumbs-up sign and tentatively made his way over the injured to sit beside his one-eyed copilot. In minutes he was revving up the engine for a short-field takeoff and then was rushing the far bank like a high-school hockey player dead-set on getting the puck. He cleared the trees by a matter of eighteen inches, and a miner at her side let out a long, low whistle. "Don't make flyboys like that anymore."

"Come on, Doc," George said, coming to her side. "We're a hospitable lot when we put a mind to it. Come in and we'll have ourselves some supper and then a game of cards. You play poker?"

"You *left* her there?"

"Doc's own mind to do it too. She could plainly see that she couldn't come. You know that bog. Can barely get two people in and out, let alone five," Leon defended. "She's a grown woman. Can take care of herself. Besides, I left her my .357 in case she comes up to any trouble."

"You gave her your gun," he said flatly.

"Told me she knows how to use it." Admiration shone in the older man's silver-blue eyes.

Eli sat back, thinking that one over. Bryn Bailey with a gun. Since when? Maybe the streets of Boston had proven harder or scarier than she had anticipated. Maybe she'd had a brush with a mugger or... "I can't believe you left her there," Eli said again, as angry at this feeling of insecurity and helplessness as he was at Leon. He knew he would've done the same thing, had the situation been reversed.

"Now look, Eli, I—"

"Who's the mine boss out there now?"

"Fella named George Schwender."

Eli stalked over to the radio. "Think I'll call up there now, ask to talk to her."

Leon went to the window. "There's no gettin' her out. Not till this storm blows over. She's fine, Eli. George'll look after her." He paused. "You worried 'cause she's a woman or 'cause she's Bryn Bailey?"

Eli ignored him and bent to turn the dials on the radio when footsteps on the front porch caught his attention. It was Sara, with a jar full of wildflowers and a bright smile on her face. "Thought you could use a little color on what promises to be a gray—" She sobered at Eli's look. "Eli, what's wrong?" she asked, abruptly setting the bouquet down and coming to him.

"Well, Leon just…" Eli stared at her for a long moment, then at the mike in his hand, then back to her. Quietly he set it down. "Nothing's wrong. Storm's blowing in. Want to go grab some dinner before it lets loose?"

"Sounds good," Sara said, her tentative smile returning. She looped an arm around Eli's waist, and he slipped his around her shoulders. Together they went to his desk where he grabbed his keys and cell phone.

Before exiting, Eli turned and looked at Leon with what he hoped was a meaningful glance. "Leon, check on that client for me, will ya? Just to make sure, I have this with me," he added, holding up his cell phone. "In case there's anything to report."

"Won't be nothin' to report, boss," Leon returned, "until that storm passes by and we can see for ourselves."

"Check on it anyway," Eli said, then turned away, knowing he had revealed how hung up he still was on Bryn. And the knowledge that he was being somehow unfaithful to Sara burned deep inside him.

The miners proved to be harmless, as appealing and problematic as a den of wolf puppies. They obviously longed for a feminine gesture, a word spoken in a soft voice, a flip of her long hair—lapping it up like milk. And after several shots of Jack Daniel's, the men were laughing and having a great time, their bellies full of caribou and whiskey, a fire burning brightly in the wood stove, and twenty almost-clean bodies shoved into the mess hall for a game of cards.

They had been careful to teach her the intricacies of poker—five-card stud, high-low Jacks, lowball, and other versions of the game. And then they proceeded to lose all their money to her, a fact that alternately aggravated and delighted them all. Bryn tried to ignore the choking cigarette smoke that filled the room and tried not to wrinkle her nose in distaste at the foul language tossed about. This, after all, was where Jesus would be if he were walking on earth today. Among his people who were desperate for the Word, a knowledge of their Creator, and their place in his world.

She sighed after raking in the last round, her wager unsurpassed by any around the table, and her pitiful hand—a pair of sevens—unchecked. "It's late, boys," she called, like a jovial bartender to brothers and dear friends. "I've taken your money and your gold nuggets. I think I had better call it a night. Are there any free bunks?"

"C'mon, Doc!" cried one across the table from her. "You can't quit now. Double or nothing. Give us a chance to win it back."

"That or go to strip poker," another said, leering at Bryn.

"That I will not do," she said, trying to keep her tone light. She stretched, as much to feel for the Colt in her waistband as to relieve tension, and mulled over their call for another hand. "Here's my bet," she said. "I'm wagering all this cash, other than my twenty that will go back to my shoe"—several men chuckled at that—"and these gold nuggets, that will go to Housecalls as a donation from a grateful group of miners for saving their comrades in arms. That leaves, let's see, six, seven hundred dollars that you can win back."

She studied the remaining men around the table, bent to unzip her bag, and pulled out her Bible, purchased the fall she left Alaska last. "If one of you wins, you take the money and run. If I win," she said, staring around the loop again, "you each read the book of Romans from beginning to end."

"Hey, now, you a doc or a preacher?" one complained at the end of the table. He had the rounded features of an Eskimo, like several others in the crowd.

"A doc," she said with her most winning smile. "A doc on a mission."

The table erupted in laughter. "The way I figure it," said a slim man of perhaps forty years across from her, "it's a pretty safe bet. Any one of us wins, we get all our cash back. The nuggets we can donate," he enunciated slowly, lowering his gaze to make sure she knew she was forcing that decision. "Chances are six-to-one that we won't even have to read that book of Romans."

"So you would think," Bryn said with another teasing smile. She reached for the deck and shuffled quickly. "But you're about to see, boys," she said cockily, "that the Lord's on my side, and he's not very fond of drinking too much or losing your hard-won money in a hand of poker."

"Most effective missionary I've encountered," said another. "What happens to the cash if you win?"

"Yeah. Didn't tell us what would happen to the cash," said the leering man down the way.

"I'll give your share back to each of you. Just as soon as you can answer three key questions from the book of Romans." She picked up her cards and fanned them out, delighted with the royalty in her hand and the King of kings who could make such things happen. Who would have thought? Who would have ever guessed that Bryn Bailey would be witnessing to a house full of miners in the middle of nowhere by playing a night's worth of poker?

"Okay, out with it," Sara said, reaching across the table to take Eli's hand. Rain pounded on the roof of Alice's restaurant and bar, where they had dined on fresh salmon. "You're scaring me, Eli."

"Scaring you?" Eli asked, puzzlement knitting his brow.

"It's not like you, not talking, not telling me about your day."

Eli took a sip of water, spent undue time staring at the rivulets of sweat running down the glass's beaded sides. His grandmother had had a beaded lampshade like this glass once. How old were these glasses anyway?

"Eli."

He forced his attention back to Sara, his mind not on the blonde across from him but on a beautiful brunette stuck in a mining camp, armed or not...

"Eli..."

"Sorry," he said, shaking his head as if water had dripped on him. A chill ran down his neck.

"You're thinking of her."

"Her? Who?"

"Bryn Bailey. You're thinking of her. Did you see her today?"

"No. No!" He threw up his hands. "Look, I'm making an effort to not see her at all."

"Then why are you thinking about her?"

How had Sara known? How did women know such things? He dared to look her in the eye, then looked down to the stack of fish bones on his plate before he spoke. "She's stuck," he admitted. "It's bugging me. Leon flew her in," he rushed on. "I didn't even see her, but somehow I feel responsible."

"Where? Where is she stuck?"

"Up at the old Lone Gulch mine. They had a cave-in today. Three men injured. Housecalls was on the scene, and Leon took her there. Ended up having to fly them all out, with no room for Bryn."

Sara's eyes widened, looking concerned for the first time. "So she's stuck in a mining camp? Alone?"

"Yeah," he said, warming to her empathetic tone. "Would've gone back for her myself but for the weather."

Sara was up and walking out of the restaurant before he knew that he had said something wrong.

The rain was still pounding on the metal roof, and Eli looked at the swinging door, then at Alice behind the bar.

"Better go after her," she said with a nod. "Pretty girl, ugly night."

"Make that two pretty girls," he muttered to himself. He threw down some cash and hurried after Sara. "Suddenly the night is even uglier."

The rain was a torrent, and Sara was standing at the corner in the dim light, looking up as the skies opened upon her.

"We just got back together, Eli," she said mournfully. "Why do you need to be the one to rescue her?"

"I don't. I mean… I don't know what I mean. Can we go in? Out from—"

"I don't want to give you up! I thought this was it."

"It still can be, Sara. I'm just confused. I don't know—"

"Don't know!" She waited until he looked her in the eye, struggling to see her through the drenching rain. "How can you say that? And *confused*, Eli? About us? I love you! Don't you—" She stopped, her question unspoken.

He was in agony. Did he love her? Why couldn't he say it? Right here, right now?

She moved into his arms, resting her head on his shoulder for a brief moment before wordlessly turning away and disappearing into the dark, wet night.

CHAPTER NINE

The one miner who had spooked her had been firmly escorted out at the end of the night by George, the crew boss. She was grateful for the interception. Still she had slept on the lower bunk, closest to the fire, with only five men in the bunkhouse, the others relegated to double up in the two remaining outbuildings. And Leon's Colt, tucked under her pillow, was within easy reach in case anyone else thought of making improper advances.

She had watched the hypnotic flames of the dying fire until midnight, listening to the rain pound outside and waiting until she knew her comrades were asleep, snoring like a quintet of old sea lions. Finally she succumbed to sleep herself. When she awakened she felt surprisingly refreshed.

She was first up and was trying to find the coffee in the mess hall to get a pot brewing when George ambled up beside her, yawning and stretching.

"You sleep last night, Doc?"

"Oh yes." She watched as he moved several cases of beans aside and pulled out a huge can of ground Folgers.

"That's good. Sometimes winning big will keep a body up." He turned to give her a wink that reminded her of Sam Elliott, and then he went back to his work of filling a large pot with water to heat on the stove.

"I really will give the nuggets to Housecalls."

"I believe you, Doc," he said.

She tucked her hands into her jean pockets. "Do you think it was too much? I mean, the Bible reading and all?"

He gave her a wry look. "You kiddin'? These boys died and went to heaven. You gave them something to talk about for years to come. We don't come across a doctor-missionary-gambler too often."

"I know I displaced some of them from their bunks last night."

"No worries," George said with another wink. "Pretty doc like you is always welcome to come and preach at my boys, regardless of what you're peddlin' or how much cash you win. You're like a USO girl in a camp of soldiers, I tell ya."

"Thanks. I think. Say, George, are there any other men in need of a doctor, you know, minor things that I could help with before a problem gets worse? I should've thought of it last night after Leon left, but—"

"Let's see now." George went to the propane-generated refrigerator and pulled out a large package of caribou sausages. "Keith had a run-in with a porcupine a few days ago. You might check on his hand. And Webby burned his arm on a lamp night before last. We usually tend to our own wounds around here—isn't often a doctor rambles through."

"I'd be happy to look at them. Will you speak to them, make sure it's all right?"

George gave her another whimsical grin. "Lady, these boys would go get themselves injured to get closer to you. You'll have no problem, I guarantee it."

The storm lifted by the time the blueberry hotcakes were bubbling on the griddle and the caribou sausages were sizzling in two wide cast-iron pans. Later, as the satiated group sat back from plates licked clean of the last stripes of real maple syrup, a plane roared overhead.

"There's your Cessna, Doc," George said.

A Cessna. Not a Beaver. She nodded, a bit disappointed.

Bryn rose to see to Webby and Keith, who obediently went to the bunkhouse as the others went out to meet Leon and hear the report on their comrades. She attended to Webby first, checking the second-degree burns that were easily diagnosed by their blisters. "Know those hurt. We'll leave them though. The blister acts as a natural bandage." She rubbed some Silvadene cream on the burn and wrapped it in sterile gauze.

Keith's left hand still had several porcupine quills in it. Bryn carefully cleaned the skin, numbed the area with lidocaine, and then, using a number-eleven blade with a fine, triangular tip, made tiny incisions next to the quills and pulled the fishhooklike ends out. The incisions were so small there was no need for stitches. She covered the area with Bacitracin ointment and grinned up at Keith. "All done."

"Thanks, Doc. That's terrific. Thought I'd have to live with them until they came out on their own."

"No problem. You should've said something last night. If you see any sign of infection, use more of that ointment."

"Ready to go, Doc?" Leon said as he walked up to them. He looked Bryn over from head to toe as if to make sure she had not sustained any bodily injury.

"Ready," she said, zipping her bag. She slid her hand over the rough cotton sheet and under the pillow, grabbing the Colt and then turning to hand it to Leon.

George watched the whole thing, chuckled, and shook his head.

"Nope, not many gun-totin', pretty girls who are doctors in the bush, as well as preachers."

"Preachers?" Leon asked.

"Never mind," Bryn said with a smile cast toward George and a nod at the group of men behind him. "Tell me about those patients I sent out with you yesterday."

"All of them are on the mend, Doc. That one with the spinal injury is the one they're concerned about most, 'course, but even he is supposed to be okay."

"No long-term paralysis?" They walked out to the swampy river bend, tentatively picking their way through mud that was worse than the day before.

"Didn't sound like it. Didn't check on him this morning though."

"Fine. Just curious. Thanks for getting them out, Leon. And for coming back for me."

The slim, older man turned and grinned. "You kidding? Eli was up at five, calling me on the phone, yammering about how I ought to already be up in the air comin' after ya. I hardly had a choice."

Bryn laughed, stowed her bags, then turned to wave at her new friends. They were a ragtag bunch. She still couldn't believe she'd spent the night with them all and survived. She smiled. It felt good, taking on challenges like this, exploring just what she was made of and finding out that she liked what she found.

Bryn entered the plane. "We goin' to Summit now?"

"Sorry, Doc," Leon said. "Housecalls has a whole lineup of visits for you to make. Looked to me to be at least a week's worth. The word is out on you, I guess. We'll start at Twin Lakes. There's a boy who's been running a high fever for five days."

George stepped out onto the pontoon and, before shutting the door, said, "Radio us and give us a report on the guys every day, would ya?"

"Happy to do it," Bryn promised.

Leon climbed in beside her and went through his checklist for takeoff. "More mud today," he mumbled.

"Is it safe? To go? Should we wait?"

"Nah. We're fine. Fine."

"Mind if I shut my eyes?"

"Not at all, Doc. You do what you need to, and I'll do my thing. Yep. Lotta years in this bird. Did I tell you about the time I lost a ski with a bunch of sightseers up on a glacier?"

"No. And Leon? Maybe you shouldn't tell me right now."

"Oh. Okay, Doc. Saddle up. We're on the move!"

Eli was working on the engine of the Beaver, replacing a Magnito, having lost his third client of the day because of his downed plane and Leon's Housecalls trip, when an attachment bolt broke loose. He grimaced and let out a cry of unbridled fury. He rammed his hand against the fuselage, wincing at the pain as flesh met metal. It would take the rest of the day to drive to Anchorage and pick up another. A whole day! Gone!

Could nothing go right in his life?

To make matters worse, when he looked up the grassy knoll past the office, he saw Sara's car pull off the highway and park in his lot. He didn't know what to say to her. He had already said everything he could think of! He needed some time to sort things out.

She walked down the hillside, her blond hair flying about like straw in the wind. Sara was beautiful, inside and out. *What are you doing, Pierce? What are you risking here?* As she drew closer, he could see the dark circles ringing her eyes, testimony to a sleepless night. "Tried to call," she said, with a sweet tuck of her head toward the office.

"Yeah," he said, wiping his hands on an already grimy cloth. "Been a little busy out here with the plane. Sorry. Didn't check for messages."

"What's the matter with it?"

"Broken Magnito. Then I busted an attachment bolt. Have to head to Anchorage now to pick up replacements, or I'll miss tomorrow's clients too."

Sara's eyes went to the side of the dock where Leon's Cessna was conspicuously absent. "He went after her then?"

"Yeah." Eli turned back toward the engine, not wanting her in his line of vision any longer. It was heartbreaking, this crevasse that was widening between them. But he felt powerless to stop it. "I told you I wouldn't go."

"She didn't ask for you?"

"No." He turned a screw that needed no tightening and looked for something else to busy himself with. It was stupid. Cowardly of him to avoid her look. He was more than this, more of a man than this. He sighed and stood to his full height, turned to look at her.

She studied him, and those clear baby blues seemed to see right through him. "But you wanted to go," she whispered. He couldn't deny it. Tears bulged at her lower lids, and Eli resisted the desire to wipe them away, to try to comfort her. He had no right to touch her.

He swallowed hard. "I'm an idiot," he said. "Nothing has happened between Bryn and me this summer," he said, repeating the words of last night. But he had to tell Sara the truth. "She's steered clear of me. She knew you and I were… She was trying… Sara, I'm sorry. You're nothing but perfect. But this thing, this thing inside of me…" He stopped, helpless. Where were the words, the words to describe what started when he was sixteen, the dream that had been resurrected when he was twenty-one and twenty-six, the hope that arose again as soon as Bryn showed up with her Housecalls badge and a yearning to see Summit? *Like catnip to a tomcat,* his father had once said.

Sara tried to smile as she stood up straighter, wiped her tears, clamped her lips shut for a moment, composing what she wanted to say. "You always were in love with Bryn Bailey, Eli. I hope she's worth it. Because I never want to see you again. I can't." She reached up, as if wanting to touch his face, then let her hand drop to her side. "I can't. I won't."

He stared at her for a long moment. "I'm sorry. Oh, Sara, I'm so sorry."

She looked at him for another slow breath of time. And then she turned away and walked up the bank again, not looking back.

Eli glanced up at the fast-moving, charcoal-colored clouds. "Oh, God," he groaned. "Lord God, what am I doing?" He rested his forehead against the cold metal of the Beaver, feeling feverish with fear and anxiety. "What have I done?" he muttered, the tears rolling now.

He had just let the surest thing in his life—other than his God—walk away up that bank and out of it forever. And for what? A chance at something he wasn't even sure could ever be?

It had been two weeks since her departure from the Lone Gulch mine. One Housecalls assignment seemed to lead to another, but she had finally made it to Summit for a night or two. Bryn felt mixed up inside. She knew it was best to avoid Eli, but she still missed him—particularly here, at the lake.

Ben joined her at his front window, staring down the water to where Eli had just landed.

"I miss him, Ben. Every day, I wake up thinking I want to go and see him."

"Sometimes we don't get what we want, just what we need."

Bryn kept her gaze out over the water. "He hasn't seen me at all. I know he and Sara are together, and I know we shouldn't see each other, but I feel as though he hates me or something."

"Hates you? Nah. I think he's confused. Trying to work out what he thinks. What he feels. But hate? No, definitely not hate." His words invited the question: *If not hate, then what?* "Let me ask you something, Bryn," Ben said. "What would it do to you if Eli came up here today and announced that he and Sara were engaged?"

Her eyes raced back to Eli's plane, taxiing toward the shoreline near his cabin. "Engaged?" she managed to repeat. Her throat was suddenly dry. "Why? Did he tell you he was thinking about proposing?"

Ben didn't answer. She could feel his heavy stare. "That's what I thought."

"What do you mean by that?" she asked crossly, finally looking at the older man in the eye.

His smile grew larger. "That's what I thought," he repeated.

"Oh!" Bryn cried out in agitation. "So smug! Just what do you think you know?"

Ben reached out a weathered hand and rested it on her shoulder.

She resisted the urge to pull away, concentrated on the nerve to keep meeting his gaze. "Bryn, that young man has been in love with you since you two were kids. And you've been in love with him. You better get things straight between you before it's too late. Sara Cussler's a fine woman. But you're the gal for Eli. Always have been."

Bryn felt as though she'd been struck. It wasn't anything she hadn't thought herself, of course. It was hearing the words from someone else's lips. She shook her head. "I have no right. I have no right to waltz in here. To try and take him from Sara."

Ben shook his head too. "Not sayin' it will be easy or kind or even fair. But life, as they say, isn't fair. We all have to stick to the road our Lord puts us on and follow his lead."

"You're saying God wants us together?"

Ben laughed under his breath. "Ah, no. I won't wander that far afield. I'm just a man on a lake in the middle of Alaska who raised the occasional cub. A man who for years has watched two kids look at each other as though the other hung the moon. Makes me willing to say a word to you. As I will to Eli."

The mention of his name made her take a breath, a breath she hadn't realized she'd been holding.

She couldn't make this move. No, it was up to him. If he wasn't willing to act on the electricity between them, she certainly wasn't. She'd nursed three girlfriends through heartbreak during her last years of medical school. No. Bryn Bailey was never going to be the other woman. Not if she could help it.

After he got his plane repaired, Eli asked Jamie to schedule him from sunup to sundown, which was getting to be very long days in the north country. He immersed himself in his work, striving to be the very best tour guide possible, spending an extra fifteen minutes out searching for that caribou or fox or moose for the tourists, scouting out new, remote lakes and streams for the fishermen.

He called the Forest Service station to get reports on the fire status for his hikers, called Fish and Game to get updates for his tourists. On a whim he gave a wooly fellow in town—a refugee from the seventies who referred to himself in the third person as "the man," *the man would like to build a Web site for you, dude*—the go-ahead to begin, wondering if he was forking over several hundred dollars for something that would never actually come up on the Net.

He pushed forward on his goal to raise the remaining funds for his basketball court at the outreach center, hoping to draw the locals year-round. He met with the town mayor for dinner, several influential parties for breakfast, the church council last night. "You're in a frenzy," Leon had said when he returned to the office later to work on his logs. Leon was clearly puzzled. "What's goin' on with you?"

"Nothing," Eli said with a shrug. "Busy summer, I guess."

"Where's Sara? Haven't seen her around for a while."

Eli cleared his throat nervously. "Sara won't be around much anymore."

Leon's eyes shot up in surprise. "So that's how it is." When Eli turned away to go to the docks, he added, "You goin' to be ferrying the doc around now?"

Eli paused, not looking back, giving him a half shrug. "Whoever is available. Just as we arranged with Housecalls."

That Friday Eli was changing the oil in the Beaver when Leon came in, an excited look on his face. "What's up with you?" Eli asked.

"Certified letter for the doc." He held up a white number-ten envelope. "Looks official. From a hospital out east."

Eli reached for it, turning the letter over in his hands.

"Mailman was hoping we could deliver it since she's out at Summit this week."

"I'll take it," Eli said too quickly. Leon's face split with a smile.

"Things are getting clearer all the time," he said.

Eli gave him a huff of derision and walked outside.

When the lake was in sight, Eli let out a long sigh. How could one woman have such a pull on him? Even if there hadn't been a letter to deliver, he knew he'd be here this weekend. Near her if not with her. He couldn't help it.

After setting the plane down and making his way up to the cabin, he dropped his gear and walked to the big window. As he stared across the lake, he knew he wanted to start taking her on her calls. To see Bryn in action. To be closer to her. To know if the thing he sensed, the track he was headed on, was the right one.

The CB radio behind him crackled to life, and he turned to answer the call. "This is Eli Pierce," he said as he picked up the mike and pressed the button.

"Yeah, Eli," came Leon's voice. "Housecalls wants Bryn to head out to Donner. There's a cabin about a mile from there with a woman who has a dislocated shoulder."

"Okay. Did they give us a name?"

"Think it's a guy named Harmon out there. Has a young Eskimo wife—she called it in."

"Okay. I'll get Bryn out there. Radio Housecalls for me and tell them we're on our way, all right?"

"You got it. Over and out."

Eli sighed. It was now or never.

From behind the windows, hidden safely in the shadows of the musty smelling cabin, Bryn watched Eli walk to his plane. He'd just arrived. Was he already leaving? Without even saying hello? After Eli freed his mooring lines from the trees and pushed off, he was in the plane and moving quickly across the lake. Toward her cabin.

Bryn frowned. He was coming across? In his plane? What should she be doing? She looked down at herself and groaned. Her shirt was soiled after her afternoon of raking the roof of forest debris. Soggy soil had left oval patches of mud at her knees when she bent to get the water flowing from the pump. And what did her hair look like?

What are you doing? She was not a girl waiting for her prom date! She was Dr. Bryn Bailey, on vacation for a couple of days from her work as a bush physician. She didn't have to look perfect. Eli of all people didn't expect her to look perfect. Her eyes shifted to the plane, rapidly crossing the lake, then to her duffel bag of clean clothes. No. She wouldn't do it.

Squaring her shoulders, she opened the heavy front door and went to shore to greet him. Politely. *No questions,* she silently coached herself.

At the last moment, Eli shut off the engine and neatly glided into the rounded gravel of her shore. The prop slowed. Was he going to invite her for a ride? He emerged from the fuselage and walked down the float like a tightrope artist taking to a rope.

"Hey, Doc," he said, flashing her a sweet, shy smile. "Housecalls radioed in. Wants you to head out to Donner to see to a woman with a dislocated shoulder. Since you're here and I'm here, it looks like I'm your pilot."

She gave him a rueful smile and wrinkled up her nose. "You just got here."

"No problem," he said easily, looking away from her. "Need some help with your things?"

"Nah. Let me just change into something clean, and I'll be right out. My bag is ready."

She ran inside and threw on a clean olive turtleneck, a fresh pair of jeans, and her hiking boots. Thinking of her night at the mine, she grabbed her parka. She shouldered her heavy bag and hurried to the Beaver, handing the duffel over to Eli.

He stowed it and offered her his hand to help her aboard.

"I'm fine," she said, ignoring his proximity. She wasn't going to touch him. Not if she could help it. Sara wouldn't like it.

Once they were airborne, they settled into an awkward silence. Five minutes into the flight, they started to speak at the same time, laughed together, and Eli gestured for her to begin.

"Business has been good, I take it?"

"Good, yes. I get quite a few tourists from Kenai."

"Won't Sara be mad about this? You, instead of Leon, taking me?"

Suddenly he looked nervous and straightened his airman's cap. "About Sara," Eli said. He ran his hand down the zipper of his jacket. "Oh, I forgot about this." He withdrew a letter from his pocket. "It's a certified letter. Andrew, our mailman, asked me to bring it out to you."

Bryn reached for it, noting the Boston address in the corner. When she opened it, she knew immediately what it was—the dream job she'd applied for those months before. "Eli!" she squealed. "I can't believe it!"

"What is it?"

"Only the best job in the country. Boston Memorial wants me. They were my top choice." It was thrilling, reaching this goal. But the thought of leaving Alaska to return to Boston made her oddly short of breath. She looked over at Eli. His jaw was tensed, and his gaze was focused on the windshield. Maybe this was what he'd hoped for, to get her out of his and Sara's way. Maybe it was God's hand, showing her the path.

Eli landed on the narrow, winding lake and then took her bag for the hike through heavy forest to a high mountain meadow. To one side, five llamas grazed. Bryn's eyes widened in surprise, and she noticed the fencing.

"They must raise them," Eli said under his breath. "At least those they can keep from the bears."

The sounds of arguing emanated from the small log cabin, which was sheltered by several large spruce and neatly tucked into one corner of the meadow. A woman cried out as if she'd just been struck. Eli glanced at Bryn, frowned in warning, and said, "Stay close."

They approached, talking loudly and calling out a friendly greeting.

"Hello?" Bryn added. "It's Dr. Bailey, from Housecalls."

The door cracked open. "We're fine," a gruff voice shouted. "Don't know why the wife called anybody."

"Heard she had a dislocated shoulder," Bryn said. "Since I'm here, I might as well take a look."

"I can fix it," the man said. He edged out, a hulk of a man with a beard that reached his chest. "We're fine. You two go on and head back to town."

Bryn paused. "Can't be often a doctor gets out your way. Why not let me have a look?" She gave him a sheepish smile and threw up her hands. "I'm in kind of a bind. Since the call was made, I need to check things out and make a report. If you won't let me, I'll have to tell my boss, who will have to tell the police."

"You threatenin' me?" The man came out and took three long steps toward them, his glowering expression making it clear she'd touched a nerve. Bryn fought to maintain her composure, stand her ground.

"No, no. Listen, I have some drugs with me that would make getting that shoulder back in place a lot easier on your wife. Please, let me see to her. You probably have other things you need to tend to, right?"

Eli moved up, a bit ahead and in front of her. He dropped the Housecalls bag from his shoulder. "Harmon, the doc here just wants to check out your wife. Why don't you and I go take a look at your animals while the women tend to each other? I don't know much about llamas, but from the look of them, you apparently do."

The big man looked Eli over from head to toe. "I know you?"

"I don't think we've met," Eli said, walking casually toward the man, his hand extended in greeting. "Name's Eli Pierce. My partner, Leon Wilmot, thought it was you up here near Donner. This here's Doc Bailey." He held out his hand as if Harmon had never been anything but welcoming.

Harmon stared at him for a hard moment and then reluctantly took Eli's large hand, engulfing it in his own beefy paw. "Leon

Wilmot, eh? Haven't seen him in years." He paused, obviously mulling things over. "You have an interest in llamas?"

Eli cocked his head. "I've an interest in anyone who can keep a beast like that alive up in these parts without them becoming a griz's supper." Bryn watched them walk away toward the long-necked animals, who watched them approach with wide, wise, wary eyes. Taking a deep breath, Bryn looked back to the cabin door, still ajar. No one appeared in it.

"Hello?" she asked softly, entering. She didn't want to call undue attention back to them from Harmon. "Ma'am? I'm Dr. Bailey, from Housecalls. You needed some assistance?"

A whimper sounded from the corner, and Bryn whipped her head around. A dog? It sounded like a dog. There it was again. After coming in from under the high mountain sunshine, her eyes were taking their time adjusting. Then she saw the huddled form in the corner.

"Oh," Bryn cried, and hurried over to her. "Mrs. Harmon?"

The small woman was rolled into a ball, as if sheltering herself, sobbing. "I call for help. Did not know if anyone…would come."

"I'm here. I'm here," Bryn repeated soothingly. How long did they have until Harmon came back to see what they were doing? A sense of urgency overcame her. "Ma'am, what can I do for you?"

The small woman raised her face slowly, reminding Bryn of a child wanting to say something but too frightened to speak, as if words might bring her more punishment. Bryn gasped. The woman's face had been pummeled. Her right eye was swollen shut, and there was a cut to the left of her mouth where it had been split open.

She reached for her bag and quickly unzipped it. "What's your name, ma'am?"

"Katarina."

Bryn's eyebrows shot up in surprise. "A Russian name?" Gently, she helped the tiny, round woman up and to the rumpled, unmade bed that smelled of sweat and grime.

"Yes. I am from Nome."

"What happened to you, Katarina?"

"I fell."

Bryn concentrated on looking for the Betadine, the butterfly bandages, and some Tylenol. "Must've been a nasty fall," she said innocuously.

"Yes. It was."

Bryn turned back and began tending to the facial wounds. "You have a dislocated shoulder?"

"Harmon wanted to put it back in place. That's why he was angry. Says he can do for me anything you can do."

"That's okay," Bryn said soothingly. "I'll make you a sling to rest it for a few weeks. It's best to keep it immobilized. Cold packs are good too. First things first though. I think you'll need a shot of Valium to relax these constricted muscles. It'll allow me to put the shoulder back in its socket." Bryn looked to her bag to prepare for the intramuscular injection, conscious that Harmon could return any moment. She moved quickly, giving Katarina a shot, and then another. Then, as the medicine began to work, she checked out her swollen eye, gently palpating the bones around the nose and eye looking for points of tenderness.

"You're lucky. It seems your eye socket is intact. Does this hurt?"

"Nah. Just swollen. It's this shoulder."

Bryn let her eyes drift down the woman's neck, noticed the fat, black bruises that looked like fingerprints on Katarina's brown skin.

"While I'm here, Katarina, why don't I check your lungs and listen to your heart?" She flashed the young woman a smile. "Basic checkup stuff."

Katarina shifted away, gave her head a shake. "No. I'm okay."

"Please. Gotta do it for headquarters. You know the drill. If I can't fill out all the paperwork, I get the riot act from my boss." She moved to pull her stethoscope from the bag, as well as a blood-pressure cuff. "Standard procedure," she added smoothly. "I'll just start back here with a listen to your lungs and heart." Quietly she lifted the bottom of Katarina's shirt. "Deep breath."

The woman did as directed, and Bryn raised the shirt a bit more, moving her stethoscope a little higher. "Another," she managed to say, not really listening to the lungs at all. They were perfectly clear, but as suspected, her back was covered with contusions and scars from previous injuries. The sound of men's voices approached outside. Bryn quickly placed herself in front of the woman and stared into her eyes. "Katarina, is your husband abusing you?" Bryn whispered.

A flash of fear passed through Katarina's dark eyes. "No." She pulled down her shirt as if in defense.

"Did you radio Housecalls because you need help in leaving here?"

"No!" she whispered hoarsely.

"We can help you, Katarina. Eli and I will help you. Right now. If you want to leave. Just say the word."

"I can't leave! I love him! This is my home."

"I know. I know you must love him. But he has no right. No right to hurt you like this. This is not love. Not love like it is supposed to be."

Katarina sat up a bit straighter. "This is the love I know," she whispered, just as Harmon pulled the door open.

"You 'bout done?" he asked gruffly.

"Yes," Bryn said. "The muscles should be fully relaxed now. Let me just pop this shoulder back into place and get the sling, then I'll be out of your hair. I'm going to leave some pain medication—for her shoulder—and tend to the cuts she got from her fall." Bryn kept working, not daring to look at the man, knowing her hatred for his actions would show on her face. She could feel his gaze on her back until Eli asked him another question and they stepped back outside.

"You did not say anything," Katarina whispered.

"You want me to? I will."

"No."

"No, I didn't think so. Here, let me take care of that shoulder. This is a bit awkward, but to get a good grip, I need you to lie back on the bed. And, well, I'm going to have to be pretty much on top of you. I'll need my knee for leverage." When Katarina did as she directed, Bryn straddled the woman to get a feel for the socket and with a quick movement popped the shoulder back into place. She climbed off, helped Katarina sit up, and gently set her arm into a sling. Bryn finished applying the butterfly bandages that would knit the facial wound almost as neatly as stitches.

Finally she looked into Katarina's eyes. "This is always a painful, messy situation. But you have to want to leave. If...*when* you want us to come back for you, tell him you have female problems." She cast Katarina a sorrowful smile. "A man will always back away from *female* problems. He'll let you call. And we'll come, take you someplace where you'll be safe."

Katarina looked to the window, her black eyes full of fear. "He'd kill me. You too. And I love him. I know it's crazy, but I do."

"Look at me, Katarina." Bryn waited until the woman's eyes met hers, then covered her small hand with her own. "God loves you in a way that can heal every hurt inside you. He can even heal the hole in your heart that leaving here might create. And I promise you, I would stand beside you until I knew you were safe. We'd bring the police. There are—"

"Gotta get to chores," Harmon said, returning. "Night's comin' on afore we know it."

Bryn stifled a deriding *huff*—it was maybe three o'clock—and packed her bag. "I think your wife's going to be as right as rain. Thanks for letting me tend to her. That shoulder should heal up without a problem." She rose and pushed herself to smile at the man. "How do you know how to pop a shoulder back in place?"

He shrugged, his expression lightening in the face of her praise and smile. "Learn things, out here."

"You do," she agreed, suddenly anxious to take a deep breath of the outside air. "You do. Still, popping a shoulder without meds is monstrously painful. I'm glad I could come and help." She walked past Eli and, feeling a bit safer, turned back and waved. "Give us a call if you have any more mishaps, Katarina." But Harmon was already shutting the door.

"What was going on back there?" Eli asked quietly as they strode away. "Will she be all right?"

"If she can get away from her husband. Why do people live like that? Why do they call it love?"

"She has to be the one to call it quits," Eli said gently.

"That's what I told her."

Eli nodded and then took her hand to help her into the plane. "You gave her some sort of code? Something to tell you she wants an escape route? We'd have to come with reinforcements. Harmon's not going to welcome another visit."

"I did," she said sadly. "Not that I think she'll ever call. I could see it in her eyes. She just doesn't know that there's anything else out there, Eli."

He sat down in the cockpit beside her, silently staring. Then, "No. Some people never do."

CHAPTER TEN

*T*he next couple of weeks passed by in a blur of Housecalls visits—attending a mother giving birth, delivering asthma prescriptions, giving immunizations—and gradually Bryn found herself awed by the incredible places people chose to live and the tough stuff they were made of that allowed them to make it in the bush. When she could, she made short visits to Summit.

She waved aside a giant Fern Lake mosquito and went to light the citronella candles. More and more, she was appreciating the rustic grace of Alaska and its hearty, down-to-earth people. If Bryn's last summer in the high country had opened her eyes to eternal, celestial things, this summer was awakening her to the beauty present right here around her. She found herself longing for that sense of connection to the Great Land that everyone else seemed to have. And, with a start, realized she already had it.

More than anywhere else, this was home. It didn't matter that her father was gone, off with a new little family, having forgotten Alaska and the draw it had for him, too. He would return one day. It seemed inevitable, just as it had been for Bryn. Maybe then she and her father could find their way again, reconnect. And a part of her wondered why she could no longer be friends with Eli, reconnect with him, even if he was seeing someone else. But to see him and not be with him was pure torture.

She stared at a boulder ten feet out in the river, where water tumbled down on either side. Eli was like that rock, with Sara on one side and Bryn on the other. Between the two of them, the pressure threatened to rock him from his foundations, create chaos.

Her eyes moved to the high white mountains in the distance, showing a bit more of the blue crevasses and brown rock as the summer sun wore on. They were partially shrouded in clouds of pink in the morning light. A thick bank of silver clouds rushed over Rainy Pass. She wouldn't be heading to Summit Lake today, regardless of whether or not Housecalls summoned her.

Bryn looked at her calendar watch. Sunday. She smiled in surprise. She was in town on a Sunday. There was only one thing to do. Go to church! Galvanized by her mission, she rose to shower and eat a quick bowl of oatmeal—sprinkled with raisins, walnuts, and brown sugar, her favorite—before heading out. With any luck, Eli would be out flying with a client before the weather turned sour. This morning, she wanted to concentrate on her Creator, give him thanks for bringing her back here, back home. If only for another summer before returning to Boston.

Eli flew a group of tourists over Chandalar Lake, tipping his wings at Mike, who with his wife ran a small lodge for tourists, fishermen, and hunters. He and his family were so kind, so together. Eli ached for that kind of family connection. Not just with his parents. With a loving wife at his side, a couple of kids running about.

He missed Sara. But now he knew letting her go had been right. The last two weeks had brought it home to him, again and again. In acknowledging the ache he felt for Bryn, he had finally understood what had been missing between him and Sara. *Why, Lord?* he pleaded, as he did every night. *I thought when she first came to know you that it was the answer to my prayers, but then she just forgot about me once she was back in Boston. And now these old feelings are back. Why give me this love for a woman who will just take off again come autumn?*

Maybe he was destined for a life of solitude. If that was what his God called him to, so be it. He took a deep breath, trying to honestly consider the idea. He could be happy single. He'd met lots of men in Alaska who had found peace and full lives alone. Eli shook his head. Why wouldn't his heart concede?

His thoughts returned to Bryn. He knew she was confused by his avoidance of her. But Eli had needed time to accept the fact that Sara was gone. He didn't know why he hadn't told Bryn about the breakup. After seeing her excitement over her job offer in Boston, perhaps he was just trying to protect his heart.

He knew he needed to tell her, even if there was no chance for them to be together. The fact that he was drawn to Bryn, longed for her, had doomed his union with Sara from the start. It wasn't fair to Sara to go on that way. And it wasn't fair to Bryn to keep the truth from her. He loved her. His heart would just have to take the chance.

He thought back to the couple outside Donner, the abused wife. He had no doubt that Bryn would have tried to fight off the huge man herself had his wife wanted to come out. She was a courageous woman. When they had talked about it on the flight home, she had grasped his hand to pray for both Harmon and Katarina as if it was the most natural thing in the world. And when that happened, Eli glimpsed the faith that had grown in Bryn's heart since the last time they met. He'd wanted to kiss her right then.

"Calling Beaver-four-two-six-Alpha-Bravo," Talkeetna radio called over his headset, interrupting his reverie. "Calling Beaver-four-two-six-Alpha-Bravo."

"This is Beaver-four-two-six-Alpha-Bravo," Eli returned, pressing the intercom switch.

"Yeah, Beaver, we have a request for all pilots in the vicinity to be on the lookout for an escaped convict outside of Kantishna. A state bounty is posted."

Eli glanced over his shoulder at the oblivious tourists in back and then to the one beside him who stared at him with wide eyes. "I'm headin' over to the west side now," Eli reported. "I'll keep a lookout. What's the bounty?"

"Twenty-five Gs. Guy that spots him buys for the crowd at Alice's tonight. Happy hunting, Beaver."

Eli whistled lowly and looked back at his passengers. "Must be some kind of bad guy for that price."

Bryn saw a patient five miles west of Wonder Lake and then talked Leon into dropping her at Summit.

"Don't know, Doc. Eli wouldn't like it. That convict is still on the loose."

Bryn let out a quick guffaw. "Eli Pierce has no say in the matter. I haven't even seen the man for thirteen days."

"But who's keepin' track?" Leon teased.

She gave him a warning look. "Besides, that was fifty miles from here, over rough country."

"Doc, the man's a rapist and a murderer. Used to the bush. From what I hear, you don't want to face him alone. And it's been three days since they lost his trail. It's feasible he's in this territory now."

"Got my own Colt .357 now," she said. "And I'll keep it loaded."

Leon let out a long breath. "Sure you don't want to head back to town, Doc? At least, until this fella is caught?"

"No. I want to be at the lake, Leon. Please."

He glanced at her, and Bryn knew by his admiring look she had won. She had faced bears before. She could handle some convict.

"I'm not goin' back and tellin' Eli this news." Leon surprised her. "You tell him yourself." He used his radio to contact Alaska Bush, and when Eli answered, Leon nodded and handed her the mike. When she said nothing, he moved his headset microphone away and whispered. "Go for it, Doc." His eyes had the light of victory in them.

She pursed her lips and then said, "Yeah, Eli, it's Bryn. I was just telling Leon here that I wanted a lift to Summit, and he's reluctant to take me. Tell him I'll be fine, will you?"

"Doc, that manhunt has moved to within ten miles of Summit. Come home."

His parental tone infuriated her. "No, Eli. I'm going to Summit. This is ridiculous. It isn't likely that that man would come over two more mountain ridges. He'll head to lower ground. And as I told Leon, I'm armed now. Completely safe."

"You'd have to be loaded for bear, Bryn. That guy is a monster."

"Eli, I want to go to the cabin." She paused and gathered herself. "Please."

There was a moment's hesitation, and just as she had known with Leon, Bryn felt the glimmer of hope that she had won this round. "If you're going to Summit, I am too. We need to talk."

It was her turn to pause, to glance at Leon in confusion. What had happened? What would push him to meet her at the lake when he had been studiously avoiding her all summer? Was he going to tell her that he and Sara had gotten engaged? She swallowed hard. "Okay, Eli. I'll meet you there."

"Keep that gun loaded, Doc, and at the ready."

"Roger that, boss, over," Leon interrupted. "Talkeetna radio, this is Cessna-six-eight-four-Alpha-Bravo headin' to Summit Lake now. ETA 1400 hours."

"Roger that, Cessna-six-eight-four-Alpha-Bravo."

And so it was done. Bryn was heading to Summit Lake.

And the escaped convict wasn't the only dangerous man coming her way.

Eli paddled over to Bryn's cabin that evening, content with the quiet on the lake. It was utterly still, allowing for a perfect reflection of the white peaks in the cobalt water. After a week of solid flying, it felt good to rest. Something in the air made him cautious, like a foreign scent to a deer in the wild.

Was it his fear of finally telling Bryn what he was feeling, what he was thinking? Or was it the threat of the convict so near? Eli had spent the late afternoon with Ben, cautioning him to barricade his door and keep a sharp lookout, as well as a firearm loaded and at the ready. But Ben had seen right through him, calling a spade a spade, telling Eli that he wasn't just there to protect Bryn. He was there to claim her.

Eli's heart pounded at the thought. His eyes went from the swirling water around his paddle to the sleeping bag, stowed in front of the canoe. If Bryn insisted on staying at Summit with a criminal on the loose, then he was determined to stay with her to keep her safe.

He chuckled suddenly. She wouldn't like it. She wouldn't like it at all.

The sound of a timber-splitting maul biting into soft, wet wood met his ears. A second later, he could see her, a braid swinging with every arc of her arms. She was strong and independent but still managed to be ultrafeminine. All woman. His kind of woman. How did she manage it? He smiled again. Allowing himself to formulate such a thought, after years of training himself not to think of her, was a freedom he enjoyed. It felt good, like hearing a wind gust coming through the trees and welcoming it with eyes closed, face forward. He dug his paddle deeper into the water and reached her shore.

She paused briefly, smiled at him, wiped her forehead, and gave the green wood another swing. It went only about a third of the way through. "You mind?" he asked, reaching out for the tool as he walked to her.

"Be my guest," she said, crouching and panting from the exertion.

With one neat stroke, he split the wood in two, then divided it again.

"You come all the way to Summit to chop firewood for me?" she asked, a teasing smile in her eyes.

"Don't mind chopping," he said, eyeing the next log.

"Thought we needed to talk."

"We do." He swung the ax around, cutting halfway through a large round. He pried the buried maul out of the center, aimed for the crack, met it, and succeeded in dividing it in half.

"All right then. I'll just be inside." She rose to go.

Panting now too, Eli grabbed her arm. "No, Bryn, wait."

She looked up at him, then slowly let her gaze wander up from his hand on her arm to his chest, to his neck, to his chin, and finally to his eyes. The effect was mesmerizing and threatened to suffocate him with its power. Her wide, chocolate eyes and mink eyelashes. Her long, straight nose and full lips. Swallowing hard, he threw the maul aside and took her in his arms.

This could not wait any longer.

"Eli—"

He hushed her with a kiss that spoke of his buried passion, the love he'd held back for years, the desire he'd longed to respond to. A kiss that said she was the one for him. Had always been the one.

"Oh, Eli," she whispered, staring up at him. "What about Sara?"

"We broke up." It was enough talking for him. He wanted the taste of her again, her lithe, curvaceous body against his. He pulled her to him, kissing her hard and long, wishing with every-thing in him that they were married and it didn't have to stop there. She met him this time, her hands running down his chest and then around to his back, her strong fingers digging in through his sweatshirt.

They separated after several long minutes, panting now from the passion rather than from chopping wood. When he looked at her, wonder and awe and fear and love passed through her eyes, and Eli knew the same must be sweeping through his own. He kissed her again and again and again, each time trying to assuage his need for her, yet desperate to turn down the heat of his fire for her to at least a hot-coal stage. But each kiss just led them deeper.

"Stop. Eli, we have to stop," she groaned as he covered her cheek in kisses, moved toward her neck. Bryn pushed him away, gently but firmly, and half of him agonized that she stopped him, half of him praised God that she had the strength he seemed to have lost some-where across Summit.

"You sit there," she said as if she barely had the strength to speak, her face red from his whiskers, her lips a bit more full. He forced himself to look away, to sit on the upended log she had indicated. She sat down, three feet away from him, on her own log. "I always wondered if you were a good kisser."

He grinned back at her. "What do you think?"

She pulled her head to one side. "Better than I had hoped. Better than anyone I've ever kissed before."

Eli forced himself to resist the urge to rise and take her in his arms again before she could protest. *Give me the power over this desire, Lord,* he prayed silently. It overwhelmed him, like a tsunami washing over an unsuspecting surfer.

"Eli? Eli! Earth to Eli!"

"Sorry. You got me spinning, Bryn Skye Bailey."

She smiled shyly. "I asked you why now? Why kiss me now? I tried every which way to get you to kiss me ten years ago. Was even wanting to kiss you last time I was in Alaska. But you never made a move. Why now?"

"I've told you, a kiss means something to me, Bryn. It's an announcement of my intent, of sorts. You weren't a believer until the night before you left here last time, so I knew I couldn't pursue a relationship. Then when you showed up this year, and all those old feelings came back, only stronger. Now you're..." He groaned, ran his hand through his hair and stared up into the limbs of trees that crisscrossed above him. Was he really ready to lay it all on the line? To make himself this vulnerable?

He stared back at her, so lovely, so enticing, so... "Bryn, woman, you are like utter perfection to me. I've been in love with you for years. Seeing you again, after all that time away, just made it clearer to me. I had to break up with Sara, even if you weren't going to give me a chance. It wasn't fair of me anyway, to be with her when I was still in love with you."

Bryn's eyes widened in surprise. "Oh, Eli, I am far from perfect."

He laughed at himself. "I know that. I know that's the reality. But this crazy thing I feel for you is like a Fourth of July rocket on a pitch-black night. It's exploding inside of me, and there just aren't words to describe all that I feel. It's electric, cataclysmic! Crazy making!" He rose, needing to pace to work out some of his energy if he couldn't kiss it out of Bryn. "I'm thirty-one years old, Bryn," he said turning toward her. "Please tell me I'm not in this alone. That we can start something together. In earnest."

She looked down at the forest floor and shook her head. "Oh no, Eli. You're not in this alone."

He went to her then, knelt by her side, ran his hand over her head and down her soft cheek. "I said I'm in love with you, Bryn," he said, waiting for her to meet his gaze. "I have to know. Have to know this today. Are you in love with me?"

Her eyes shifted back and forth, always on him. "Eli Pierce, I've always been in love with you."

And then she was back in his arms, beneath him on the forest floor, beside him, her dark hair blending with the land he had always loved. They kissed and cuddled and talked and picked pine needles and twigs and sticks out of each other's hair until the sun sank over the western mountains and the chill of the forest superseded even the warmth generated between their bodies.

They picked at their dinner, lost in staring at each other across the candlelit table, each dizzy in the discovery of love. Shoving aside his plate at last, Eli reached for her hand. "Pray with me, will you, Bryn? I'll start, you finish?"

She smiled, pushed her own half-eaten trout away and took his hand in answer. He stared at the simmering beauty of her in the dancing candlelight, just a moment longer before bowing his head too. "Father God, thank you for this woman. This thing that has started between us. We ask for your hand in our relationship, that you will guide us and lead us and pull us away from anything you don't want us to do. Please, Lord, we ask that you help us draw the lines on our passion for each other. We want to honor you in all things, including this."

"Yes, Father," Bryn added, a smile in her voice. "I thank you for Eli, too. What a blessing he has been to me, throughout my life, but especially this year. Lord, I'm afraid. Afraid of this wrenching open of my heart, afraid that it will be left open and bleeding. Protect us both, lead us, but make us brave and courageous, too. Help us to follow your call, wherever it leads. We ask for these things in your name, Jesus. Amen."

"Amen," Eli echoed.

She met his eyes then, and they stared at each other for several long minutes. Eli felt as helpless as he had when he had fallen for Chelsea Thompson. Except worse. Or better. He laughed.

"What?"

"Nothing. Well, I forgot how great—and terrible—it feels to be in love. It's all tangled up inside me."

"I know the feeling." She covered his hand with her other, and he did the same. "I just can't believe that all *this* was just beneath the surface."

"Me neither. In a way. But then I think I knew it all along. Just wasn't acknowledging it."

She nodded, glanced to the window. "Eli..."

He followed her look. In the corner of a window pane was the faintest stripe of neon green on the far horizon.

"Do you think?" she asked, nodding toward the lake.

"Could be. That would be the perfect ending to a perfect day. Let's go."

Wordlessly she went for her parka and then opened the door. "Separate canoes?" she asked.

"Probably would be safer for us," he said with a laugh. "Otherwise we might end up making out in the middle and fall in."

She shivered. "That would be cold. I'll make you a deal. You stay on one end of the canoe, and I'll stay on the other." She stuck out her hand, and with a grin Eli shook it.

Her eyes moved from him, back to the night sky. "Oh, Eli, they're coming. Hurry!" He laughed at her girlish zeal and nodded for her to step in and go to the front of the canoe. When she was seated, he pushed off and sat in back. In minutes, they were in the center of the lake, watching as the aurora grew along a serpentine path that was almost identical to the one they had seen five years before.

But this time as it neared, the rays crisscrossed above them in shades of purple and green. Again and again the lights rolled past, as though the Weaver was at work on a heavenly loom. It reminded Eli of a plastic disk he'd had as a child, filled with multicolored sand that created new patterns each time he moved it.

Bryn turned her face from the light to Eli. In the dim glow of a sinking quarter moon, he could see that her cheeks were as wet as his own from the tears of joy and awe. The northern lights were always so magical, such a vivid reminder of the majesty of his Creator, the power at his hand. "Oh, Eli," she breathed. "It's God's blessing. A blessing on our love."

He wished he could reach out to her then, hold her. "Yes," he agreed, looking back up. "Yes, it is."

Bryn rose early the next morning, stretched luxuriously, and then lay back to stare at the ceiling and think about Eli. She didn't know where they were going or what would transpire between them; for now, this was enough. This fabulous feeling of knowing that every last nerve cell was awake, that she loved and was loved in return.

After about twenty minutes, she pushed herself out from under the warm Hudson's Bay blanket and to the stove. She frowned at the empty woodbin and then chuckled to herself. She had gone out yesterday to fill it, but a certain man had diverted her attention.

Bryn grabbed the wood carrier and headed out to the door, which stopped abruptly when it banged up against something solid outside. "What—"

"Uhh," said someone in pain.

She peeked around the door and discovered Eli in his sleeping bag. "Want to tell me what you're doing here?" she asked. They had said their good-nights on shore, after the aurora had faded away into the night, leaving behind only its imprint in her mind.

Bryn had assumed Eli had gone home.

"That manhunt," he explained, sitting up and rubbing his hip where the door had connected. "Five miles south of here. Over the ridge."

"Still don't think I can take care of myself, Eli?"

"Let's just say I don't care to gamble that you could. I just kissed you last night, Bryn. I don't want anything to happen to you."

She considered his words for a long moment, then gave in. "Thanks, Eli. For caring. How'd you know he was so close?"

"Went home after we said good night, heard the report, and came back over. I had thought to sleep over here earlier, but after our kisses"—he smiled at her appreciatively and rubbed his jaw—"I knew my days of sleeping inside your cabin and not in your bed had come to a close."

"So you took to my front porch. Very gallant." She bent over and kissed him lightly. His face was as cold as the morning air. "Why don't you come in? I'm getting some firewood, and we'll soon have a pot of coffee on."

"Sounds good." He climbed out of his sleeping bag, still fully clothed in jeans and a blue wool sweater, and took the wood carrier from her hand. "Let me get that."

"Okay," she said with a shrug. She followed him out to the woodpile and watched him gather a handful of kindling and an assortment of larger pieces.

"What would you have done, Bryn? If he had come here, I mean?"

"I guess he would've met my friend here," she said, pulling the revolver from the back of her waistband.

"Leon told me you were carrying it. Is it loaded?"

"Not much good without a bullet, is it?"

"Can you shoot it?"

"Dad taught me how to shoot a rifle."

"Can you shoot *that?*"

"If I show you, will you sleep in your own bed instead of on my front step tonight?"

He paused and stared hard at her. "Maybe."

She turned, aimed at a tree twenty feet away. "See that knot-hole?" she asked, still aiming.

"I see it."

She shot then, and the bullet zinged just an inch right from the hole, embedding itself in the old tree limb.

Eli went over and touched the bullet flattened in the wood. He looked back at her with open admiration. "A real bed *would* be preferable to that front stoop."

CHAPTER ELEVEN

*A*fter spending the entire day hiking and fishing and stealing kisses, Eli had finally torn himself away from Bryn and tossed and turned through the night, worrying about the escaped convict, wishing he had camped on her porch again. Even with a girlfriend who was armed and dangerous herself. He rolled to his side and stared out the bedroom door to the front window, where he could see just a smidgen of the lake. He smiled at his use of the term *girlfriend,* even in the privacy of his thoughts.

Bryn Bailey was his girlfriend. She was his. She loved him! He grinned like an idiot, happy beyond all measure. *Dear God,* he prayed, *thank you for this. For all this bounty. Bryn is a treasure beyond belief. You're so good to me. Thank you. Help me to be a faithful steward of this gift. Amen.*

A helicopter swept overhead suddenly, and then another, wiping the smile from his face. He sat up abruptly and craned his head toward the window. State police choppers. The convict! The chase was coming closer! He hurried over to the window, looked around, but the helicopters had zoomed out of his line of vision. The lake was still. A gentle curl of gray smoke emerged from Bryn's chimney—she was up and eating already. His smile returned a little. *I think I'll just go bum a cup of coffee from her, keep her company.* He'd feel better being with her, even if she did have a gun.

He was just turning away, going to heat some water for a brief bath, when a shot rang out across the lake.

Eli's head whipped around toward the window, and he wondered if he had misplaced the gunshot's report. No, he was sure of it. It had come from the direction of the Bailey cabin.

Bryn.

"Get out of here!" Bryn shouted. The black bear was at her window, snuffling about through the broken panes as though she was fixing her blueberry pancakes for him instead of Eli. He had come around before, and by his radio collar, she assumed he was one of Ben's orphans, come home to roost. But he had never been this forward, usually shying away when she banged some pots together or yelled.

When he came to the door and started pushing against it, making it shudder with his weight, she moved forward with two cast-iron skillets, clanging them together in hopes of shaking his interest. He just kept pushing at the door—was he rubbing his back up against it? Sure enough, his up-and-down momentum succeeded in raising the latch bar. The door swung open. He rolled inward on his back, as surprised to see her as she was him.

That was when Bryn pulled out her revolver and, shouting, shot at his feet, hoping to scare him. The bear immediately turned tail and ran outside, but he didn't get far. The fish drying on racks high above him caught his attention and he turned, still looking for an easy breakfast.

Eli paddled madly across the lake and, for the first time ever, wished for an outboard motor. Despite the early-morning chill, sweat broke out across his brow. What if he was too late? What if the rapist had already gotten to Bryn? He paused for half a second, listening for the sounds of a scuffle, a scream, but he heard nothing. As he neared, he could see that Bryn's cabin door was open, alarming him all the more. With her constant battle with squirrels, there was no way she would leave such an open invitation to them.

I should have stayed with her, obeyed my instincts. He cursed himself as a fool for believing she could take care of herself. *A woman out here, alone, unprotected.* He dug in deeper, willing every muscle to work to get him across the lake faster. *Please, God,* he prayed. *Please, God.*

It was then that he saw Bryn with two skillets, banging them together. His eyes tracked through the trees, in the direction she was looking. A bear. A black bear. He stopped paddling, his arms and shoulders and back aching, and almost felt like laughing. A bear! Bryn could handle a bear!

She looked up at him then. "Good morning! Think he's one of Ben's!"

Eli nodded, out of breath, his heart still pounding.

In formation, the two helicopters roared back over the lake, heading in the direction of Anchorage. The sound apparently scared the bear, and he ambled off with the lumbering, rolling gate common to all bears.

Bryn shook her head and walked down to shore to greet Eli. "I thought about shooting him, but Ben would've never forgiven me. The rascal has become a regular pest—" She stopped abruptly and stared at him. "Eli? What's the matter?" He knew he must be as white as a ptarmigan in winter.

He lifted one hand helplessly, looked away. "I heard a shot. Thought…" He shook his head and gave her a rueful look. "I was worried. I came as fast as I could."

Bryn stared at him and then looked to the sky, where the helicopters had disappeared. She crossed her arms. "Haven't been listening to your radio this morning, huh?"

"No," he said, slightly irritated by her smug manner.

"They caught him, Eli. Over the ridge, near that old mine you and I hiked to once." She waved him in, grinning. "The only intruder I had to deal with was a bear our neighbor raised." She pulled the canoe front onto shore and hugged him when he disembarked on shaky legs.

He held her tightly and kissed her forehead. "Thank you," Eli whispered skyward.

"What?" Bryn asked, looking up at him.

"I was just giving thanks that you're all right. Regardless of who was on the attack. I haven't been that scared since we encountered the poachers."

Over the next weeks Bryn and Eli became inseparable. Eli flew her on every Housecalls mission he could, and they often stayed up into the wee hours of the morning, talking, kissing, and snuggling on her porch or his.

So when the old phone rang in her Talkeetna cabin one early morning, Bryn was none too happy. Exhausted, she groaned and forced her eyes open. "This relationship is going to be the death of me yet," she groused. She reached for the receiver and pulled it to her ear, allowing her eyes to shut again for one blessed second. "Bailey here," she mumbled.

"Bryn? Bryn, honey, it's your mother."

Bryn sat up straight in bed. She hadn't heard from Nell all summer long. "Mom? Are you okay?"

"I'm fine, honey. It's... I'm afraid I have bad news. Your father called today. He tried to reach you last night, but you were out, I guess. He's in Boston. Your Grampa Bruce is very sick. Honey, they don't give him long to live. Maybe a day or two."

"Oh." Bryn's hand went to her mouth.

"Can you go there? To see them, I mean?"

Bryn shook her head as if to empty it of the water that seemed to be drowning any thought. "Yes. I mean, I have to check with Carmine, but, yes, I think I can. Will you?"

"Oh no, honey. I have no place there. That's your father's family. He'll be there with... No, I'll stay here. But I'll keep you in my thoughts. Let me know where you are, will you?"

"Sure, Mom. Thanks for calling. For letting me know."

"Of course. Call me, honey."

"I will," Bryn promised, staring at the phone for a long moment after. Her mother had actually sounded caring and loving. She hadn't even called Ashley "that woman," as she usually did. Bryn supposed Nell cared about her grandparents too. They had been her own in-laws for over thirty years. A person didn't just throw away thirty years without a thought, regardless of how distant the relation might be or how much your ex-husband hurt you in leaving.

Bryn picked up the phone again and dialed Eli's cell. Her tears started flowing then, at the thought of saying good-bye to her grandfather and in fear of finally seeing her dad again after so long. It had been a couple of years, with the excuses of being cross-country from Bryn and raising two young sons with Ashley. They'd been married almost five years, Bryn figured, counting in her head.

"Alaska Bush," Eli answered, sounding as though she had awakened him.

"Eli, I'm…s-sorry," she said through her tears. She choked on her sobs.

"Bryn? Bryn, what's the matter?"

"It's my gr-grandfather, Eli. He's dying. I have to go to Boston."

"Boston?" He sounded surprised.

"I have to see him one last time, before it's too late," she sobbed.

"Of course you do. I'll be right there, sweetheart. You get your stuff together. I'll get you to an airport right away. And, Bryn?"

"Uh-huh?" she managed, wiping her nose.

"I love you. Hang on to that, okay?"

"Th-thanks, Eli."

By the time Bryn got to Anchorage and down to the Lower 48, then all the way across country, it was midnight in Boston. When she emerged from the plane, she saw her father in the terminal, a washed-out expression on his face, and she knew.

"Oh, Dad," she wept, sinking into his arms.

"I'm sorry, Bryn Bear," he said, holding her tightly. "He knew you were on your way. We told him. But he died this afternoon."

They stood there together, clinging to the love they had shared for a man now gone, clinging to each other. Finally her father pulled away a little and kissed her forehead. "It's for the best, you know. He hasn't been in good physical shape for a long time. He was ready to go be with Gramma."

Bryn nodded. "I know. The people left behind are just never

ready." She had seen it herself a hundred times at the teaching hospital. The deceased let go, and the bereaved wanted to hold on.

Peter let one arm drop and then guided her forward, toward baggage claim, with his other arm wrapped around her shoulders.

"How's Aunt Luanne?"

"Struggling. It will do her good to see you. Trevor's here too, down from Maine with his wife."

Trevor Kenbridge, her cousin, was as close as a brother to her. "Did he get to see Grampa before he died?"

Peter smiled sadly and cocked his head. "Yep. That Trevor always could get your grandfather to laugh. He got his last smile out of him."

She nodded, looking around. "Dad, is Ashley here? And the kids?"

He glanced at her. She could tell he was trying to cover his surprise at her asking about them. "Yes. At the hotel. Bret's still napping a lot, and Matthew is a whirlwind, always on the go. We try to give him a little space." There was an element of pride in his voice, and Bryn felt a flash of grief for allowing her own pain to keep them all separated. Her father deserved happiness. They all did. Life was too short to hold on to anger and bitterness and sorrow over what once was.

"I'd like to see them. While I'm here."

Peter smiled tentatively. "I'm glad to hear that, Bryn." He stopped and turned her to him. "I've missed you, honey." They embraced for a short moment and then resumed walking, each wiping tears from their eyes. "So you're back in Alaska," he said, changing the subject.

"You know me. You started that whole five-year-cycle thing. Life just doesn't seem right until I hit that fifth year and go again."

"You likin' it? Working up there, I mean?"

"Oh, Dad. It's so good to be back."

"Got a card from Ben. Told me your fireplace is still standing. I'll have to get up there soon and see it."

"I'd like that," she said. "Maybe you could bring Ashley and the boys. Let them see a little of your history, our history." She ignored his misstep at her words, his hesitation as she broke free and walked toward the baggage carousel, which spun around but had no bags to deliver yet.

"I thought," he said, joining her and staring at the empty silver slats before them, folding and opening as they rounded the corner, "I thought you wouldn't want Ashley there."

Bryn turned to face her father. "Dad, it hurt when you left Mom."

"I know. I'm so sorry, Bryn—"

"No," she said. "It's okay. Something's changed for me, Dad. Something big. I think I'm finally ready to forgive you. And Mom. To gather up my family, however ragtag they may be, and take what I can get. Grampa always said that life's too short. I think I'm finally inclined to agree. Let's move on, Dad. Not forget about the past. I think we can learn from it. But let's move on."

He stared at her then, and Bryn noticed the gray at his temples, the slightly receding hairline. He was still handsome, and the joy that sparkled in his eyes after hearing her words made him practically glow. It was so good to see him again. What had taken her so long? "I love you, Dad," she whispered.

Peter pulled her back into his arms, kissed her temple tenderly. "I love you too, Bryn Bear."

After the funeral and reception at the house, Bryn went to a coffee-house with her cousin Trevor and his wife, Julia, and her old college roommate, Christina Alvarez—now a nautical archaeologist—to catch up. The Kenbridges had let Christina know about Bryn's grandfather's death.

"It means so much that you came, Christina," Bryn said, look-ing over at the beautiful Spanish-descent brunette across the table. "I was so surprised to look up and see you there. It's been, what—two, three years?" The two had corresponded off and on since college but rarely had the chance to see each other. Between residency demands and Christina's world travels in her own graduate work, they were hardly ever in the same place at the same time.

"Three," Christina said with a smile. "And I was honored to be there. Your grandparents were good to me in college. I'll never forget those Sunday night dinners at the big house. Ham, pot roast, turkey…"

Bryn smiled and stared at her coffee, which she had been stirring for a solid minute. With slow movements, she removed her spoon and set it beside the huge cup on the matching saucer. It seemed ages since she had sat in a coffeehouse instead of Alice's café and bar, drinking truck-stop coffee out of chipped white mugs. Or from her own cup at the cabin on the river, or with Eli at Summit.

"Bryn?" Trevor asked. "You okay?"

"What? Oh. Yes, fine. Just thinking."

Christina and Julia exchanged a knowing glance. "She's got that look," Christina said toward Trevor and Julia, still staring at Bryn. "Doesn't she?"

"What look?" Trevor asked, knitting his brows and staring hard at his cousin as if she had a disease.

"The Look," Julia said, nodding.

"Who is he?" Christina asked. "Where'd you meet him?"

"There are twice as many men in Alaska as women," Julia put in.

"You're in love?" Trevor asked, catching up.

Bryn laughed and shook her head. "Shouldn't we be talking about Gramps? Reminiscing?"

"Nah, we've done that," Trevor said. "Gramps would be as interested in this as we are, Cuz. Who is he? "

Bryn felt heat rise up her neck. She was blushing, for Pete's sake! "Eli Pierce," she said, giving in.

"Eli Pierce?" Trevor repeated.

"Eli… You mean Summit Lake Eli?" Christina asked, putting old stories together with the new. "Across the lake, the handsome neighbor, Eli?"

"That's the one," Bryn said with a smile.

"Who's across-the-lake-handsome-neighbor Eli?" Julia asked.

Trevor sat back in his chair and smugly crossed his arms. "Just the guy she always claimed she was never in love with."

"He's been our neighbor on Summit forever," Bryn explained to Julia. "We've been friends since we were kids. This year, everything just clicked."

"Clicked, huh?" Trevor said, putting an arm around the back of his new wife's chair.

"Clicked," Bryn agreed.

"So are we losing you to Alaska forever?" Julia asked.

Her question caught Bryn by surprise. She thought about the letter from Boston Memorial still unanswered on her dresser in Talkeetna. She had been so taken up with Eli, with this love they were discovering, that she hadn't stopped to consider what autumn would bring. She'd wanted to savor each day, remember each moment, enjoy the present and let the future work itself out. And yet he hadn't exactly proposed to her yet.

"Uncle Peter said you got a great job offer from Boston Memorial. If I know you, there are ten more hospitals out there ready to hire you."

"There are probably hospitals in Alaska," Julia said wryly.

"But," Christina broke in, "you've worked so hard."

"I don't know what I'm going to do," Bryn said, considering Christina's intimation that accepting a job in Alaska would be the equivalent of throwing in the towel. She took a long, slow sip of coffee. She had worked hard to be at the top of her class, shine above all others to get the prime job offers after residency. Was she willing to throw away all those years of sleepless nights spent studying or at the hospital for a minimum-salary, minimum-prestige job in Alaska?

"Love is worth a lot, Cousin," Trevor said gently.

"It is," Julia concurred, taking his hand. They had been a mismatched pair from the start, from different worlds—Julia the heiress who wanted a home, Trevor the traveler. But they were so right for each other. They were so *together*.

"I don't know," Christina put in. "She could be making over a hundred thousand next year. Does it make sense to throw all that away?"

"Love doesn't come knockin' very often," Trevor said.

"I just broke up with a boyfriend who wanted me home every night," Christina said. "I love my work. To cut that off would be like cutting off a part of me. What if Housecalls goes under? Where would you work then? And I know you. You don't need just any job. You need a job that stimulates your mind, challenges you."

"Housecalls has done that for me."

"For a summer. What are they paying you?"

"Room and board. My loans," she said, holding up a hand to her friend's unspoken question, "are on deferment for a few months." She looked around the table sheepishly. "Guess I ought to figure out what I think about it, what my options are, huh?"

"If you're serious about this guy," Julia said.

"If you want to stay in Alaska," Christina said.

"Bryn," Trevor said, taking her hand and waiting until she looked at him. "Just promise me one thing."

"What?"

"If this is love, don't let it go. You've cared for Eli for a very long time. If something magical is happening, don't walk away. I did, once," he said, staring at Julia. "And I had to turn back around and break up a wedding to make things right. Don't get yourself into a bigger bind just because it might be hard to make things work. If God is in this, he'll see you through, make a path. Loans and all," Trevor added assuredly.

"You think?" Bryn asked, knowing the answer, just needing to hear it again from someone she knew and respected and loved.

"I know."

"I know this is it," Eli said, pacing in Ben's house. "This is the real thing, Ben." He looked out toward the other end of Summit, where he'd left three tourists to fish at the river.

"The question is, what are you going to do about it?" The older man stared at his radar screen, trying to pinpoint the marauding bear's position. The young male would have to be moved far outside any populated area.

"I'm going to marry her."

That brought Ben around, his eyes sparkling with delight. "You think that girl will marry a lout like you?"

"I hope so." He shook his head, ran a hand through his hair. "I'm in love, Ben. Worse than ever before. Having her all the way in Boston—it's about to kill me."

"She'll be back soon."

"Think I ought to have gone with her? Been there to support her?"

"It happened so fast. You've got a business to run, and she could get a bereavement ticket. Yours would've cost at least a thousand."

Eli stared out at the lake. The river wasn't the best fishing around, but it had given him the excuse to come and see Ben. And the scenery was spectacular. Hopefully his clients would catch a decent load and deem the entire outing worthwhile.

"Why hasn't she called?" he asked for the hundredth time, as much to himself as Ben.

"She's busy with the memorial service, taking care of her family, catching up with long-lost relatives and friends that she doesn't see unless somebody gets married or dies."

Eli sighed and nodded, crossing his arms. "I just feel so helpless, having her out there. Outside, I mean."

Ben rose and stood by the picture window with him. There was a strong wind, sending foot-tall swells down the lake toward them. Ben put a hand on the younger man's shoulder. "Eli, if you can't trust her to go to the Lower 48 and return, either you're not ready to marry her or she's the wrong one for you. Unless, that is, you're ready to move where she goes."

Eli winced, pulled his head sideways. "Can't imagine that. My business—"

"She's a doctor now. Where is she going to get work up here?"

"Housecalls might hire her on. Talkeetna has a clinic."

"Doesn't pay much. Doctors these days head out of school owing more money for their education than it takes to buy a house. Especially those Ivy League–educated docs. Besides, Talkeetna has the doctors they need on staff, I'd wager."

"Willow, then. Anchorage!" he said, getting irritated. Did Ben not want things to work out between them?

"Just want you to be thinkin' realistically," Ben said, dropping his hand. "Got your head up there in the clouds. With your mom and dad Outside on their RV expedition, I'm thinkin' I'm your only voice of reason. Me and the Man upstairs."

"I thought you said God would work it out."

"He will. I'm just thinking there're more places to live than here—for the right woman."

Eli let his forehead bump up against the cool windowpane. He didn't want to think about reality. He and Bryn had just discovered each other, allowed themselves to revel in newfound love. Couldn't they just enjoy that for a while? Wasn't it enough to think of marriage itself? Couldn't their happily-ever-after come later?

What if she did decide to take that job in Boston? Could he really leave to be with her?

Bryn said good-bye to her coffeehouse companions and walked through the park, watching lovers in the swan boats and wondering about Eli. It was sweltering hot, and Bryn found herself longing for the cool, refreshing northern summer air of Alaska, to be out of the crowds, walking on trails that maybe only two or three others walked along over a given summer. She longed for a friendly hello from a passerby, a look that said she had been seen, not merely taken in with the rest of the landscape.

"Lord, a little direction, here," she whispered skyward. She wiped her temples and upper lip of sweat and then opened the huge phone book, looking for Boston Memorial's number. What was the name on that letter? "Make it clear, Father," she said. "Show me what I should do."

CHAPTER TWELVE

*B*ryn consciously dropped her hands to her sides and let them swing, as if she was feeling comfortable, relaxed, instead of all tied up in knots inside. She was nervous—*nervous!*—about seeing Eli again. She turned the corner in the Jetway, and a bit of the Anchorage terminal came into view. And then she saw him, carrying a bouquet of roses and grinning as if she were the Chugach Mountain Range on a lovely Sunday afternoon.

She hurried to him, feeling shy, wondering what it would be like to hug him again, but when he swept her into his arms and gave her a long kiss, she knew her nervousness had been foolish. He loved her, would always love her. He ran his hands over her hair and down her back and kissed her again, his lips soft and welcoming, his scent of cinnamon and wood smoke washing over her.

This was home. This place, under the curve of Eli's chest and arm, walking side by side, feeling all warm inside, smiling at each other as if they had just been given the grand prize from *Reader's Digest.* Bryn's chest felt tight with glee at the realization that she was in love, truly in love, and that Eli was in love with her too.

"It's good to have you back, Doc," Eli said, staring at her tenderly.

"It's good to be back."

"Tell me about your trip. How're you doing? Your dad?" They began making their way to baggage claim.

"'Fair to middling,' as Grampa Bruce would've said. I get teary thinking I won't see him again for a long time. I'm going to miss him! But I'm glad he's reunited with Gramma in heaven. They were so in love. So it's good, too. All my life, I've wanted a marriage like theirs."

Eli pulled her close again. "It's good to see that marriage vows can last until death, isn't it?"

"Uh-huh. And my dad's doing pretty well. I spent a little time with him and Ashley and the kids. It was all right. There was something about going back, seeing him, something about Grampa's passing. I just finally realized that I was punishing him for making a new life without me. For finding happiness with his new family when we could never seem to get it together ourselves. It was just as much my fault as his that we haven't been close. Got to see my baby brothers—they're very cute. And somehow, it was all okay."

"I'm glad to hear that, Bryn. Everyone needs their dad."

"Yeah. After my last summer in Alaska, I thought I could make it on my own, look to God as my heavenly Father. Get what I needed from him. But Dad's still alive, and, well, I had to forgive him. For myself as much as for him."

Eli nodded. She glanced into his warm hazel eyes and then away, tucking her hands into her jeans pockets. Talking about this felt good, but it also made her feel vulnerable. "We'll never have that lovey-dovey, father-daughter relationship that everyone always talks about. But I think that's okay. My dad is a good man. I'm just now remembering that."

"And seeing him the way our heavenly Father does," Eli added. "With a measure of grace."

"He got a charge out of finding out you and I were…together,"

Bryn said, feeling shy again. She stood up on her tiptoes and gave him a quick kiss.

"I bet he did," Eli said. "There's your bag." He lifted the heavy case off the conveyor belt with ease, and the two headed out to the open-air parking lot. A thick cloud bank covered Anchorage that day, making it seem later in the day than it was.

Eli opened the truck door for her and put her bag in the back. He hopped in and pulled her to him for a long, searching kiss. "I missed you, woman," he growled, kissing her again.

She giggled and put her arms around his neck. "I missed you too, Eli."

"Don't go away again."

"I won't. For a while, at least." The two eyed each other, aware that the summer was rapidly coming to a close. She only had three weeks left on her Housecalls commitment. What then? Eli turned away and cranked the key in the ignition, obviously not ready to talk about it yet.

"Mind if we stop at Housecalls? It's just a mile from here," she said.

Eli didn't like the way Dr. Carmine Kostas's eyes lingered over Bryn, the way he perused Eli like a thrift-store aisle with no decent goods. The doctor was plainly interested in Bryn and disappointed she had arrived home accompanied by a man. Last summer Eli and Carmine had hit it off. This summer they were in opposite corners like two prizefighters, separated by Bryn, the referee. Eli supposed he'd have to get used to other men being interested in his girlfriend. Bryn Bailey was a knockout and smart to boot. A guy would have to be from another planet not to look twice in her direction.

A drenching rain began as they sat in Carmine's office, each drop pummeling the old warehouse roof as if knocking to get in. Carmine looked in Bryn's direction mostly, solicitous in his care in asking after her family. Once they had caught up, he turned to a series of maps behind him and flipped to the one that covered Bryn's Housecalls territory.

"I'm assuming you're ready to get back to work."

"Yes," she said.

"Good. We had a couple of calls. Sent one emergency helicopter into a McKinley base camp with climbers suffering from altitude sickness. There might be a few more calls like that if the Park Service can't handle it themselves. They only call us when they're maxed out elsewhere, like yesterday when they were battling a western flank fire. Now with rain like this, I wouldn't expect them to need us for a while. Yet with the season coming to a close, there will be more climbers attempting the ascent. Be prepared."

He turned back to his map. "We had a call relayed in yesterday from a family near Webster's hot springs. The dad's a UCLA professor studying what it's like for a family to be living in primal conditions. His six-year-old son isn't faring well. Been sick for weeks. Might be pneumonia."

"They didn't want to come out right away?"

"The father is reluctant to break their study period. He wanted to wait for you to come back. Thought his son would be fine until today."

"Temperature?"

"A pretty constant 102 degrees."

"I'll go in with some Rocephin just in case. Check him out and hopefully knock that infection back or bring him into town, if necessary. Dad can stay put." She shook her head, obviously thinking the man crazy to be placing his studies ahead of his son's welfare.

"It's not flying weather," Eli said, rising and walking to the window. The rain was coming down in torrents. "And you're beat." He turned toward Carmine. "She just got in."

"I know," Carmine said. "I'm hoping that the rain will let up before you reach Talkeetna," he clarified. "Bryn, I know you must be tired. But I'd rest easier tonight knowing you'd seen the boy."

"Me too," Bryn said, her eyebrows knitting together.

"You sure you're up to it?" Carmine asked. "I could radio—"

"No. It'll be fine. We'll get in and out and be back home."

Eli raised his hands. "Guess you're back to work, Doc. Want to head out?"

"Are we done here?" she asked Carmine.

"Yes. That's all I have. Be careful in this weather. And radio in, let us know if you're headin' to the hot springs tonight. I'll pray that the weather lifts."

"Will do, boss," Bryn said, rising.

"You make the call about the weather. We appreciate you two and wouldn't want to lose you," Carmine said, shaking Eli's hand.

"Don't worry," Eli said confidently. "We'll be fine." He hoped Carmine understood his use of the word *we*.

Kostas's eyes shifted from Bryn to him. "Good," he said.

⁓

"Weather Service says we have a break. A few hours though at the most. It will take an hour to get to the hot springs and an hour back. That leaves you half an hour with the kid. Will that be enough?"

"Better than not seeing him at all," Bryn said. She looked over her Housecalls bag's contents, making sure she had everything she needed. "Let's go."

Eli took the duffel from her, the consummate gentleman. She shook her head. It was endearing, his care of her. She followed him down the slippery bank to the plane. The clouds were low, but at least it had stopped raining.

"Are those clouds high enough for you to have good visibility, Eli?" Bryn asked, warily surveying the horizon.

"We'll be fine. I once flew a hundred miles right over the tree-tops, low over waterways, so I could see," he said. He stowed her bag and helped her in. "You packed your rain slicker plus your parka, right?"

"Check."

"Waterproof boots? We'll have to hike a ways to get to Webster's."

"Roger that."

He gave her a smile that told her he knew she was teasing him. "I just don't want to get you up there, Doc, and have you whining about wet feet or something."

"Have I ever been a whiner, Eli?"

"There's a first time for everything."

Eli flew over the Donnelys' cabin to pinpoint their location, tipping his wings to let the family know that help was on its way. The rain started up again just as he was lining up for his landing.

Bryn closed her eyes.

"We'll be fine, babe," he reassured her, not taking his gaze from the windshield. They were a hundred feet up, seventy-five, fifty, twenty-five, and then skidding to a stop on the pond.

Bryn blew out a breath of relief. "You bush pilots really are the best, aren't ya?"

"Was there ever any doubt?" he asked, cocking a brow at her. He ran the plane straight toward the bank, pushing forward on the pontoons. "Expecting some wind with this storm," he said, nodding outside. "Want her firmly ashore."

Eli climbed out first and shoved his arms into a rain slicker, then flipped the hood up. He shouldered her bag and helped her out and into her own slicker. They sat on the edge of the pontoons, under the wing and out from the rain, to yank on their waterproof boots. Then they set off for the Donnelys' cabin.

In ten minutes they were there, and the professor was outside, dressed in a bearskin blanket and beaver cap. He shook their hands and waved an arm toward the open doorway. "Come in, come in," he said.

Eli and Bryn entered the dark, tiny, one-room cabin. It still smelled of fresh-hewn wood and had a dirt floor. A pine-bough bed was in one corner with a child stretched out on it, and a narrow bed in the other corner doubled as a couch during the day. Along one wall stood a fireplace that resembled Bryn's, with a cast-iron crossbar that allowed a pot to simmer over the coals. Bryn was glad she wasn't hungry. Whatever was cooking did not smell good.

"Thank you so much for coming. I'm Susan," said the mother to Bryn. She looked haggard and worn, like countless other mothers of sick children. "I've been so worried."

Bryn followed her over to the corner and examined the child. "Can you bring that lantern over here?" she asked.

"Yes, yes," said Susan. She hurried away to the central table and back. The men settled on the two chairs to watch, silent.

"What's his name?"

"Jason."

"Hi, Jason," Bryn greeted him. "I'm Dr. Bailey. Can you open your mouth? I want to see your throat." Obediently the child did as she asked. He was pale and, from the look of his lips and skin, a bit dehydrated. She used her penlight to check his tonsils, but there was no sign of enlargement or infection. He was wheezing, and she guessed his parents' diagnosis of pneumonia might be right.

"Here, sweetie," she coaxed softly. "I'm just going to take a quick look in your ears and then take your temperature again." His eardrums were not inflamed. In three seconds her digital thermometer beeped, and she had the result—102.5.

"Running a zinger of a temp there, bud," she said. Bryn looked to the mother. "Any Tylenol?"

"Aspirin, every four hours. That's all we've had to give him. It's the most I could talk *him*"—she tilted her head disdainfully at the professor—"into letting me bring here. That and a thermometer."

Bryn ignored the barb thrown at Professor Donnely. Right now her focus was on the child. She brought out a stethoscope and listened to Jason's lungs. She could hear rales at the lower base of one lung. He was clear everywhere else.

"How long has he been sick, Susan?"

"Started with a cold. Two, maybe three weeks ago. It wasn't that bad, it just never got better. Then about five days ago he got this sick."

"I think you're right. He has pneumonia. I'll give him a shot of a powerful antibiotic. Should get him feeling better within twenty-four hours. And I'd like to run an IV while I'm here. He's a bit dehydrated. Is he allergic to anything?"

"No, he isn't," she said.

"Good. You should see a remarkable change in him in the next day. If not, I want you to either bring him out of the bush or call me back."

"We can't leave here," Professor Donnely said. "It's only our fifty-eighth day!"

"Professor," Bryn said calmly, rising. "This is your son. I don't care how important your research is. You can do it again next summer. You don't get a second chance with a life. And what Jason has is potentially life-threatening."

The man opened his mouth as if to retort and then closed it. Opened it, and then closed it. He reminded Bryn of a trout dying on a bank. He knelt down and placed a reassuring hand on Jason's shoulder. Bryn turned away to clean the back of Jason's hand and then insert the needle for the IV bag. "You'll feel a prick, and then it will sting a bit, Jason." She nodded for Susan to hold the child. "I'll move quickly so it'll hurt less."

"We shouldn't even have you here," the professor muttered to Bryn. "The pioneers never had IV bags and prescription drugs. I told Susan we could find the herbs to treat him, that he would make a recovery in time."

Bryn took a deep breath to steady her nerves. "You made a wise choice, Susan," Bryn said, looking into the mother's eyes. "Your responsibility is to him," she added in a whisper, nodding at the child between them. "The IV's just saline solution. Nothing too twenty-first century," she said to the father.

"Couldn't find that plant, Dad," said an older child, suddenly appearing in the doorway. "Sorry. Looked everywhere."

"That's okay, Son," the professor said woefully.

"Can I go see their plane?"

"No plane. By having visitors here, we've already jeopardized the integrity of my research."

"Aw, Dad," the boy said. He came in and pulled off his bearskin coat and beaver cap.

"You can go out with us when we see them off," the professor said.

"How's Jason?" the boy asked, kneeling beside his little brother.

"He's going to be all right," Bryn said. "I'm Dr. Bailey. What's your name?"

"Seth."

"Nice to meet you, Seth. Want to do me a favor?"

"Yeah."

"Hold this IV bag, right about here."

The boy obediently took the plastic sack, looking with wide eyes down his brother's arm to where the needle entered the back of his hand. Bryn turned to her Housecalls bag to fish out some children's Tylenol. The IV fluid was on slow drip, but it was entering the child's system quickly. He already looked a little better.

She turned to Eli. "I'd like to wait an hour, see if we can get this temp down a bit."

"We can't wait that long, Doc," he said, staring at her with warning in his eyes. "Not unless you want to spend the night here. That storm system is coming in fast."

Staying the night was certainly an unappealing idea. If she had to spend more than a couple of hours with the professor, she really would let him have it. And their living conditions were truly rudimentary. To add two visitors would infringe on the family's comfort, to say nothing of Bryn and Eli's. Suddenly all she could think about was her big bed in the river cabin.

"We might have to come back tomorrow," she warned.

"Fine by me. Can't do better than you for a flying companion."

"What about your schedule? Leon said you had a full roster tomorrow."

"They'll have to understand. Cancelled on behalf of a sick kid in the bush. It will be something for them to talk about at the lodge over their moose steaks."

"Eli, that's kind of you."

She looked down at the sick boy, running her hand along his feverish brow.

"Bryn, let's do what's best for Jason. You need to stay here for an hour to make sure he's going to get better, let's do that. I've slept in worse places," Eli said, eyeing the floor. "Besides, maybe the storm will wait for us."

Bryn sighed. It wasn't what she wanted, but it was the best plan. "I really would like to stay for an hour. I won't sleep at all at home if I'm worried about him."

"Done," he said, nodding once. He stepped away, giving her room, and she took the IV bag from Seth.

By the time they left the Donnelys', Jason's temperature had dropped to 100.8, and he was more responsive. The IV fluid had definitely helped. With strict instructions to administer the Tylenol every four hours and monitor the child's temperature at least three times a day, and to radio if he showed any signs of becoming worse again, Bryn bid the family farewell.

Eli led the way, splashing through puddles and eyeing the sky. He was practically running.

"Eli, wait," she said. Even though Eli was carrying the Housecalls bag for her, it was tough to keep up with his long stride.

"Gotta get out of here if we're to have a chance at getting home," he said over his shoulder.

"Maybe we should just stay here."

"If we can make it, I'd like to. As you pointed out, I have that full roster tomorrow."

"Okay." She concentrated on following in his footsteps through the muck. The rain had let up, but even the air was pregnant with moisture, and the pewter clouds were low in the sky. "Think we're gonna get more rain, Eli?" she asked nervously.

"Could be. Worst-case scenario, we set down on a remote lake and snuggle in the fuselage until dawn." He paused to wink over his shoulder.

"That sounds like a recipe for a fall," she said, shaking her head in amusement. She wouldn't mind kissing until dawn, if they could just stop there.

"We'll get home," he said.

When they reached the plane, each pushed on a pontoon to dislodge it from the muddy beach, and once it was turned for takeoff, Bryn climbed aboard and stowed her bag. Eli climbed in after her and radioed Talkeetna.

"Beaver-four-two-six-Alpha-Bravo calling Talkeetna."

"This is Talkeetna radio. Go ahead, Beaver."

"Talkeetna, we're headin' home. Comin' from the hot springs."

"Roger that, Beaver," came the crackling response. "See you soon."

With one last worried look to the sky, Eli ran through his routine flow check and took off into the wind.

Fifteen minutes later they left the high valley and headed south toward Talkeetna. The clouds lifted, and Bryn breathed a sigh of relief. They were going to be okay. She had rarely felt uneasy in the Alaska skies, but today there was a tickle on her neck, a vague unease in the pit of her stomach. What was the matter? She decided it was all in her head, that the combination of her red-eye flight to Anchorage, the drive to Talkeetna, and the late visit to the Donnelys' cabin had simply driven her to exhaustion.

"You're quiet all of a sudden," Eli said, looking her way.

"Tired. I just realized how tired I am."

"You must be. I'm bushed, and I didn't get up at three o'clock."

"Boston time," she reminded him.

"Boston time," he repeated with a nod. "Gotta get you home and into bed, Doc." He reached out and rubbed her neck. "You okay?"

"Yeah. Mostly."

"You handled the professor well."

"Can you believe that guy? I just don't understand…" Her words trailed away as she looked to Eli and noticed the concern etched on his face. She followed his gaze, noticing the angry steel-gray curtain a dozen miles ahead. "What's wrong?"

"Multicell thunderstorm. Unusual in this area. We'll have to go back and wait it out."

She sighed as he banked the de Havilland into a smooth turn east and radioed Talkeetna again. Beneath them were miles and miles of unbroken forest. "Back to the Donnelys'?" she moaned.

"Rather find that hidden lake," he teased, waggling his eyebrows.

She hit him on the shoulder playfully. "Guess the Donnelys' is the best place for us."

"You'll be so tired, even a dirt floor will look good," he said. "Or you can sleep in here, and I'll go to their place."

"That could wo—"

A fluttering form darted into view immediately ahead, and Bryn choked on a gasp. Then another to the right, a huge—

"Geese!" Eli shouted, as if using a swear word. He kicked the rudder pedals and rolled the Beaver hard left, but two geese dived in the same direction, grew larger for an instant, and with a bone-chilling crash one pelted into the windshield.

The airplane jolted, and the propeller flickered to a stop. *It can't be,* Bryn thought. *This can't be happening.* A sickening silence, broken only by the rushing wind, fell over the cockpit's interior as Eli's hands flew over the instrument panel, trying to restart the engine.

"Come on," he ground out through clenched teeth. "Come on!" He turned the ignition key again and again, so hard that Bryn was afraid the key would snap. He swallowed hard, his Adam's apple bobbing in profile. He keyed the mike as he settled the aircraft into a smooth, shallow glide toward the forest below.

"Mayday. Mayday. Mayday. Beaver-four-two-six-Alpha-Bravo. Bird strike. Engine failure. Two souls on board." He dropped the radio and gripped the wheel with both hands as the entire plane fought him.

The trees below loomed closer. "Eli," Bryn said, trying not to scream. He didn't respond, merely pulled a thick blanket from behind her seat and shoved it into her lap.

"Here. Get this between you and the panel." He pushed her forward, and she heard him unlatch her door. "Just sit tight like that. Keep your muscles loose."

The Beaver slid inexorably downward. There was no choice but the trees, no waterways visible in a land of rivers and ponds and lakes.

"Dear God," Bryn cried softly. "Dear God!" No other words came to her other than the cry for help.

"Some sort of lake up ahead. If I can just hold her a few hundred feet," Eli said, still clenching his teeth, every muscle flexed as if defying gravity by sheer will alone.

He leveled off the airplane, letting the speed bleed now as branches and trunks rose into view. He muttered to himself, as if repeating an old instructor's demands. "Slow down as much as possible, let the wings take the impact, keep a level flight attitude..."

The treetops brushed along the bottom, sending a chilling scratch along the fuselage, and then there was a deafening *boom* and the scream of tearing metal as the wing next to Bryn was wrenched away. She looked up to see the dull silver gleam of water, and she shut her eyes as the windshield shattered. She found herself thinking of her river cabin, of Summit, of Eli, of Grampa Bruce, of keeping her muscles loose...before all went black.

CHAPTER THIRTEEN

*B*ryn came to and dimly realized that they had come to a stop. The seat belt was digging into her hips, and the throbbing in her head made her feel as if she'd been hanging upside down for hours. She could hear the rush of liquid and looked around to see water rising in the fuselage. Painfully she turned her head to the window, trying to make sense of it all. Her thoughts were fuzzy, as if she were drunk. They were in shallow water. Eli had been hoping to reach water. *Almost made it,* she thought ruefully.

"Eli," she said, turning toward him. He was out of his seat belt and crumpled into an odd curl at the control panel. Clearly, he was still unconscious. His skin had a deadly pallor to it. "Eli!" she yelled.

There was no response.

Bryn struggled with her seat belt, and with a *click* it finally released her. "Eli," she said urgently, studying the curve of his spine for signs of a broken neck. There was blood everywhere, but his spine seemed intact.

Her thoughts were clearing now. Did Talkeetna have a way of tracking their last known position? Would there be a helicopter coming for them any minute? The Civil Air Patrol? With teeth that already chattered from being in the glacial temperatures, she righted Eli and dragged him between the seats and to the side door. At least the water was working for her that way—it would be difficult to manage his two-hundred-plus pounds on shore.

Most of the blood seemed to be coming from a cut on his face and another on his head. From the way the bone in front near his chest caved in, it was obvious that his shoulder was dislocated. And his arm was broken, maybe the clavicle, too. But right now, Bryn focused on getting them outside and to shore. He needed to be covered, sheltered. The rain was beginning again, and Bryn groaned. With a swift kick she opened the door, and more water rushed in. Once it had leveled off, Bryn dragged Eli out and to shore.

It was difficult to see in the pounding rain, but Bryn headed toward the biggest tree she could find, with the branches lowest to the ground. As she suspected, it was rough going on the beach, and she could only drag him about ten feet at a time. Whenever she stopped to rest, she would check his pupils, his breathing, and then shout, "Eli! Eli! Talk to me!"

But there was no response.

With a last heave she made it the remaining fifteen feet to the towering white spruce and lifted a low-hanging branch. She pulled Eli to the covered place, blessedly out of the rain. Then she ran back to the plane. She needed her Housecalls bag, the emergency kit, anything she could lay her hands on that might be of use. She had heard enough stories about these woods to know that they could be as deadly as they were beautiful, especially if one was caught unawares.

She waded into the silver waters again, rain pelting the lake with a million little splashes. If she kept at it too long, she knew she would be suffering hypothermia herself. She had to get what she needed quickly, build a fire, get them both dry, review Eli's wounds to make sure she wasn't missing anything critical, get his shoulder back in the socket, set the broken bone. Her teeth chattered as she entered the

fuselage of the downed de Havilland and searched through the floating debris.

Her Housecalls bag was within easy reach. Then she took their
rain slickers and the soaked blanket that Eli had placed between her
and the control panel, and, giving up on the emergency kit as lost,
she returned to shore. She was shaking violently and fell several times
en route back to their tree. Everything in her longed to lie down
beside Eli, to try to seek some warmth next to him, just for a
moment, but she knew that if she lay down, they both would die
there.

She struggled to keep her hands steady enough to grab the zipper
and open her bag. The rain was still pouring and the temperature was
descending. Soon it would be night. There would be no rescue party
until morning. If they were to survive, it was up to Bryn.

Dear God, she prayed, *give me the strength to do this. Help me!
Help us!* She fought the urge to weep in her frustration with the
zipper, and then her fingers found the metal clasp and worked it
downward. Inside, it was surprisingly dry. She turned to Eli, checked
his pulse and breathing—they were faint but consistent. He was
trembling now too.

Briefly she did an assessment on herself. She knew she would do
neither of them good if she ignored something critical about herself
and in her shock lost consciousness. She felt bruised around her hips
and abdomen where the seat belt had cut into her, and there was a
laceration on her forehead. The blood seeped down her face and
into her eye. But otherwise she believed she was all right. She'd
check for blood in her urine later to be sure the seat belt hadn't
caused any kidney damage. But for now she'd focus on Eli. He was
the crucial concern.

The first thing she needed to do was try to warm him. She stripped off his soggy boots and dumped the water from them. Then she took off his wet jacket and shirt to examine his arm. She could clearly see the dislocated shoulder, and after administering some muscle relaxants, she knelt above him and popped it back into place. She set the broken ulna—a clean break, thankfully, that hadn't pierced the skin—using three wooden slats from her bag and adhesive tape.

The wood and tape would suffice until they got to town and could cast it. Then she wrapped him up in the rain slicker, peeled off his jeans, and, with nothing else dry, tucked his legs into her Housecalls bag, which she had emptied beside him. The bag and slicker weren't exactly warm, but at least they weren't wet. With shaking hands, she unraveled the space blanket that looked like tinfoil folded into a tiny three-inch square, but happily unfurled to cover three by eight feet. It was flimsy, meant for a one-time use, but it would do the job. She covered Eli with it.

She looked through the remaining contents of the duffel and pulled out more wooden slats, and she grinned at the sight of the lighter she carried for quick sterilization. She grinned and in doing so, again noticed her own chattering teeth. "Thank you, Lord," she whispered toward the tree branches. She gathered up pine needles, old dead branches from among the larger ones above, then braved the rain to rummage for more fuel. She pulled up dead logs to reach drier, dead wood beneath and returned in a hurry. It was a start.

The needles crumbled and bent in a feeble black-and-red attempt, then suddenly caught fire, making the pitch-rich twigs crack as soon as the heat engulfed them. The wooden slats were excellent as kindling and kept the fire going long enough to catch the larger twigs and logs above, set in a tepee fashion, and spread into a smoldering fire. In another minute the fire was safely rolling, allowing Bryn to leave it for a moment to gather more fuel.

She used a large, serrated surgery blade to cut through the branch directly above Eli, sacrificing the increased shelter from the rain in order to keep the growing fire from consuming their shelter at large. The tree was so wet that there really was little danger, but she would keep an eye on it anyway.

Bryn laid the branch on the ground and cut several more, remembering from the pioneer book at Summit Lake that many had slept on beds of pine boughs and used the same for blankets. They would keep the cold from seeping up and into Eli from the earthen floor. When she had created a sufficient bed, Bryn dragged him onto it, even nearer the fire, and covered him again. To protect his bed from catching fire, she poured a line of gravel around him.

When she had wrung out the wet wool blanket as best she could and hung it from the tree branches—next to their coats to dry near the fire and using it at the same time as a kind of ceiling to hold in some of the heat—she sat back on her haunches and gnawed on a hunk of moose-meat jerky she had found in Eli's pocket. She had to keep her strength up. She was actually warm from all her working, but she knew as soon as she stopped the cold would return. She placed another log on the fire, watched grimly as the damp wood smoked until it finally caught, then stripped to her silk undershirt, wrapped up in her own slicker, hung her sweater and turtleneck up to dry, and climbed under the blanket with Eli.

"Eli," she whispered, cuddling up to him. Two were better than one when it came to warding off a chill, and another's body heat was the best way possible to combat hypothermia. If only he would come to, tell her it was all right, joke that he had gotten her that alone time on a deserted lake…tell her the date, the president's name. "Eli?"

But still he didn't answer. She peeked over his chest to the water. The rain had stopped as night had descended, but something different was in the air, something odd on the wind, just now picking up.

Bryn swallowed past the lump in her throat. It was snowing, blowing hard across the water in a diagonal slant. *Snowing.*

She began to cry.

Eli winced in the dim light as consciousness claimed him. He relived the last harrowing moments of the crash, the panic and pain, the realization that they were somersaulting, the lost sensation of going under, and then the rising sensation of coming to. He awakened with a start, wondering where Bryn was, if she was dead.

"Eli? Eli!" she moaned, right beside him then, in his arms. It was a miracle! She was alive, and nestled right here, with him, not locked far away, trapped in an airplane as she had been in his dreams.

She lifted her head and smiled in the dim light of dawn. Her breath clouded before her face. "You're all right," she said.

"You're all right—," he tried to reply, but in the effort to rise, realized he was injured. "Ou-ouch," he managed to add.

"You have a broken arm and a dislocated shoulder. By the bruising, I'm guessing your collarbone is broken too."

"Anything else?" he asked, closing his eyes. He hadn't ached like this since the high-school football championships. Or the time he was moose hunting and a bull charged, sending him scrambling down the river and over a few too many boulders.

"You were out for some time. Probably a concussion. Thank God you didn't go into a coma. The cold would have claimed you for sure then." She rustled through the medical supplies on the ground and pulled out her stethoscope and her blood-pressure cuff. "What day is it?"

"I'm not sure."

"Who's the president?"

"Bush. By a hair."

"What's my full name?"

"Bryn Skye Bailey. The love of my life."

She smiled then, finally, apparently appeased. "Head must be okay if you remember that. I'm tired of your having concussions," she groused. "How 'bout we quit this cycle?"

"I'm game. Are you all right? Other than freezing?"

"Nothing broken, by some miracle."

"You have a nasty cut here," he said, gesturing above her eye.

"Guess it will be my souvenir."

"You're still beautiful, Bryn." He shook his head. "I'm so glad you're okay." The thought of losing her brought tears to his eyes.

For the first time, Eli chanced a look about. They were under a giant old white spruce, their clothing and a blanket stiffly hung from the branches—frozen, maybe—and there was a pitiful fire smoldering to his left, giving off a little heat, but not much. "How, how'd you do all this? What happened?"

Bryn recounted her memories of the night before, of getting him to shelter, returning to the plane for supplies, of attempting to build a fire and keep them both warm. "They'll come for us now, right?" she asked, nodding toward the edge of the tree where light was warming a solid blanket of glistening, unbroken snow.

"I would imagine," he said, trying not to scare her. With the low cloud ceiling, it would be difficult for anyone to fly. "I don't… Bryn, before we crashed, did I get a location out with my Mayday?"

"I don't know. It's all kind of a blur."

"For me too. I think I had to give up on the radio transmission to keep the plane aloft. The thing is, with this snow, we might be in for a wait."

"Just our luck that we'd get snow in August."

"It won't last long. We must be at a higher elevation. And conditions must've been right last night. The plane?"

"Went down in the lake. The trees ripped off the pontoons and wings, but they are still hanging on by their rigging, it looks like."

"So it can be salvaged?"

"I guess. If you can salvage a partially submerged fuselage." Clearly, getting back in the plane was the last thing on her mind.

"What about the radio?"

"Under water."

"Emergency kit?"

"I couldn't find it. But I was getting so cold, and you were under this tree in wet clothes—"

"Shoot. There was a flare in there. And some decent fire starters. Maybe I can—" Heavy footfalls through the brush caught his attention then, making him wonder if a search party was almost upon them. Eli craned his neck to see, hoping that they would soon be in a litter, covered in blessed wool blankets, being carried to safety. But a giant black bear snuffled into view. Eli's eyes widened. The bear was maybe forty yards away, lifting his nose and grunting. *The blood. He smells our blood.*

Eli tried to swallow, his mouth suddenly dry, and whispered to Bryn, "You have your gun?"

"I do." He heard the safety release, saw out of the corner of his eye as she aimed at the bear. It was at that moment that the bear spotted them. He was about to charge. Eli could sense it. The bear stared them down for an impossibly long time and then rushed.

"Shoot it," he whispered hoarsely, the bear thirty yards away. The shot echoed across the lake as the bear roared, fell, rolled to its feet, and ran toward them again, closing the distance impossibly fast.

Bryn shot again from twenty yards. The bear tripped and then rose again, nipping at its wound.

Eli grabbed for the gun, knowing the next shot would be their last chance, but his shoulder and arm screamed in pain. "Make it count," he groaned, almost losing consciousness.

Bryn grabbed the gun back and shot again. The bear was maybe ten yards away now. Eli feared Bryn had missed. But the bear stopped suddenly, and then curled into a collapse, like a waning whirlwind. He huffed a few times with labored breaths, and then his chest ceased rising.

The gun was still pointed at him, and Eli noticed Bryn's trembling hand. Gently this time, he reached out to take it from her. "You did it," he whispered.

"I did it," she repeated, as if to convince herself. She laid down beside him, reminding Eli of the bear's collapse. "I had to go and fall in love with a bear magnet," she muttered. She gasped for breath as if she had been holding it for the last thirty seconds.

"A bear magnet that smells like fresh moose meat," he added.

Bryn just groaned. She was trembling again, her teeth chattering.

"We gotta find some heat."

"My fire," Bryn defended.

"Ain't doing much. How 'bout that blanket? And our clothes? Are they dry?"

Bryn struggled to rise and felt them. They were as hard as sheets of ice. "Fr-frozen," she said.

"It was a good thought. Just not warm enough to dry them. Come back here. I'm already colder without you."

She snuggled up against him.

"Are we going to die out here?" she whispered.

"I hope not. Pray with me, would ya?"

She nodded against his chest.

"Father God, we're in serious need of a miracle here. Please, Lord, we pray that you will guide searchers to us, as soon as possible. In Jesus' name. Amen."

"Amen."

Bryn awakened, trembling so hard her head hit the ground. She stared over Eli's chest to the bear she had shot. A thin layer of frost covered each hair of his fur, leaving him looking as if he had bleached the ends of his hair. Unbelievable. It was still amazing to her that she had shot it. She had been ready to shoot Ben's bear when he broke into her cabin. But he had been more of a rummager than a hunter. This one had been so close, so clearly intent on killing them for a meal. She shivered, double-time.

Her movement roused Eli from his slumber, and he looked at her, then to the tree limbs above them. "Shh. Listen. Hear that?"

"What?" All she could hear was the faint breeze sweeping through the stands of alder and the tree above them. But then, a faint whine...

"C-130," he said with a grin.

Her eyes widened in delight, and she returned the smile. Pushing herself up on all fours, she rose. On shaking legs, she exited the tree foliage to look upon the lake for the first time that day. There was still a solid cloud ceiling, but it was high enough now for planes to be out and searching.

"Two de Havillands, coming behind her!" Eli called, too wounded and weary to join her. "Quick, come get a rain slicker, something to wave at them!"

She hurried over to him as the C-130 loomed closer, the churning of its giant engines reverberating in her chest. It was coming fast and low. She scrambled under the tree and grabbed the slicker, then hurried back to the beach, panicked that she might fall and blow their chance at being discovered. Their downed plane was covered with snow, so it would look like a jetty from that distance, not a fallen aircraft.

The large plane burst over the treetops, not a thousand feet above ground. And trailing behind, a half-mile distant on either side, were the Beavers, painted orange and white. The Anchorage Civil Air Patrol. They passed in a vivid display of air power, like planes at the Air Force Academy's stadium on game day. "We're here!" Bryn screamed, waving her slicker. *"We're here!"* she yelled after them, as if her cry could pierce the metal sheathing of their fuselages and bypass the engine noise.

"I missed them, Eli!" she cried in despair, wanting to kneel and weep. "I missed them! They didn't see us! I was too late!"

"They'll be back," he said calmly from his perch beneath the branches. How could he be so calm?

Bryn moved five feet to the left in order to see the planes until they disappeared. It was cold, so cold. How could they survive here?

None of the planes turned; they continued to canvass the landscape beneath them as they flew northward. "Oh, God," she cried. "Please, Lord, I can't take another night. Please, Father, lead someone to us!" Tears ran down her face. "Please, Lord," she begged, falling to her knees and bowing. "Please."

"Doc?" Eli asked a moment later.

"Y-yes?" she said, wiping her face and rising.

"A Cessna. Heading our way. Wave that slicker, honey. Wave it as hard as you can."

CHAPTER FOURTEEN

When the rescue team landed on the tiny mountain lake, Bryn sank to her knees again and gave in to the trembling of hypothermia that she had staved off for hours—like a grad student succumbing to a cold on the day after finals. Soon after they arrived, Bryn dimly recognized a helicopter, a medevac from Anchorage or Willow. She was picked up and placed in a sleeping bag, with heating pads in her armpits and an oxygen mask over her face.

"Eli," she moaned. "Eli!"

"Shh," said an EMT beside her. "They're bringing him, too. He'll be right here beside you in a minute." The medical technician checked her fingers and toes.

"Fr-frostbite?" she mumbled.

"Maybe," he said grimly. "I'm more worried over your core temperature."

"What am I running?"

"Ninety-one." A body temp of 89 degrees would bring coma.

"And Eli?" she asked, as a litter was placed beside her with a rough-and-tumble clatter. Almost immediately she felt the chopper lift into the air and a cold rush of wind through an open doorway. She blacked out before she could hear the EMT's answer.

Bryn awakened in a hospital and recognized the warmth of blankets as nurses piled them on her. She was still trembling violently and had been laid on a board attached to chains that were hooked to a ceiling hoist. With a start she realized that they had catheterized her and there were intravenous needles in both arms. The nurses were pumping warm fluids into her, urging her body back to its normal temperature.

Meanwhile they began to lower her into a warm bath, gradually increasing the heat. After her second dip, her mind cleared enough to think about Eli. Where was he? Was he in worse shape than she? Had he…died? He had been injured far worse than she had, and he'd been so cold for so long. "Please," she said, grasping a nearby nurse's arm. "Eli Pierce. He was brought in here with me. Is he all right?"

The nurse gently pried Bryn's icy fingers from her forearm and placed her hand back under the warm blankets. "He's doing all right. He's next door, in a room identical to this one."

Bryn gasped for breath and realized she'd been holding it, waiting for the nurse's answer. Tears ran down her cheeks. What would she have done had he died? What would her life be like without Eli?

"Dr. Bailey?" said another nurse in concern over her tears. "What's the matter?"

"Nothing," she said, trying to smile through her chattering teeth. "Nothing at all." *Thank you, Lord,* she prayed silently. *Thank you, thank you, thank you.*

They lowered the platform again, and the nurses pulled away the towels. As the warm waters surrounded Bryn, she knew she had been plucked from the edge of eternity for a reason.

Eli shook his head, relishing the warm blankets that covered him from chin to toe, but he was unable to quit shaking. His head kept a steady beat on the padded gurney. He chided himself for his weakness and asked the nearest nurse about Bryn.

"For the seventh time, Dr. Bailey is doing better all the time. Just like you."

"When can I see her?"

"When the doctor says it's okay."

"When Dr. Bailey says it's okay?"

"No. When Dr. Albrechtson says it's okay. Rest. Get warm. Let us assess how you are faring. You'll see Dr. Bailey soon enough."

Eli doubted that. He thought about what they'd just been through. They were alive! And recovering! In a hospital where there was a good chance of saving fingers and toes. "Thank you, Lord," he whispered. Leon had passed a message to him via a nurse that they were already working on salvaging his Beaver. With any luck, he'd have his girl and his plane both in one piece within the week. Or the month anyway. The month…

It was August. Bryn's Housecalls contract ended in a matter of days. Eli had seen Carmine walk past his window, to see Bryn, he presumed. Of course, the Housecalls director hadn't stopped to check on his volunteer pilot. *Ladies first*, Eli grinned. *Think again, Doc. The lady's taken.*

As the medical team raised his litter and lowered him into the warm pool, he thought about Bryn and their future together. What could he offer her here? He had built a business, a life, in Talkeetna. Was the crash God's way of getting his attention, of giving him a wake-up call that all he had built could easily be taken away? Maybe Bryn deserved someone better than him, another doctor, like Carmine Kostas.

No, that mind garbage didn't ring true to him even in his sorry state. He was in love with Bryn, and she was in love with him. There had to be a way to be together. There had to be. But if he pressured her to stay here when she didn't truly want to, it would only lead to trouble later. Perhaps a rift that they couldn't bridge. He couldn't bear for that to happen.

Would she walk away? He wasn't a fool. He knew she had that Boston job offer on the line. A prestigious position like that would pay off her "mountain of school loans," as she called it. Did he make enough at Alaska Bush to help shoulder that debt? He sighed heavily. One thing at a time. One thing at a time. There would be plenty of opportunities for fretting, considering, hoping. For now he would simply appreciate the warm liquid that surrounded every inch of his aching body and revel in the fact that he and Bryn were alive at all to fret, consider, and hope for a new day.

It took them another forty-eight hours to leave the hospital, but both did so on their own two feet. Bryn had a few frostbitten toes that concerned doctors and five Steri-Strip closures on her forehead, but she was otherwise okay. Eli had a broken clavicle, as Bryn had suspected, a dislocated shoulder, and a broken arm. The fingers on that arm were still numb, also a concern, probably due to the lack of circulation and the cold. He and Bryn hoped that with time and prayer all would be okay. "Even if they have to come off, I'm so glad to be alive, I'd call it a small sacrifice," he said, putting his arm around her. "You can love a one-handed man, can't you?"

"If you could love a woman who's missing three toes," she said. They kissed and walked outside into the dark night, where Leon had parked his sedan, ready to take them home to Talkeetna. It was icy cold, and they each pulled their warm parkas a bit closer; Eli resolved never to take warm clothing for granted again.

"There's a definite nip of winter in the air," he said, pulling open the car door for Bryn.

"Winter? It isn't even fall yet!"

He shut the door and went around to the other side. "You blink in Alaska, and autumn has rolled on by."

"I can't wait to see the tundra," Bryn said, staring out her window into the inky darkness. She turned to Eli suddenly, but he couldn't see much of her face, just a vague outline in the glow of the dashboard's gauge lights. "I asked Carmine for the rest of the season off. Told him I wanted to spend my last days at Summit."

"Oh," Eli managed. "What'd he say?"

"He agreed. Asked me to come back next summer."

Eli swallowed hard. "What'd you say to that?" he asked, trying desperately to keep his tone light.

"I said I'd think about it."

Eli refused to add anything. He didn't want to sway her decision. She had to do what was right for her. If they were meant to be, the way would be made clear. Somehow.

Why didn't Eli ask her to stay? Did he not love her enough to marry her? Did he not know yet? Because Bryn knew. After nearly losing him in the water, under that tree, to that bear, there wasn't a single doubt in her mind.

"You ready to ride in a plane again to Summit tomorrow?" Eli asked.

She shook her head, trying to focus on what he was saying. "Wh-what? Oh yes. I thought about it a lot in the hospital. Back in the saddle and all that." She turned back to her dark window, to watch ghostly silhouettes speeding by.

"Want me to fly you up there?" Leon volunteered, looking up into his rearview mirror as if he could see her.

"That would be great." She turned toward Eli, taking a risk. "Can you come too? I don't want to spend my last days in Alaska without you. But I know you've been away from the business an awful lot. I don't know if Leon—"

"Yes," he interrupted her. Tenderly he took her hand in his good one and lifted it to his lips. Against the drone of the car engine, he softly kissed one finger and then the next, and then the next, sending tingles of delight up Bryn's arm and down her spine. How could she leave this man? Ever?

When he kissed her on her river cabin doorstep and left, his parting felt like a tear in her flesh, from the inside out. Did he feel this ache, this longing to remain together and never part? His lips were soft and warm, and his breath covered her face for a long moment as she memorized the feel of being in close proximity to Eli Pierce. Would another man ever move her like he did? Could she ever find this connection, this friendship with another?

"Good night, Doc," he whispered, kissing one eyebrow and then the other, and then finally giving her a last, soft kiss on the mouth. "Better go in now," he quipped. "It's cold out here."

She stared into his eyes. "I love you, Eli Pierce."

"I love you, Bryn Bailey."

"See you in the morning?"

"Yeah. Say, nine o'clock? Think we both could use a good night's sleep."

"Yeah. See you then." She gave in to the rending then, the laceration of her heart.

She placed her hand on the cold pine door as she listened to

Leon's car drive away. "God be with you, love," she whispered. "God be with me." She hoped her Savior would draw closer than ever before, that she could let him in, that he would guide her, lead her, teach her. Because Bryn Bailey had some big decisions to make.

Eli and Bryn flew to Summit Lake the following day. There were some high clouds, but it was mostly sunny. The tundra was alive with autumnal colors—russet and gold and olive. The birch were every shade of ripening squash, from a light green to an orange yellow. And the lake was as pretty as ever, a curvy mass of mercury amid the tundra and trees. Arriving on Summit always felt like a homecoming to Eli. He grinned over at Bryn.

She had handled the flight well, more quiet than usual, but generally fine. He had held her hand with his good one, content to sit in back with the more limited view in order to be near Bryn. Leon sat alone in the cockpit like a chauffeur in the front of a limo. He made a smooth landing and dropped them both at Bryn's cabin.

"Smoke rising at your place," she said, nodding across the lake.

"That's my folks. Back from their travels, I guess. The people at the hospital tried to reach them but had no luck."

"I'm glad they're here." She disappeared through the doorway. "I'd like to see them. There's something I'd like to ask them."

"What?"

"You'll see."

"Okay, surprise girl. Why don't you take an hour to yourself? I'll go catch up with the folks, and then you can join us for lunch."

"That'd be good, Eli. Really good."

He leaned down and kissed her, turned, and then shook his head, laughing under his breath. Feeling foolish, he turned back to her. "I don't have my canoe here, and even if I did, I wouldn't be much good with one arm."

She giggled and stood on tiptoe to kiss him on the cheek. "Give me half an hour, and we'll go over together, all right?"

"Okay," he said, giving her a rueful smile. "I'm gonna go sit on the porch."

"All right. I'll put on a pot of tea."

The two struck out across the lake half an hour later. Eli was eager to see his folks, eager to show off Bryn and see how they would feel about seeing him and Bryn together. His dad's words of all those years before came back to him—"Like catnip to a tomcat." He smiled. "Can't you paddle a little faster?" he teased, throwing the comment over his left shoulder.

"Can't you get out and swim?"

He grinned. Up ahead, his cabin emerged from the trees, and his parents walked onto the porch and then down the steps to meet them.

"Eli Alexander Pierce," his mother said in surprise, "What have you done to yourself this time?"

"And why Leon's plane? Where's the de Havilland?" his father put in.

"Had a little accident. We'll tell you all about it over lunch. Welcome home, by the way," he said.

"I told you we should have gotten that cell phone fixed," Meryl said to Jedidiah while she reached out to give her son a hug and to greet Bryn. "My, haven't you turned out lovely! And I hear you're a full-fledged doctor now. Your parents must be so proud."

Bryn smiled shyly and then hugged Eli's father. "Yes, my dear, you've grown up real fine," Jedidiah said. "Prettier every time I see you. No wonder my boy is head over heels."

"Not any more than I am," she said. Eli grinned back at her.

"Well, come in, come in," Meryl said. "I have tomato soup on, and in a few minutes we'll have cheddar sandwiches to go with it."

"Sounds great, Mom," Eli said.

Eli spent the next hour telling his folks about their ordeal. His mother could say nothing but "oh my" and kept a hand over her mouth. Jedidiah looked over at them both and said, "Thank God you two are all right. I'm sorry we weren't within reach."

"I'm glad we didn't know," Meryl said, rising and clearing the lunch dishes. "Spending a whole day not knowing if you were alive or dead is something a mother doesn't wish to endure."

Eventually the topic of conversation switched to the Pierces' cross-country trip in the RV. Eli relaxed and sat back, watching his parents interact with Bryn and get to know her again. They had a natural way with each other, like old friends. And Eli noticed that his mother leaned in, as if wanting to be affirming, whenever Bryn spoke.

When they all finally rose again, Bryn helped his mother wash and dry the lunch dishes, then clean up the kitchen. Eli chatted with his dad, but his eyes were on Bryn. She was so incredible. And she fit so well into his family.

She and Meryl were obviously discussing something intently, speaking in hushed tones and smiling. His mother wiped tears from her rounded cheeks and then reached up to tenderly embrace the taller girl. What were they talking about?

When they came out, Meryl handed a sack of cookies to Eli. "Your father brought an outboard motor for the rowboat," she said. "Why don't you go fire it up and run these down to Ben?"

"I'm not sure he's there, Mom. It looked pretty quiet."

"Go and check. I don't want the cookies to get stale. You know how Ben loves chocolate chip."

"All right," he said slowly. Were they trying to get rid of him? Besides, Eli was more in the mood for a nap than a run down the lake. But the prospect of the outboard motor roused him. If it worked, he'd be able to get to Bryn's and back without escort.

"Want to come with me?" he asked Bryn. His mother sat down beside his father and whispered something in his ear.

"No. Thanks. I think I'll just stay here and rest. It's been a big day already."

"I know what you mean," he said, rising as she sat down. He went to her and gave her a quick kiss, conscious of his parents' approving grins and careful to ignore them. "Dad? You want to come?"

"Uh, I'll get you started. A nap sounds good to me, too."

Eli looked around at the others. What was cookin' here exactly? They all stared back at him with innocent expressions.

"Come on, Son. You'll be back before you know it. We'll just stay and chat with your girlfriend a little more, maybe catch a little shut-eye." He gestured toward the door, and Eli went for his coat, picked up the cookies, and left with a curious smile toward Bryn.

"So, what do you think?" he asked his father as they descended the steps toward shore.

"Of Bryn?"

"No, Dad. Of the weather."

Jedidiah chuckled. "You and Bryn were always meant to be together."

"Why do you say that?"

"Because when I sat there drinking with her father—back during my drinking days in Germany—we were feeling as close as brothers, me and Peter." He laughed and shook his head, rubbed his neck with one hand and then looked his son in the eye. "Pledged our firstborn to each other. You and Bryn, being our first—and only—children were a matched pair from the beginning. An arranged marriage, we called it."

Eli stared at him in disbelief. "But—"

Jedidiah waved at him and smiled. "We were only kidding, of course. But I'd wager that Peter will be as pleased as a fox in a warm winter den if you two would make it official. I would be." He bent to lift the small motor and place it on the back of the rowboat.

"I'm thinkin' about it, Dad. But I don't know. I don't want to push Bryn into anything."

"Bryn doesn't seem like the type of woman that anyone pushes into anything. Not unlike your wonderful mother," he added with a wink.

"Yeah," Eli said with a sigh. "Bryn's terrific. I'd hate to lose her."

"You wait for that moment. It'll come if this is truly meant to be."

"That's what I figure." He watched as his dad put gasoline into the engine and got it going with a strong arm. He cranked the throttle, letting it run high for a moment, then climbed out of the boat and past Eli. "Give my best to Ben. Tell him to join us for dinner if he's available."

Eli smiled. "Will do." He climbed in. "What's with the engine? I thought you were against anything but canoes up here."

"I am. But your mother said she'd come with me to the lake more often if we could go for afternoon rides and she wouldn't have to paddle."

Eli took Bryn home in the rowboat that night after dinner, letting the canoe drift behind them on a rope. It wasn't as peaceful and idyllic as paddling a canoe, but it was faster.

When they crunched to shore, she climbed out and turned around. "Can you sit with me for a little while, Eli? There's something I need to talk over with you."

"Sure," he said, trying to sound casual, not overly curious. He turned off the motor and climbed out, then turned to pull the boat higher up on the rocky bank.

"Let's go in, build a fire."

"Sounds good." He followed her inside and she lit eight vanilla-scented candles. "It drowns the must and mothball smell," she said as she set them around the room. Eli laid the fire and struck a match to the pile of kindling and needles at the bottom. Within minutes it was crackling, and Bryn set several blankets, the bearskin, and pillows on the floor in front of it.

With a grin Eli sat down across from her, cross-legged as she was. The fire lit half her face, leaving the other in deep shadow. He was reminded of the days when she had cared for him after the grizzly incident at the river. "I'm so in love with you, Doc," he whispered, raising a hand to caress her face.

"Eli," she said, taking his hand in hers and pulling it to her knee. She swallowed slowly, her eyes, big and luminous, searching his. "I took a job," she said carefully.

Her words robbed him of breath. "Oh," was all he could manage. He tried to put on a brave front. "I hope it's not in Boston. Please tell me you're at least on the West Coast."

"At least," she said dryly. "It's in Willow. I'm going to work at the hospital there, continue on with Housecalls in the summertime."

"You-you *what?*"

"I took a job in Willow. I'm staying here," she said slowly, lowering her eyes at him as if something were wrong with his ears.

"You're…you're staying here?"

"Yes."

He let out a breath in relief and then grinned from ear to ear. "That's, that's so great. I mean, I had wondered…I had hoped. Oh, Bryn. Thank you. Thank you for staying." He pulled her to him for a quick one-armed hug. "I'm so glad, sweetheart. I'm so glad you're not going away again."

"Not for a while," she said, smiling now too. "Especially if you answer the next question right."

"Which is?"

"Eli Alexander Pierce," she said, "I asked your parents for their blessing this afternoon, and they gave it."

"Blessing for what?"

"On our marriage."

"Our…what?"

She laughed then and touched his face. "I know it's unconventional. But I love you, Eli, and I don't want to wait another day, wonder for another moment. I want you, forever. As mine and mine alone. Would you do me the honor of becoming my husband?"

He joined in her laughter and then shook his head. "Bryn Bailey. Always have to do things in your own time, your own way, don't you?"

"Yes." She looked at him with sheepish, hopeful eyes. "I can be a problem that way, I guess. I'm still hoping—"

"Of course I'll marry you, Doc. You'll make me the happiest man in Alaska. You already have."

And then they kissed and hugged and caressed and cuddled for hours. "We're going to spend our wedding night here," Eli said lowly, kissing her softly on the nose. "On the floor, in front of the fire, when there are no boundaries anymore. You'll be mine, body and soul, and I'll be yours."

"Let's wed soon," she said, urgently kissing him again.

"You're the boss, Doc." He laughed quietly and pulled back to peruse the beauty of his intended bride. "Why do I get the feeling you always will be?"

She answered him, not with words, but with another kiss. She was smart and savvy and sexy beyond belief. And Eli knew they were on a path to love, fulfillment, and happiness. "I'm gonna marry you, Bryn Skye Bailey, the day your family can get here. I will wait no longer."

"Now who's bossing whom?" she asked playfully.

"I'll let you wear the pants in our family once in a while. But don't you forget, I'm the man."

"I can never forget that, Eli," she said softly, pulling him to her again. "I've thought of you as a man since I was fifteen."

"Lots has happened in the years since then."

"Good and bad. But mostly good. You're one of the best parts."

"As are you."

"Eli?"

"H'm?"

"Should we pray? Ask for God's blessing?"

He sighed, long and hard. Praying wasn't heavy on his mind, but she was right, it should be. He smiled. "You start, Doc. And I'll finish."

ACKNOWLEDGMENTS

*T*his book would have been impossible without a quick trip to Anchorage and Talkeetna. The people there were wonderful and treated me like an honored guest, particularly Peggy Beal of the Kingsview Bed and Breakfast (www.kingsviewbandb.com) on the Anchorage hillside, who also read my manuscript; the gracious people at the lovely Copper Whale Inn of Anchorage (http://anc-biz.com/copperwhaleinn); Elbert Sturgis, my very efficient pilot at Alaska Bush (www.ak-biz.com/alaskabush/) outside of Talkeetna who flew me out to meet the Nickols family, who own the Caribou Lodge (www.cariboulodgealaska.com). If you want to see the Alaska bush yourself, talk to Elbert and go visit Caribou Lodge for the night! Elbert's assistant, Karen, was wonderful in helping me coordinate the whole last-minute research trip that I am so glad I took. She sent me to the kind and helpful Nickols family rather than to visit a very lonely bush man who was eager to spend "a week" with a romance writer.

I also leaned heavily upon my father and my brother, Jim and Ryan Grosswiler, who are both pilots and helped me write all those scenes aloft with some degree of authority. It was the medical side of my family who once again bailed me out on the technical things. On Christmas Eve Day, Drs. Cecil Leitch, Nancy Leitch, and Paul Amundson helped me get all those medical traumas right.

I gleaned a lot of my information—and a couple of scenarios I used in my own novel—from books written by Alaskan authors: Larry Kaniut's *Cheating Death,* Joe Rychetnik's *Alaska's Sky Follies,* and Sam Keith's *One Man's Wilderness* among them. I was thankful to discover these excellent and fun resources on Alaska life and adventure, past and present.

Cheryl Crawford prayed me through the process and read the manuscript, as did Nancy Leitch and Rebecca Price. Traci DePree, beloved friend and editor, sacrificed much to get this book done on time. I am grateful to them all.

Dear Reader,

Thank you for reading *Pathways*. It was fun to return to the romance genre and find a fresh spin for yet another of my intrepid couples. As I sit and consider what I want to share with you today, I find that gratitude is most heavily on my mind. I've been blessed over and over, and it makes me weep when I stop to consider how much God has done for me. Just look at the book in your hands now! I am well aware of the doors God has opened, going before me, always and forevermore.

I took an amazing trip to Alaska last fall and had an experience under the northern lights similar to the one Bryn had when she finally "saw the light." I was saved years ago, but when I stood outside and watched that aurora dance, I was reduced to tears and a laughter that I can only describe as the joy of the Holy. For I was truly witnessing the power at the Maker's hand. And once again, he was gifting me with a vision that would help make my book shine, as well as an experience I'll never, ever forget.

I pray that each of you might find the time and the inclination to seek the miraculous in your day-to-day life. God seldom appears in the celestial way he did to me over Talkeetna that night, but more often in the soft call of my two-year-old's "I love you, Mama" from the dark recesses of her room at night, my five-year-old's concern over Jesus "getting cold in my heart since I'm freezing" (it's winter here!), my husband's unfailing support, or the warm lights of our home greeting me when I return in the evening. God has given each of us much, yes? I am overwhelmed by all I have in my life, all I've been given. I hope you, too, find cause to be so.

Every blessing,

Lisa Tawn Bergren

Write to Lisa Tawn Bergren
c/o WaterBrook Press
2375 Telstar Drive, Suite 160
Colorado Springs, CO 80920

or e-mail her through her Web site:
www.LisaTawnBergren.com

If you enjoyed PATHWAYS, *be sure to look for other books in the*
Full Circle series, available at your local bookstore.
The following is an excerpt from one of those books, TREASURE.

PROLOGUE

JULY 1627
THE GULF COAST

Above the high-pitched scream of the wind, Captain Esteban Ontario Alvarez heard the wails of his passengers below, but he had too much on his mind to worry about a contingent of overindulged Castilian merchants. He squinted his eyes against the constant spray of the sea and struggled to maintain hold of the helm with the help of his first mate and a soldier.

The wind was relentless in its drive back toward the coast. Soaked to the skin after battling the storm on deck for four hours, the professional sailors were losing the war. *"Jesucristo,"* the captain grunted through clenched teeth. *"Sálvanos, por favor."* Jesus, please save us.

"¡Capitán! ¡Capitán!" Screaming over the wind, Alvarez's cabin boy struggled valiantly to make his way across the deck to his superior. He fell, was swept against the ship's starboard railing, then picked himself up and pushed forward once again. Esteban watched

out of the corner of his eye, his heart in his throat, but was unable to leave the wheel. They barely had control of *La Canción.*

"¡Capitán!" The boy pointed frantically, unable to say anything else as terror overwhelmed him.

"*¡Sí! ¡Sí! Qué…*"

But he saw what struck fear in the boy's eyes. *Tierra.* Land. They would break apart on the reef if he didn't slow them down quickly. "*¡La ancla! ¡La ancla!*" he yelled at the boy, wanting with everything in him to release the wheel and run for the anchors himself.

The boy clung, monkeylike, to the torn sails, railing, masts…anything he could grab as he made his way forward to the one thing that might save them. The ship, a giant that weighed over three tons, rocked chaotically. So steep was the incline from starboard to port, the boy feared that they might capsize even if they did manage to slow their rapid advance.

He heaved against a door in the floorboards and scowled at a frightened sailor clinging for his life belowdecks. "¡La ancla!" the boy screamed. The grimy man nodded, climbed the steep stairs, and helped the boy release the huge iron hook.

The six-hundred-pound weight sank quickly, pulling with it yards and yards of chain. It struck the ocean floor in under a minute, dragged across sand and loose rocks for a moment, then sank its teeth into a massive coral reef.

The ship lurched at the force of the anchor's braking power, throwing every loose object and body aboard. Captain Alvarez and his men gave the ship's wildly spinning wheel room and searched for rope with which to tie it off.

Belowdecks, *La Canción's* hasty building schedule was telling.

Mahogany ribs, weaker than oak, strained under the burden of heavy seas and a taut anchor chain. Planking popped as boards requiring ten nails each broke free of their scanty two. Waves gnawed at the interior clamp that held the anchor to the ship. It took only one more watery monster to yank the teeth from their sockets.

"We're moving again!" Alvarez yelled in the Castilian accent of aristocratic Spaniards. "Sound the warning: Abandon ship!"

Seeing that they were drifting, his man on the fo'c's'le deck swiftly threw a second anchor, unaware that the interior clamp was gone, that there was nothing below to keep the anchors from merely sinking beyond the wounded ship. He threw a third. A fourth. Holding the last one, he gazed frantically from the quickly approaching rocks to the chain in his hand, knowing that all was lost.

JULY 1986

THE GULF COAST OF TEXAS

Mitch had rarely scuba-dived with visibility as great as this: eighty feet in any direction. He looked left to his friend Hans, provoking a moray eel with a stick, then right to Chet, meticulously studying the coral reef and its inhabitants. He smiled around the regulator in his mouth. As far as he was concerned, this was heaven.

Catching sight of a lavender-and-gold striped Spanish grunt fish, Mitch stroked through the water with powerful legs, coasting after the beauty with ease. Over the rise of coral he discovered a huge pile of rocks and moved to investigate. Such exploration had lately become the focus of Mitch's dreams. On each dive he imagined finding vases, ballast piles, anchors: the beginning clues of valuable and ancient wreck sites. Ever since his introduction to Nautical Archaeology 101, he'd had nothing else on his mind, much to his parents' chagrin. Mitch knew that they were just biding their time before bringing up law school again.

He tried to dismiss the thought of actually finding a wreck on a casual dive off Galveston, but as much as he tried to banish the idea, he found himself returning to it again and again. It would only take one wreck to convince his dad. Mom might have to have an emerald necklace that once belonged to Queen Estuvia or a Celtic cross that once hung from a devout monk's neck to convince her there might be a way to make a living in such a business.

He smiled. Then. Then they would not keep hounding him about the cost of a "perfectly good education squandered away on a schoolboy's dreams." *Just one. Come on, God. Think of the ministry potential! Such success could open all kinds of doors!* He laughed at himself, recognizing that one could not bargain with God. Yet he felt that a life of searching the underwater world was a personal calling and that the Lord would reward his following the call.

Mitch fully realized that his chosen course might leave him poor, chasing the siren call of one ship after another for the rest of his life. Yet it was not wealth that enticed him to this life path. It was the anticipated thrill of a find. The spark that lit each successful treasure hunter's eyes when telling of that special dig. *Just one, God.*

The Spanish grunt darted away, and Mitch turned his attention to several multicolored queen angels, their heavenly wings waving to him as they ate from the pile of ballast stones on the ocean floor. *Ballast stones.* Mitch caught his breath and held it. He closed his eyes slowly and then opened them, expecting the pile to disappear.

It did not. He rose fifteen feet—to a depth of about forty-five feet—eager to catch the attention of his buddies. Hans spotted his wave first and dragged Chet away from his studies and toward

Mitch. Seeing his Texas A&M pals en route, Mitch moved back to the pile, carefully examining each rock—without moving them—as Professor Sanders had advised.

Sometimes the kind of rock could help a diver narrow down the ship's port of origin. *If this really is a ship,* he chastised himself silently, willing his excitement back down. He dusted off the rocks but could not tell what kind they were. Chet, better at such things than he, was already studying the color and texture. Mitch moved on.

Thirty feet away, in the direct line of the current, he found another large, lichen-covered pile. After investigation, Mitch discovered that the pile was made up of hundreds of earthen jars, such as the kind crews once carried, filled with fresh water or delicacies, like olives. Many were intact, even covered with marine life.

Mitch abandoned the vases to see what else might be nearby. As he swam over the next rise, his breathing became labored, and he wondered if what he was seeing could really be true. There, scattered between what was clearly the rotting remains of a ship's timbers, lay thousands of sparkling gold coins.

His friends soon joined him, and the trio excitedly filled the "goody bags" at their waists with as many coins as possible, then swam to their raft thirty feet above. Clinging to the sides, they laughed and shouted while throwing their bounty on board.

"Well, boys," Mitch said, grinning broadly, "I think I finally know what I want to do when I grow up."

AUGUST 1994

OFF THE COAST OF MASSACHUSETTS

Trevor leaned toward Julia and kissed her gently. "I love looking over at you and saying, 'There she is. My *wife.*'"

"I love looking over at *you* and thinking, *my husband*. Husband, husband, husband. It will take awhile before that word rolls off my tongue."

"We've got years to get used to it. I didn't expect it to become second nature in the first month."

Julia lay back, soaking in the sun and the sights of Martha's Vineyard. It was the perfect honeymoon destination. Quiet if a couple wanted it to be so, social if they wished it to be otherwise. She and Trevor had been drawn to the solitude and stayed close to the small cottage they had rented for the week.

Trevor looked lovingly at Julia, then gazed down the beach. She followed his line of vision and nudged him indignantly. "Hey, no looking at other women on your honeymoon…or ever."

Trevor smiled, but his eyes remained on the attractive woman walking toward them on the beach. "It's just…she looks like someone I should know…"

"Who? A swimsuit model from *Sports Illustrated*?"

"No. You know I never read those."

"Yeah, right."

He kissed her soundly. "I think it was Paul Newman who said, 'Why go out for hamburger when you have steak at home?'"

"I always liked that guy," Julia said, smiling at her new husband.

The figure drew closer.

Trevor looked up again and scrambled to his feet, leaving a bewildered Julia sitting alone. "It *is* her," he mumbled in explanation as he walked toward the other woman. "Christina! Christina!"

The woman came to a stop, turning at the sound of her name, and when Trevor drew near, took his hands and gave him a quick, friendly kiss. Trevor pointed toward his new bride, and Julia grimaced as they made their way up the sandy hill.

She suddenly wished that her swimsuit could magically turn into a turtleneck and sweats. She was in good shape, but women like the one next to her husband always made her feel hopelessly inadequate.

Trevor smiled. "Honey, this is an old friend, Christina Alvarez. Christina, meet my new wife, Julia Rierdon-Kenbridge."

Christina gave her a broad grin and shook her hand warmly. "I always wondered who would finally get a ring on this guy's finger." She turned and playfully punched Trevor's muscular arm.

"I was the one that had to work to get a ring on her finger," he said, smiling down at his new bride.

"Sounds like there's a good story behind that one. But I know you're on your honeymoon, and I don't want to interrupt. I'm working off the coast of Massachusetts. Maybe I can stop by sometime."

"We have an inn in Oak Harbor, Maine. Why don't you come and spend the night?" Trevor offered.

"I'm afraid I just have ten days of shore leave, then it's back to the grind for another month of intensive salvaging."

"Well, we're leaving the Vineyard in five days," Trevor said. "Why don't you come see us next Tuesday? I'd love to catch up with you and for you to see our home."

"Are you sure? It sounds like a lot of fun." Trevor and Christina turned to Julia.

"We're sure. Please, come." Julia felt none of the grace her tone displayed.

"Fantastic! I'll see you two next week!"

CHAPTER ONE

*J*ulia pulled the kitchen curtain aside and shoved the wave of jealousy out of her mind. She was unaccustomed to getting anything but Trevor's complete attention, and he was definitely not thinking about her now. Instead he was held captive by their newly arrived guest, Christina Alvarez.

She narrowed her eyes as she looked out at the two and said a quick arrow prayer for an unencumbered heart. She left the kitchen with a pasted-on smile, her chin stubbornly raised, and carried tall glasses of iced tea out to the porch to her husband and his ex-girlfriend.

"Oh, that looks great," Christina remarked, spotting the thin frosted glasses topped with sprigs of mint and slices of lemon.

Julia tried to smile graciously. "It seems to get hotter every year," she said, making an effort at conversation. "My grandparents always had a huge container of iced tea ready for guests. I thought it would be fun to make it a Torchlight Inn tradition."

"Sounds good," Christina nodded. "You guys have done a remarkable job on the house; I didn't get a look at it before all the work, but I've rarely seen a more inviting home. I tell you, after fourteen days on a houseboat off the coast, it feels good to sit on a porch and talk with friends."

"Tell Julia what you're doing, Christina."

Christina looked a little embarrassed at being put on the spot.

"I'm heading up a team of nautical archaeologists; we're diving and recording the Civil War wrecks off the New England coast."

"How interesting!" Julia said, warming a little to the stranger. "How many are there?"

"Fifteen that we know of. We've been working all summer with student teams and will probably do so again next summer and the summer after that."

"Sounds time consuming. What do you do down there?"

"We spend a lot of time clearing silt off the wrecks so we can study them. We are very careful not to disturb the ships; they're like time capsules, and we don't want to pollute the sites."

"How exciting!" Julia's mind was on her great-great-grandfather Shane Donnovan's ship and how wonderful it would be to see what remained of it. Shane had been lost at sea in the prime of his life. *It'd be interesting to find out what happened to him.*

Christina and Trevor continued talking about her work and what he'd been up to in the five years since they'd gone separate ways. Studying the two, Julia decided that they must have parted amicably.

That night, while peeling carrots for dinner, Julia looked out the window as their beautiful guest walked from one flowering bush to the next, bending to smell and study each one. Her long, dark brown hair blew lightly in the breeze, and her olive skin shone under the early evening sun.

"She's absolutely stunning, Trevor," she said, trying to keep her voice even. "Why did you guys break up?"

Trevor placed his arms around her waist and kissed the back of her head. "She and I were never meant to be more than friends. God had you in mind when he created me."

Somewhat mollified, Julia smiled and continued peeling. "So

you and I were destined for each other. Still, how'd you ever pull yourself away from her? She's smart, she's beautiful, she's adventurous. What went wrong?"

"You're asking a lot of questions. You know, curiosity killed the cat," he teased.

"Careful, I've got a peeler in my hand. If you prove to be difficult, it could get ugly."

"I love a woman who resorts to threats of violence to get the information she wants." He sighed. "As I said, we were just meant to be friends. When we tried to be anything else, it just didn't work. I appreciate people who go after their dreams…like you. But she's consumed with her desire to find her ancestor's ship. She doesn't have time for men and won't until she finds it."

"That's it?"

"And she's got a Spanish temper that can wither the most valiant of men. When we became more than friends, she got very uptight."

Julia nodded.

"Are you all right?" Trevor asked, turning her around to face him. "Really, I do think she's attractive. But to me, you're more beautiful all around. You're the woman who will have me, body and soul, for the rest of our lives. Okay?"

"Okay," Julia said, raising her lips to meet his.

That night at dinner the conversation revolved primarily around the topics of shipwrecks and innkeeping. As the evening drew on, Julia found herself liking their adventuresome guest more and more. After chatting briefly with the four other guests and making sure they were settled for the night, Julia and Trevor joined Christina around the kitchen table with bowls of ice cream and talked of her future plans.

"Where will you go this fall?" Trevor asked.

"I've completed my degree program with my graduate thesis on the Spanish sea traders and the importance of the port of Veracruz—"

"Ah, the long awaited Ph.D. has finally been attained," Trevor teased.

"Yes, at last! As for this autumn…well, I've still got those doubloons and family folklore on my heart and mind. I want to know if *La Canción*—"the song"—existed as anything other than a figment of some ancestor's imagination."

"So you still think it's true," Trevor said gently.

"I do. At least part of it. I've been to Seville and spent weeks in the Archives of the Indies."

"The Archives?" Julia asked.

"Yes. El Archivo de las Indias. It's the best resource that treasure-ship seekers have today. Unfortunately, it's also in the worst shape. There used to be records kept of every Sevillian ship that came back from the New World loaded with gold. The records themselves are highly detailed, but poorly kept. The basement of the archive building is filled with old documents in stacks five feet high. It's a disaster, but I rolled up my sleeves and went after them with the help of a friend, Meredith Champlain. She's an expert in the field of translating Spanish documents dated from the fourteenth century on."

"And you found another clue," Trevor said.

"I did," Christina said, her eyes bright. She didn't say what it was, however.

"Well if you ever give up on your ancestor's *Song*, maybe you could find my great-great-grandfather Shane Donnovan's final resting place," Julia said after a long moment. "I don't know if he carried anything of great value at the time, but he was last seen leaving Rio.

They think he was caught in a storm. All hands went down with the ship."

"I know of the Donnovan Boatworks," Christina said.

"You do?"

"Yes. I've actually been a part of a team that dove a Donnovan wreck site and recorded it."

"Not my great-great-grandfather's last—"

"No. The location wouldn't make sense. It was off the coast of California. Shane Donnovan was into the Gold Rush, wasn't he?"

"Yes. It's really what made him a success. Would you like to see his logs?"

"I'd love it!"

For the rest of the evening, Christina pored over one old, weathered leather-bound book after another. Trevor and Julia soon gave up on her and went to bed, telling her they'd talk in the morning. Christina barely raised her hand and mumbled a good-night.

Julia was struck by her uncompromising passion for her work. Trevor shook his head as they walked up the steps, his arm around her waist. "That's how I knew Christina. Always with her nose in a book. When I'd demand she spend more time with me outside the library, she would start feeling tied down. She needs someone who shares her passion, who understands it."

One of their first guests sprang to Julia's mind. "What about that guy who stayed with us? What was his name..."

"Who?"

"He was in Maine for his sister's funeral. The treasure hunter..."

Trevor remembered the sad, roguish man who had stayed at Torchlight. "Mitch Crawford?"

"Yes!"

"Oh no, I don't think it would ever—"

"You never know," Julia cut in, sliding into bed. "Don't you say a word when I mention him to her tomorrow."

"I don't like the idea of matchmaking, Julia."

"Think of it as networking," she said with the impish smile he could never resist. "I'm merely going to put one professional in contact with another."

"Good morning!" Julia was surprised to see Christina up before any of their other guests. "What time did you get to bed?"

"One. Those logs are terrific! If I had something similar on my own ancestor's ship, I'd be able to find it right now. If I didn't have this burning desire to seek ancient Spanish wrecks, I'd love to pursue the romance of younger ships, tracing their stories."

"So maybe someone will go after Shane's ship one day?"

"Maybe," Christina grinned, helping herself to one of the mugs in the stack and pouring herself a cup of coffee.

Julia smiled at the woman, whose shiny, dark brown hair was pulled back in a French braid. "Now how can you look that terrific after six hours of sleep?"

"It must be the bed. This is a great place. I admire you and your dream. You've made it happen."

"Not without help. If Trevor hadn't come along, I'd have been in deep weeds."

"Somehow, I think you would've made it all right." The two studied each other, each admiring the independent woman she saw in her companion. "I think Trevor married well, Julia," Christina said softly. "It's good to see him so happy."

"It's good to be this happy," Trevor said, coming in to kiss his wife. He grinned at Christina. "Although I never pictured myself as settled down as this. An innkeeper. Can you believe it?"

"It suits you, Trevor." Christina felt a pang of loss and turned away, busying herself with a muffin and preserves. *Will I ever find this security, this peace, this love?* Somehow, she knew Trevor hadn't been the man for her. But he was terrific. If he hadn't met her needs, who would?

As they sat down to eat, Julia looked at Trevor mischievously and asked Christina in a casual voice, "So you found something in the Archives. Can't you go after your ship now?"

"We found one document that mentions *The Song*. There have to be others, but I ran out of time and money. I'll go back when I find a partner and investor."

Interest made Julia's eyes sparkle. "So you're looking for someone to work with?" she said, ignoring her husband's light pinch under the table.

"I am," Christina said, pouring a fresh cup of coffee for herself and topping off Julia's and Trevor's.

"Well, then, we had a guest here about two months ago who you should know about…"

CHAPTER TWO

*M*itchell Crawford lay awake in his bed, an unhappy man. He had failed to find sleep's peace the night before, consumed as he was by thoughts of his only sister's death. Each time he dropped off for a moment, he had been awakened by his niece's incessant crying.

As the little girl let out another wail, he glanced at the clock—5:05 A.M. Mitch threw a pillow over his head and willed the voice to go away. He had his own grief. Even his trip up the coast of Maine had failed to distract him from it. How could he deal with the sorrow of two small children? *Heck, I don't know the first thing about kids.*

Talle, the Cuban who had been his maid for five years, opened his door without knocking and went straight to the long vertical blinds. She drew them back from one dramatic window, then went to the next to do the same.

"Talle!" he barked. "I'm trying to sleep!"

Talle looked back at him and pulled the third window's blinds. Then she paused, took a deep breath, and gazed out at the ocean.

"It is a beautiful day, sir. The children would like to go out and play with you." Her English was nearly perfect, each syllable carefully enunciated.

Mitch sat up, rubbing his face in irritation, trying to focus. "They said they want me to?"

"No. But you see, sir, I cannot take care of them all the time *and* clean this huge home *and* cook." She busied herself with picking up his clothes from the night before, gathering them in a wicker basket.

"It's not forever, Talle—"

"It's been two weeks. The girl cries all night and will not allow me to comfort her. The boy is sullen, angry. He sneaks food like a little thief and throws mud into the pool."

"They're just kids—"

"Kids who need a full-time keeper. I cannot do all that you've asked of me. You must hire a nanny. For now I can arrange for my niece Anya to come. She can stay through the summer."

"Fine," Mitch said wearily. "Just get her here within a couple of days, okay? If I don't get some sleep, I'm gonna scream."

"Certainly, sir. I've taken the liberty of calling her already. She'll be here tomorrow." That said, she left the room.

Mitch shook his head. Even though she made him feel as if he were the boss, he knew Talle orchestrated his actions as smoothly as she ran the house.

Mitch rose and walked to his window. Kenna had stopped crying at last. He looked out over the blue-green Caribbean sea, in the direction of the big island, San Esteban. The palm trees lining the beach swayed in the trade winds, sending the salty, musty smell of the water to his nostrils. He loved the tiny island. But was it the place to raise his sister's kids?

"Oh, Sarah," he said sadly. "What were you thinking in sending them to me? I don't know what to do with your kids!" His fist struck the window sill. *How could she have given me this burden? Couldn't she have made her friends their guardians, people who knew them? Knew how to care for children?*

Kenna and Josh had stayed with the Johnsons, Sarah's friends, for the two months that Mitch needed to finish work on his current dive site and decide whether to take them. Maybe he had made a mistake agreeing to take them. They needed a mother. And a father with more patience than he had.

He left the window and went to take a shower. The hot water did little to alleviate his angst. He stood under the spout, thinking. *Why, God? You took my whole family! Why saddle me with a couple of kids? Especially now?*

Mitch heard no answer. He felt very far from God, as if even his loudest cry would never reach the Father's ears. Glumly, he turned off the water, toweled off, and dressed. There were bigger things to worry about than the kids, he decided resolutely. *Like locating another find.*

It had been over eight years since Mitch and his friends had happened upon the mother lode of treasure ships, *La Bailadora del Mar. The Ocean Dancer.* Since then, he and Hans had established Treasure Seekers, Inc., while Chet had chosen to pursue an academic career. So far, Treasure Seekers had located and salvaged sixty-two ancient ships. None had held such wealth as the first, but the excitement of the work and the substantial potential riches to be gained drove them onward. They made a nice living and had chosen for their headquarters the island of Robert's Foe: a tiny spot on the map, amid a chain of islands northwest of Cuba.

On Robert's Foe, their modest wealth went a long way. Mitch's home sat on the crest of a hill that sloped down a hundred feet to meet white sand beaches. The house had been built by a drug baron who was caught by international agents, and Mitch had purchased it for half of its worth. He loved it, and Robert's Foe became his personal playground and private paradise.

Paradise, except for the loneliness. Hans had married a loving Cuban girl named Nora some years back, but Mitch never had time to date women, let alone marry one. His work consumed him. Nothing was more important than the next find. When he was lonely, he sought solace in his library, scavenging facts from ancient ship logs, tracking down valuable clues, and studying the maps that lined the room's walls.

But this morning, after another long night, the loneliness hung on him like a soggy fur coat. He sat down at the breakfast table and sullenly helped himself to a freshly baked roll and the exotic fruits that were typical fare on Robert's Foe—papaya, banana, kiwi, and star fruit.

"Good morning!" Hans's booming voice startled him. Mitch scowled over his shoulder at his friend and partner. "Do you always have to be so cheery, Hans?"

"Sure! There are many reasons to be happy. You are a father now!" The big man slapped Mitch on the back, nearly causing him to choke on the bite of roll he was swallowing.

"He's not my father!" Joshua yelled from the corner, his small four-year-old fists at his side. "He's not!"

Both men turned to the boy and housekeeper, who had quietly slipped into the room.

"Joshua…," Mitch said, rising and moving toward the boy. But Josh ran around Talle's skirts faster than he could reach him, escaping down the marble hallway.

Mitch sighed, sitting back down. "Hans, this father stuff is getting to me."

CHAPTER THREE

*T*hree days later Mitch and the household had not fared any better at getting some sleep. Exhausted, crotchety, and roaring with anger at the late arrival of Talle's niece, Mitch ripped aside the gauze living room drapes when he heard the boat launch.

"Finally! She had better have a good excuse!" He hurriedly dressed and strode down to the launch, where he would take the upper hand with Anya.

As he neared the new nanny, her beauty took the edge off his anger. She was slim and well proportioned, with long, dark hair pulled back in a ponytail. When she grabbed her big backpack and a duffel from the boat captain and turned to Mitch with a friendly smile, he faltered and took an odd step. *Still, she's late. She's lucky I'm not going to toss her right back on that boat.*

"Hello," she started and held out her hand. "I'm—"

"—late," he finished for her, ignoring her outstretched hand. "You agreed to be here three days ago, and because of your lackadaisical attitude, I have lost three solid days' work. Do you know what that means financially?"

Christina was flabbergasted. "I don't think you understand…"

"Save your breath. You're here now, and we'll just make the best of things. If I had any other option, you'd be outta here so fast it'd make your head spin." Mitch whirled around and began climbing the hill to the house, not offering to help carry her things.

"Of all the rude, ridiculous ways—," she began, but her words were cut off by the engine's roar as the boat reversed and sped away. Christina looked helplessly from the retreating launch to the back of the proud man who strode away. Swallowing her anger she swung her backpack up onto one shoulder and followed, resolving to straighten things out at the house.

Upon reaching the mansion, she paused to catch her breath, her inquisitive eyes catching every detail. Huge windows opened to catch the fresh breeze off the ocean, and some downstairs walls opened completely, creating an easy, airy feel. The effect was one of a luxurious tent, strewn with soft, welcoming couches, chairs, and overstuffed pillows. *Whoever decorated the place had great taste.*

"Don't stand there and gawk. You've got work to do."

"Now just a minute—"

"I don't have time. I've had work on the back burner for weeks now. After you get settled and get the kids in line, then we'll talk. Until then—"

"Kids? What kids?"

Mitch looked at her, puzzled.

Christina set down her bag, seeing that the man had finally calmed down enough to listen. He was arrogant, haughty, and out of line, but she noticed despite herself that his furrowed brow made him appear incredibly handsome.

"Allow me to introduce myself. I am Christina Alvarez. I've come to talk business, not to baby-sit."

A slow blush crept up his neck as he realized his faux pas. He turned and walked to the window, swallowing hard. "Ah, the famous Dr. Alvarez."

Mitch knew very well who she was. In the short time she had been in the business, she had become famous for her work on the Civil War ships. But he had to take care of his family first. He couldn't think until then.

"I've tried to reach you several times on the phone. I've left messages."

"I didn't return them. I already have a partner."

"I know. The least you could've done was call me back and hear me out."

"If the idea's so good, why'd you come all the way to me? Why not try someone else?"

"I think you know why. Treasure Seekers is the only company that has unlimited access to the Florida Keys, Texas, or Mexico. You even have limited access in Cuban waters. Ask for a permit, and it's yours. If I ask for a permit, it will take three years."

He turned to look at her. She was pacing, clearly excited about the prospect of the find. And she was gorgeous. She spoke quickly, and her passion was contagious.

"I've been after this for years, Crawford. It's my ancestor's ship, and I've got insider evidence that no one else can touch. I've been to the Archivo de las Indias and found one document. If I went back, I bet I could find more. I've got a friend there who would help me. I know where the wreck is."

"Which wreck?"

"*La Canción.*"

Mitch drew in his breath. "No way." The ship was a fable; she was every treasure hunter's dream, full of gold and a wealth of archaeological information. But nobody had any idea where she was. Mitch and Hans had decided years earlier that she didn't exist.

"I'll show you what I have if you make me your partner, sixty-forty."

"*If* we ever took you on as a partner, it'd be seventy-thirty, our way. We're the ones who have the equipment, the access to permits—"

"I'm the one who has the information that will lead you there."

"Look," Mitch pulled his hand through dark blond hair that reached past the nape of his neck. "I'd go broke if I chased every pretty girl's dream. As I said before, I don't need a partner. I have one."

Christina was stunned into silence by his words, and Mitch instantly regretted them. But he had too much on his mind—his heart—for this.

"Of all the ridiculous, closed-minded—"

"I'll call the launch back," Mitch interrupted. "It'll take a few hours. Please make yourself comfortable while you wait."

She took a step toward him, really angry now. "You listen for just a minute. First of all, I am not just some girl chasing a dream; I am a woman who has a doctorate in nautical archaeology. Second, never before have I met such a pigheaded man. I wouldn't willingly put myself in a working relationship with you unless I had to, but you're my only option. Somebody else might find her by the time I get around the politics!"

He looked at her, smiling. She was fired up, her eyes huge, her cheeks taut. *A Spanish beauty's anger is best avoided,* he remembered reading on an ancient ship's cannon graffiti. Out of the many slogans he had seen carved into ships by sailors long dead, that was the one that had stuck in his mind.

"I need a nanny, not a colleague."

"That's not what I hear," she shot right back. "You need some new money to fund your operations."

A small girl's wail echoed down the hallway. Mitch ignored it.

"What do you know of my business?"

"Word travels fast, Mitch. I know how Treasure Seekers is faring." She winced as the girl's wail turned into an angry scream.

Mitch looked over his shoulder angrily. "Talle! Could you keep her quiet for just a minute?" He turned back to Christina. "Look, I don't have time for this. Hans and I are close—real close—to something big. If I could get a little peace and quiet around here, I could concentrate enough to peg it. But between the kid's crying and people like you barging in on me, I can't do squat."

"Well, pardon me. I'd heard of your reputation for arrogance, but had hoped that it was purely rumor. To think the Kenbridges told me such nice things about you… If you'll call the launch, I will leave. I look forward to the day when you eat crow and I have the sweet joy of finding *The Song*."

"Gladly," Mitch said. His head hurt already from their confrontation. *Women. Useless distractions.* He walked to a phone that was hidden in an attractive mahogany cabinet and dialed. "No answer," he grumbled after several moments. "Make yourself comfortable and I'll try again in a minute."

With that, he stormed out of the room, leaving a frustrated Christina in his wake.

Christina paced the room for half an hour, feeling helpless and angry. *How could he not even hear me out? Who does he think he is?* The child's incessant crying only made her more anxious. *Whose kid is it anyway?* The Kenbridges had never mentioned Mitch having children, and she had not heard anything about it in the industry scuttlebutt.

The girl's sobbing continued. *Is no one watching her? Comforting her?* Christina found it impossible to ignore the frantic wailing. She made her way down the marble-floored halls, following the sound of crying.

The ceilings were high, lending a palatial, airy feel to the building. As she peeked into the individual rooms, Christina noticed ocean breezes blowing through gauzy, fluttering curtains and well-crafted floors of wood and stone. *So he's a rich man, but can't be bothered with his own children,* Christina thought resentfully. *Just another guy who wants to pawn his kids off to a nanny and take no responsibility. Where was their mother?*

The cries grew louder. Christina turned a corner and watched as a Cuban maid walked stiffly down the hallway in the opposite direction. Christina peeked into the room from which the woman had apparently come. There, on a small bed covered in white eyelet, a little girl lay on her side, sobbing. A little boy sat beside her, patting her hand, repeating over and over, "It's okay. It's okay."

"Hello," Christina said with a big smile. The older child's face shot around to search hers.

"Are you the nanny?" he asked quietly.

"No. I'm a…friend of your father's."

The boy looked puzzled. The little girl momentarily stopped her crying.

"You know where my dad is?" the boy asked suspiciously.

"Well, of course. He's right down at the other end of the house."

The boy turned away to look at his sister, his expression unusually mature for a child of his young age—four, Christina guessed. "He's not my dad. He's my uncle."

"Oh," she said, faltering for a moment. "Well, I'm Christina. What are your names?"

"I'm Joshua. This is my sister, Kenna."

"Joshua, it's good to meet you. You, too, Kenna."

Joshua nodded his head solemnly. Kenna sniffled and took a deep, shaky breath.

"Why are you guys cooped up in here?"

"'Cause Talle doesn't want us unnerfoot, and Uncle Mitch doesn't want us outside and inta trouble," Joshua replied.

"Is that why Kenna's been crying?"

"No. She's sad 'cause Mama died."

Christina tried to not let her pity show. "And you don't know where your dad is?"

Joshua shook his head gravely.

"I see. Well, why don't we three go out and explore? I promise I'll keep you out of trouble. I think we'll all feel better if we get some fresh air."

Mitch and Hans were arguing vehemently when the noise ceased. Hans noticed it first. "Sh, sh, sh. Listen! The girl's stopped crying. It's a sign."

Mitch snorted. "A sign? That Christina is a God-sent messenger waiting to take us to the treasure marked with a big red X?"

"That she'll be good for you, maybe in more ways than one…"

"Hans, I don't need a wife…I need a nanny. And *you're* my partner. Why would you want somebody else—especially some Ph.D. twit—to step in between us?"

"She wouldn't be between us. Our twosome would just become a threesome. If it doesn't work out, we can just say good-bye to Dr. Alvarez. And if it does work…"

"I've never seen a threesome work. Particularly when there's a woman present."

Hans leaned back in his chair. "I think it would be good for Treasure Seekers to add a 'brain' to the team, even temporarily. At least hear the woman out."

"No way. I've got enough to worry about without a Spanish hothead on my team."

"Mitch…"

But Mitch turned away and dialed the boat launch on the big island again. "I said no way. Where's that boat captain? He should've been back at San Esteban an hour ago!"

One body…One community…One shared search for a lasting love.
THE FULL CIRCLE SERIES
by Lisa Tawn Bergren
Available now at your local bookstore!

REFUGE (Book 1) • When Rachel Johanssen dared Beth Morgan to answer a personal ad in *The Rancher's Journal,* she never thought her citified friend would become a rancher's wife. Now, Rachel, too, is falling in love with the glorious Elk Horn Valley—and with Dirk Tanner, a rugged Montana rancher who makes it his home. Rachel's young friend, Jake Rierdon, has taken a shine to ranch life as well—and to beautiful young Emily Walker. But shadows from the present and past threaten to destroy both couples' chances for a future.

TORCHLIGHT (Book 2) • After inheriting her family's lighthouse and mansion on the coast of Maine, heiress Julia Rierdon—sister of Jake Rierdon *(Refuge)*—sets out to restore the estate with the help of a mysterious stranger. Motorcycle-riding Trevor Kenbridge is gorgeous, infuriating…and just the man she needs to help her renovate the home. He may also be the right man to claim her heart.

PATHWAYS (Book 3) • Doctor Bryn Bailey—cousin to Trevor Kenbridge *(Torchlight)*—has come to Alaska to tend those who cannot reach healthcare through the traditional routes and, with the aid of bush pilot Eli Pierce, begins to take trips into remote areas accessible only by plane. Then one evening during a freak storm their small plane goes down in the wilderness, putting Bryn on a desperate search for pathways back to civilization, to God…and to love.

TREASURE (Book 4) • Ever since she roomed with Bryn Bailey *(Pathways)* at Harvard, nautical archaeologist Dr. Christina Alvarez has been obsessed with finding her ancestor's sunken treasure ship. Only one man—Caribbean treasure hunter Mitch Crawford—can help her, and he refuses to do so. But Christina's fight to win Mitch over may lead them both to a treasure more valuable than either of them ever dreamed.

CHOSEN (Book 5) • As supervisor of the Solomon's Stables dig in Jerusalem, archaeologist Alexana Roarke—grad-school friend of Christina Alvarez *(Treasure)*—knows she is in significant danger. Yet she will let nothing impede her excavation, not even the concern of handsome, world-renowned news correspondent Ridge McIntyre. Her stubbornness, however, could cost Alexana her life—and a future with the man she loves.

FIRESTORM (Book 6) • As a forest-fire-fighting crew boss, Montanan Reyne Oldre—friend to Rachel Tanner and Beth Morgan *(Refuge)*—once led a team of courageous firefighters into a blaze that ended in tragedy. Now that the flames of love have begun to flicker between her and smokejumper Logan McCabe, Reyne must face the fears from her past and battle the raging firestorm that burns in her soul.